Faerie Born

TITANIA ACADEMY BOOK 3

Also by Samaire Wynne:

Mad World series:

#1: EPIDEMIC
#2: SANCTUARY
#3: DESPERATION

ROMANOV series:

#1: ROMANOV – Vengeance Never Dies
#2: (title coming soon) (2021)

The Paladin Princess series:

#1: The Pirates of Moonlit Bay
#2: The Pirate Queen
#3: The Lost Treasure
#4: The Pirate Prince
#5: The Death of the Queen (2021)
#6: The Fountain of Youth (2021)
#7: Magellan's Tears (2021)

Titania Academy series:

#1: Faerie Misborn
#2: Faerie Elemental
#3: Faerie Born
#4: Faerie War

Faerie Born

TITANIA ACADEMY BOOK 3

Samaire Wynne

Black Raven Books

This is a work of fiction. All of the geography, characters, organizations, and events portrayed in this novel are either products of the author's imagination or are used fictitiously.

Black Raven Books

The text was set in 12-point Californian FB

ISBN-13: 9781948594394

First Edition: June 2020

10 9 8 7 6 5 4 3 2 1

Dedicated to the dogged perseverance uniquely present in all heroes.

Faerie Born

Chapter One
The Perfect Day

August. The start of a new school year.

In the beginning, we had no idea how bad it would get. We had no idea all of us wouldn't make it out alive.

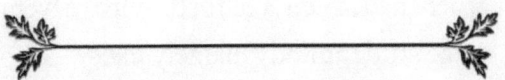

It was a sunny day, the Saturday before fall semester started at Titania Academy, and we were all in high spirits, celebrating my birthday.

I couldn't believe how the summer had gone.

The fire that was consuming the Academy had been extinguished, and work had soon begun on its restoration. With everything aided by magic, it seemed like it had been done in no time.

It had been months since the castle had been repaired, and restoration efforts had just been completed the week before.

One of the best things to happen since the attack on the school was that Professor Ó Baoghill had been recalled early from her sabbatical. She had been hard to locate, but when she heard of the destruction, and of interim headmaster Merryweather's actions toward me, she gladly returned.

"I cannot believe how you were treated, Miss Ó Cuilinn! Completely against school rules and general propriety! My goodness!"

I had felt, in a small part, vindicated. Especially when Merryweather had been charged with several crimes against the fae student body, namely me.

He was now being held at a remote facility.

I just hope he never gets the chance to retaliate.

Still, I breathed easier now that the summer was nearly over, and everything had been put to rights.

I hope.

My friends had insisted that we celebrate my birthday with a big party on the fresh, green lawn in front of the castle, and everyone in the school had been invited.

It was late morning, and Liesl and I lay on the warm grass, our eyes half-closed in the sunshine. A long blade of grass held between my lips, I faced Liesl and grinned.

"Jack has ..." She blushed and dropped her eyes.

"Jack has what?" I asked quietly, raising my eyebrows.

She grinned. "He's asked me out."

I sat up, my mouth open in surprise.

"Well?" I asked. "Tell me everything!"

Liesl sat up as well, and we faced each other, both of us sitting cross-legged, so close our kneecaps touched.

Girl talk.

"Well," Liesl said, bending forward. "He's been gone for most of the summer to Mallorca, visiting his grandparents. So last week, I saw him in the market. He actually saw me first."

I smiled expectantly.

Liesl continued.

"I was looking at the Magical Blossoms Shoppe, staring in the window. You know that shop?"

I nodded hurriedly, wanting her to continue.

"Well, he came up behind me. Tapped me on the shoulder." She giggled, remembering.

"What did you do?" I asked, breathlessly.

"I turned and saw who it was." Her face was getting redder, if that were at all possible.

"Anyway, he said 'hi', and I said 'hi,' and he told me he'd been on holiday, and was just now getting back."

"And did he touch you — other than tapping you on the shoulder?" I whispered.

Jack was a Savannah Fae, blond and feather-coated when not in a glamour. Well, very fine, tiny feathers. Feathers than looked almost like a fuzz on his golden fae skin.

Liesl had a deep crush on Jack, but had been hiding it. Unsuccessfully, it turned out.

"He did not touch me," Liesl said softly.

If he had, he would have shared his emotional state. Something Savannah Faes are loath to accidentally do.

"So... what happened?" I asked.

"He made a bit of small talk about his grandmother's garden. Then he paused for a few seconds, kind of staring at me. Oh my God, Holly, he had this thoughtful smile on his face, and his lips were so adorable..."

"Yeah?" I grinned.

She giggled. "And then he asked me to go have dinner with him. Tonight. In the forest."

"At the new faun café?" I asked.

She nodded, grinning so widely her dimples stood out.

The fauns living in the forest had gotten together and opened a small three-table café next to an enormous oak tree, just a few dozen feet into the forest. It was the first of its kind on the school grounds. They'd had to get special permission from the council: It has only been approved because of the need to boost morale, according to Professor Farryn. I had yet to see it, but it was reputed to be the perfect spot for a dinner date. The tables even had magical flowers growing on them, according to Chance.

"Liesl, you're kidding." I said.

"I am not kidding. I nearly fainted." She turned suddenly, and her expression changed to one of mild shock. "There he is!"

I turned to look.

Jack was trotting onto the lawn from behind the castle, three of his buddies following him. There were all Savannah Fae, with deep golden hair, bleached white on the tips from the summer sun. They were in soccer uniforms, having just finished practice, I surmised, and the white T-shirts and black shorts showed off their summer tans so well they almost looked like burnished gold in the bright daylight.

Liesl reared up on her knees and waved shyly.

Jack saw her, and grinned and nodded, then all three boys trotted off to the side and began a game of foot-and-ball.

We settled back down.

"Well," I said after a minute of contemplation, the grass blade between my lips waving up and down as I spoke. "You could do worse." I laughed.

Liesl put her hand to her chest, and her eyes swooned. "Oh, I know, right? He's so cute!"

I chuckled. "You've got it bad, roomie."

Just then, Liesl glanced toward the front steps leading up to the Academy.

"Speaking of having it bad, look who's done with his meeting," she said.

Chance was coming down the steps with Professor Farryn, both of them deep in conversation.

"He looks taller," Liesl said.

"I think he's grown a few inches over the summer," I murmured.

Chance was definitely taller. Not only that, but his shoulders were broader, and his arms had become more muscular.

He was filling out. I had definitely noticed.

We watched the two finish their conversation, both of us remaining silent. Professor Farryn looked adamant about whatever he was saying.

"I hope everything's okay," I said quietly.

Liesl glanced at me and put her hand out to touch my forearm. "I'm sure it is, Holly. Today is your day. Don't worry about anything else."

I glanced at her. "Is there anything to worry about? What have you heard?" I sounded slightly manic, even to my own ears.

Liesl laughed. "No, I haven't heard anything. I'm trying to reassure you, nothing's going on. Well, at least nothing worrisome. As for later tonight, I'm hoping you have a nice birthday dinner with Chance after the party." She grinned.

"Oh, yeah." I murmured, calming down. Chance was making me dinner in his dorm room, just the two of us. He'd mentioned us dining up on the castle balcony, next to the parapets.

Should be nice.

I stared at Chance, daydreaming.

I'd been doing a lot of that lately.

"I can't believe you're fifteen years old, sweetheart," I heard behind me.

That sounded like Aunt Clare's voice!

I swung around sharply, but there was no one there.

I'm going nuts.

A shiver rose up my spine and made the hairs on the back of my neck stand up.

I felt my face grow cold.

Liesl put her hand on my arm, it felt warm.

"You okay, Hol?" she asked in a quiet voice.

I let out a breath of air and glanced behind me again.

Nothing was there except the grass, the sunshine, and the summer.

Suddenly, I felt myself again.

"Yeah, I'm okay," I answered. "Just thought I heard my Aunt Clare there, for a minute..."

"That happens to me sometimes," said Liesl. "I'll hear the voice of my ancestors, when nothing's there. I think it's the spirits trying to help me. Either that or my own subconscious being a brat." She shoved me playfully and laughed.

I grinned and turned back to look at Chance.

"Hmmm," said Liesl softly. "We have some fine students here at Titania Academy."

I glanced at her, caught her staring at Chance. Grinning, I shoved her shoulder playfully.

"Hey, stick to Jack." I laughed.

She grinned.

"Hey, I can appreciate a beautiful sight," she laughed.

That was all it took.

We both laughed louder and louder, falling into the grass, giggling madly.

Must be the sunshine.

Chance wandered closer, and both Liesl and I lay back on the warm grass and watched him approach.

He is fine, indeed.

I closed my eyes and chuckled to myself, then opened them when I heard his voice.

"Holly! Come here!" Chance called.

I jumped to my feet and ran to him across the lawn, past the balloons and the cake on its table.

I jogged up to Chance, grinning. He caught me in his arms and swung me around him, his eyes sparkling with merriment.

"Ready for the three-legged race, birthday girl?"

Professor Farryn had suggested party games from the world of humans, since that's where I had spent my first fourteen years. Problem was, in his research he had neglected to study the era from which he chose the games.

Since he was coordinating the party, we hadn't discovered this until we'd arrived at the event.

The result was an olde-fashioned birthday party, the first I had ever had, and it was fabulous.

I grinned as he set me down, and we raced hand-in-hand to the side where flags had been planted in the ground and gunny sacks were waiting for pairs of runners.

"Let's run together," said Chance.

My cheeks pinked, and I laughed happily.

We quickly put one leg each in the sack, and, holding it so we could move, lined up at the start line.

"We're gonna beat you! Just watch and see!" Liesl and Renée said from a few feet away. Then they dissolved into a giggling fit and fell over onto the grass.

Chance grinned at me.

"Looks like the secret to winning the race is not laughing until you fall over," I said, smiling.

"Looks like it," he replied.

Aspen and Tundra, my two familiars, bounced in happiness on the lawn. Nearby, Jade and Snowbear, Renée and Liesl's familiars, were in a mock battle, rolling over and over, jumping apart and coming back together in their own game. Chance's hawk flew overhead, keeping an eye on her master.

Professor Farryn walked up with a white-and-black-checked starter flag.

"Is everyone ready?" He called out as he lifted the flag above his head.

There were seven pairs of runners altogether. We all cheered in reply to the mountain gnome, a favorite teacher at our school.

"Ready?! Set?! GO!" He brought the flag fluttering down, and we were off!

We all ran as best we could, but it was more of a hobble than an outright run.

Several pairs tumbled to the ground after just a dozen feet.

Chance and I stumbled a few times, but were able to right ourselves and run forward toward the finish line ahead: a red ribbon stretched across the grass about fifty feet in front of us.

Liesl and Renée had a rhythm going and passed us.

A few other pairs on our other side passed us as well.

We surged forward, determined to catch them.

I glanced back and saw two pairs of runners behind us, then looked forward again to the four that were ahead of us.

"I think we'll be okay. Just gotta make a strong push to pass..." I stumbled, tripping over the flap of the bag.

Chance grabbed me around my waist and hoisted me up on his hip. I was now mashed up against my boyfriend. I could feel the muscles in his arm as he carried me effortlessly.

Oh my God...

I felt hot. I just knew my cheeks were flaming.

Chance was sprinting now, carrying me on his hip, my legs dangling. His face was an inch from mine. He looked so determined.

We passed two of the running pairs.

Then another.

Now we just had to overtake our friends.

Liesl and Renée were nearing the finish line.

Renée glanced back and saw Chance sprinting toward them, and turned and said something to Liesl, who looked back to check on us. Her eyebrows shot up her forehead in surprise, and I started to giggle.

And that was it. I was lost in a laughing fit.

Chance now looked grim, and he hoisted me farther up on his hip and surged forward.

I couldn't stop giggling.

Chance's legs were pumping hard.

He's been working out, all summer...

We passed Liesl and Renée.

Chance let out a roar as we hit the red ribbon and won. I caught the fluttering streamer as we surged forward.

A few steps beyond the finish line, Chance finally stumbled on the sack and we went down in a heap.

At the last moment, Chance turned and fell underneath me, and I plopped down onto his arm with an "Oomph!" and then fell to the side.

"You okay?" I heard him ask. "Holly?"

I opened my eyes and saw the back of his head.

I had landed behind him.

I was fine, still giggly, and I sat up quickly as he turned on the grass. I leaned over his shoulder, laughing.

He turned around, grinning.

"Guess so," he murmured, laughing with me.

I fell back down on the grass as Professor Farryn trotted up, a large blue ribbon fluttering in his hand.

"The winners!" The small but mighty teacher called out, and stuck the ribbon onto Chance's shirt as he sat up.

I lay back on the warm grass and watched Professor Farryn congratulate Chance on carrying me the last half of the race.

Chance thanked the teacher, then turned to me. He stared down at me, and I grinned back up at him.

I suppose I should have felt self-conscious, but I was having too much fun.

The sun was bright in the blue sky, and fluffy white clouds passed overhead. I closed my eyes, still grinning.

The bright sunlight was cut off suddenly, and I opened my eyes to Chance bending over me and blocking out the direct sun rays.

"There's grass in your hair," he laughed, and plucked out a few green blades, then placed them on my nose.

I sneezed lightly, closing my eyes and grinning some more.

"You're beautiful, Holly."

My eyes popped open again. I stared at him.

I felt a rush of heat like nothing else.

There was a look in his eyes, almost as if...

Chance lowered his lips to mine.

"Holly?" I heard my name called and tried to open my eyes. I didn't want to. Chance's lips were so warm and nice...

"HOLLY??!"

I opened my eyes. I was lying on my back in the grass, Chance was crouching over me, as well as Liesl and Farryn. They all looked very concerned.

Chance held a small bag of ice against my temple.

"Hey. Hey, kiddo, you okay?" Professor Farryn knelt at my head, staring into my eyes from a few inches away.

I groaned and put my hand up to my forehead.

"What happened?" I mumbled, trying to sit up.

"We conked heads, that's what happened," Chance said, sounding worried.

A wave of dizziness washed over me, and I fell back to the grass again.

"Take it easy, there," Farryn said. "Just rest. I'll go get you some water." He jumped up and ran off out of sight.

"Holly, try to sit up again," said Liesl gently, her hand behind my shoulders.

I sat up, unsteady, with her help.

"Thanks," I whispered. I glanced at my roommate, my best friend. "Hey, did you see the kiss?" I asked.

Liesl's eyes went wide. "Kiss?"

"Yeah," I closed my eyes and sighed, then opened them again. "Chance and me, we fell, then he kissed me..."

Liesl bent to my ear. "He didn't kiss you. You've been out cold for several minutes, Hol. When you two fell, your heads smacked together, and you went down for the count."

I reared back a few inches and fixed her eyes with a questioning look.

She nodded.

Oh, great, I imagined the kiss while I was unconscious.

Professor Farryn ran up with a cup of water and knelt down on my other side. "Here, Holly, take a sip of this. You'll feel better."

I took the cup and bent my face to it, sipping its contents. The cool water felt good going down my throat, and it helped to bring me back to my senses.

My head throbbed.

"Holly, you okay?" Chance bent down and patted my shoulder. "We knocked heads pretty solidly."

I felt my forehead. No knot, thank goodness. I took another sip of water. The headache was already fading.

Chance sat down cross-legged in front of me.

I sipped water and watched him over the rim of the cup.

Liesl still had her arm around my shoulders.

"How many fingers am I holding up?" Chance asked, holding up the first and second fingers of his right hand, in the 'peace' gesture.

His lips were pursed, and his face looked worried.

I grinned in spite of myself.

"Two."

His face relaxed.

Liesl smiled.

I drained the last of the water and stood up with Liesl's help, no longer feeling dizzy.

Chance stepped closer to me, brushed my hair off my forehead and blew gently where his head had hit mine.

"Aw," his voice was low and mellow, "You're fine." He leaned in and kissed my forehead. "There, all better."

"Mostly," I said, cracking a grin, dipping my head to the side, then lifting my chin, closing my eyes, and puckering my lips.

Chance kissed me gently, then pulled away when the gathered crowd began to hoot.

I opened my eyes and grinned. "Now I feel better."

"Guess there *was* a kiss," Liesl laughed.

Renèe ran up just then. "Classic kiss, you two."

I grinned.

Suddenly, I heard a low whooshing noise. I glanced overhead. A streak of white was slowly arcing over the trees from the east. I watched, open-mouthed in astonishment.

It was a boiling puff of dense white cloud, traveling too slow to be a plane.

Besides, planes never cross over fae land: It's enchanted and hidden from the human world.

The cloudy train made a slow gentle arc, and descended toward the castle.

Is this an attack? Should I be worried?

Professor Farryn, not three feet from me, glanced overhead, saw the cloud trail, and didn't seem alarmed.

I glanced at the others on the lawn: Some were adults, nearly everyone had noticed the cloud arc, and no one was reacting to it with anything stronger than mild surprise.

They know what it is.

I felt insanely curious, and at the same time, not a little worried.

"What is that?" I finally uttered, feeling shocked at the sight.

"Visitor from the outer lands," Renèe whispered, her eyes pinned on the cloud trail. "Rare, but not unheard of."

I gasped involuntarily.

"Not seen for years, but Renèe is quite right," said Professor Farryn. "Foreign visitor."

I couldn't help myself: I stared, watching the plume of white descend to the top of the castle.

I stared hard, trying not to blink.

After a minute, my eyes started to burn.

I blinked.

"Weird," said Chance. "I've never seen one of those. I have heard of them, but... like Renèe... rarely seen."

"Wonder what it's all about?" Liesl said in a quiet voice.

Chapter Two
Presents and a Surprise

That evening, we all gathered in Professor Farryn's study.

"Ó Cuilinn," Farryn's voice slurred slightly, "you are my brightest second-year, and I want you to know this gift is the best I could imagine for you." He handed me a sheaf of papers, tied with brown twine.

I set my glass of water on the table next to my chair and leaned forward to take them.

Farryn was the perfect host. He had made sure we were all quite comfortable in his private offices, and each of us sat in a seat brought especially there for us.

Farryn sat comfortably in an ornate gothic chair that would have been a tight fit for anyone else in the room.

Brendan was there, as well as the enigmatic Jess. Chance, Liesl, and Renée sat sharing a comfortable couch. Professor Ó Baoghill, her cheeks flushed, was on her second sherry, quietly rocking back and forth in the glider chair she'd settled into, a faint smile on her face.

I had been given an ornate yet diminutive throne-like settee, a soft afghan across my legs, and a small yet treasured pile of gifts next to me.

I studied the writing on the top page of the papers Farryn had handed to me.

"Oh!" I looked up at my favorite professor. "Thank you! This is fantastic!" I waved the sheaf of papers aloft. "Look everyone! Private lessons on Concealment!"

"Oh, that is useful."

"Oh, Holly, you're going to love those lessons."

"Wow!"

"Oh, gosh, I am envious."

Murmurs of appreciation rose as I read the rest of the top page.

My God, this is major.

"Professor," I looked up into his warm eyes. "Thank you. I... thank you, very, very much." I smiled a watery smile.

"We can start right away, tomorrow, if you'd like," Farryn said, sounding pleased.

I nodded vigorously.

"10 a.m. good for you?" he asked.

"Yes. I will be there," I answered.

I studied the sheaf of papers for a few more minutes while the others talked about Concealment lessons and what talents a student would have to possess to be able to learn well.

I tucked the sheaf of papers next to my leg, patted them, satisfied they were secure, and reached for the small glass of half-drunk water again.

Taking a sip, I smiled, feeling happy and warm among my friends. I felt very content to listen to them talk together.

The atmosphere of the room was warmed by several flickering candles, and a small fire crackled in the fireplace next to Professor Farryn.

The sherry was very good, and several bottles were being passed around to refill the tiny glasses Professor Ó Baoghill had provided upon her arrival at the small gathering.

"Holly," Chance touched my arm. "Here, this is from Liesl, Renée and me." He handed me an envelope, and Renée handed me a long box wrapped in a filmy dark green material.

As she was handing me the box, Renée whispered, "Holly, Liesl and I made this for you by hand. It took us a month."

My eyebrows shot up, and I glanced at Liesl on my other side. "Really?"

She nodded.

I took the box and the envelope. "You guys, thank you. You are the best friends anyone could have."

Chance chuckled. "Well, open it before you say that, though."

I grinned at him.

The box was actually made of rolled and formed hardened leaves. As I unwrapped it, I was in awe. "This box and material are fantastic!"

"Yeah, but look inside," said Liesl, smiling.

I unwrapped their gift. It was a massive staff, at least seven feet long.

I stood up, lifting it into the air, and hit myself as well as Chance in the head as I did so.

"Here," Chance said, laughing, "I'll help you."

I sat back down, and he placed the staff next to my leg.

"Tuck it next to your arm, like this," he instructed.

"Liesl, Renée, this is amazing," I murmured.

"The wood is from Jess's tree," whispered Renée. I glanced over at the Lacewing Faerie, who felt my gaze and winked at me.

"We had to coax the tree to give us this branch," said Liesl. "It took two days."

I laughed in delight. They had gone to so much trouble for me.

"We sanded it and polished it and imbued it with magic," said Renée. "It's been soaking for two moon cycles."

I raised my eyebrows. "Two?!"

The moonlight imbued extra magic into natural objects. I stared at the staff, and it glowed softly in my hand.

"I can feel it: It's humming with power!" I exclaimed.

Liesl and Renée nodded happily.

"Open the envelope," said Chance.

I balanced the staff against my leg and carefully opened the envelope and withdrew the single piece of paper within.

I read through the words on there, and my heart softened.

"Oh, Chance!"

He had given me lessons as well: He was going to train me in how to use the staff weapon.

"And, like most magical weapons, it goes invisible when you want it to," Renée said.

I patted my other sleeve.

I could feel my stick tucked back into my shirt, safe and sound, and invisible.

I'll never get used to calling my stick a 'wand'.

I grinned to myself.

I could not believe all the gifts these wonderful people had given me.

Chance had told me earlier that the Fifteenth Birthday was a huge celebration in the Fae World, much like the Sixteenth Birthday was in the human world I had grown up in: New York City, in America. So they had made an especially big celebration for me.

I felt wealthy beyond my years.

"Don't forget, Miss Ó Cuilinn, tomorrow morning at ten o'clock!"

I smiled at Professor Farryn. "I won't forget. In fact, I might get there early!"

Tomorrow was Sunday, and there were no normal classes on the weekend. We could spend half the day in the classroom.

"Holly," Chance said beside me. "I'm going to teach you not only how to defend yourself with the staff, but also to fight offensively, too."

I could not wait.

The next few weeks are going to be crazy!

"Sometimes it's good to fight offensively, trust me," said Renée, smiling.

I gave her a look. "You bet. I am learning that the hard way."

I suddenly thought of something and looked over at Professor Ó Baoghill, who was sipping from her refilled glass of sherry and studying her own hand.

I leaned over and whispered to Renée and Liesl.

"Have we heard anything about the white cloud streak arcing over to the castle during my birthday celebration?"

Liesl shook her head.

Chance shrugged.

"The headmistress doesn't know?" Renée asked in low tones.

I lifted my eyebrows. I had no idea.

Chance glanced over at Ó Baoghill, studying her.

"She doesn't look like she's that concerned. Then again, I heard she's extremely upset about what happened last spring," Chance said, turning back to me. "I would be, too, if it was me."

I took a deep breath, deciding. "Professor? Professor Ó Baoghill?"

The older woman looked up from the study of her hand, her own eyebrows going up in a question as our eyes met.

"Professor, that cloudy mark in the sky this afternoon? The one over the Academy?" I asked.

"Yes, Miss Ó Cuilinn?" She answered.

"Did you find out if it was indeed a visitor? I'm just curious," I finished.

"Miss Ó Cuilinn, I actually just got back this morning, and came directly to your party after dropping my bags off at Jess's," the headmistress said. "I have not even been to my office yet. It's actually still in command of the Academy Council. They hand it over tomorrow, I'm told." She struggled to sit more upright in her chair. "Miss Ó Cuilinn, I want you to know I am very upset with how the school was run in my absence. I don't know if I will ever trust the council enough to leave again." She took another sip of sherry, draining the small glass.

Dr. Farryn immediately offered to refill it, and the professor nodded.

"So kind of you, Farryn, really," she said softly.

"My pleasure, Minerva," he said as he tipped the ornate bottle and deposited more of the rich, rosy amber fluid into her glass. It filled up quickly, as the sherry glasses only held about two ounces.

I looked at my own glass, sitting next to me on a small table. It was half drained. I'd found the cold water tracing a line of coolness down my throat when I took a sip.

"Do we know if it even was a visitor to the castle?" Liesl asked.

"Could've been. Not sure," Chance said. "I didn't go check. Was having too much fun at Holly's birthday party."

I blushed.

"You were having too much fun smooching Holly, you mean," Renée murmured, giving him a look over the rim of her own water glass as she took a sip.

My blush deepened; I actually felt my cheeks grow hot.

Chance looked at me, a slight smile on his lips.

"Get a room, you two," Liesl laughed.

"Oh, god, I need some fresh air," I got up and stretched my arms overhead.

Sometimes you need a deep breath of cold air.

I turned to Professor Farryn. "Sir, which way to the window?" I asked.

Farryn's quarters were covered in tapestries, so it wasn't clear where the outer castle wall lay.

"I'll show you, Miss Ó Cuilinn." He got up and carefully made his way through the many people, until he was on the outer reaches of the room. "Right over here," he gestured.

I followed him down a short hallway and into a study lined with old books.

He made his way to a tall double tapestry, grasping the edges with each hand and throwing the cloth back to expose a small alcove. Then he turned toward me and gestured.

But I was mesmerized.

I stared at the old tomes, some bound in leather, others in silk. I reached out to a particularly large book nearby; its binding was a rich purple silk.

"Professor, these are amazing..."

He walked over. "I'm glad you think so, Miss Ó Cuilinn. This library is my pride and joy. I've been gathering this collection for nigh on eighty years."

I swung my head sharply. "EIGHTY YEARS??"

He nodded, grinning broadly. "Yes. I've been assigned to the university for nearly a century. It has been my privilege to teach Titania Academy students for a very long time."

I blinked in wonder, staring at the books.

"Weren't you afraid the room would burn in the fires?" I asked.

The summer attack on the school had been fierce and violent.

"Yes, I was. But I have taken precautions," he winked.

"Precautions? What kind of precautions?" I was curious.

"Well, beyond fireproofing of the room conventionally" — he indicated the walls and ceiling — "spells here and... here." He gestured to the doors. "Each and every book in my quarters is also magically protected by a spell."

"A spell? A fireproof spell?" I had so much to learn. Fireproof spells on books: amazing!

"No, no, no. Although that would work, too. No, the spell I have on my castle possessions, which are mostly the books and scrolls, is one of transportation. If they grow too hot, or too wet, they are instantly transported to my home in the remote mountains of Sweden."

Oh my god!

"Professor, that is fantastic!"

"Indeed." He brushed his hand across the spines of the books shelved next to him. "Luckily, the fire did not spread this far." He turned to look at me. "Thanks to you, Miss Ó Cuilinn."

He smiled generously.

I dipped my head. "It was my pleasure."

"Well," he gestured out the alcove. "Fresh air awaits. If that was indeed what you were seeking."

"Yes, I actually was." I stepped out onto the curved balcony. The cool night air blew gently against my hair. "The closed room made me feel warm."

"Yes, it has that effect on the very young." He fell silent.

I closed my eyes and inhaled. I thought I could smell the honeysuckle vine in bloom. It grew up the side of the stone castle in abundance.

Professor Farryn cleared his throat gently. "Uh, Miss Ó Cuilinn."

I kept my eyes shut and made an inquiring sound, "hmmm?"

"Are you and Mr. Mac Craith, uh, erm... how do I put this. Are you two mated? Erm, I mean... committed? Uh, dating?"

Dating!

"Oh! uh, well, I'm not sure. I guess so." I glanced down at him. "How, how does one tell? I've never, uh..." I fumbled, feeling embarrassed.

Farryn chuckled. "Has he made a statement of your relationship yet?"

"A statement?" I asked.

What is he talking about?

"Has he... er..." Farryn paused as the sound of a voice clearing came from the room behind us.

"Holly?" Chance called out softly. "You in here?"

"Out here, Chance," I answered. I glanced at the small professor with the big heart. "I guess we can find out now, eh, Professor?"

"Oh, oh no no, no, no no I would never... er... that is..." Farryn stumbled over his words.

Chance poked his head around the tapestry.

"Ah, there you are," he smiled.

Professor Farryn blushed, and ducked back out of the balcony, mumbling: "I'll just go check on uh, on my other guests, while you two, er... confer..."

And he was gone.

"What is with that guy?" Chance murmured.

I giggled.

Chance stepped out onto the balcony and stood next to me. "It is really nice out here," he said.

I took another deep breath. "It sure is. My head is clearing and recovering from the stuffy room."

He grinned. "Farryn is a great host, but his quarters can be stuffy, eh?"

I nodded.

Chance breathed the heady scent of the honeysuckle in. "Whoa."

"You got that right."

We stood out in the fresh air for a while.

It was lovely.

After ten minutes, I felt Chance take my hand. All of a sudden, my face was warm again.

"Holly?"

"Mmm?" I answered.

"Happy birthday."

I grinned.

"Chance?"

He turned to me and kissed my cheek softly. "Yes, Holly?"

"Are we, um, boyfriend and girlfriend?" I asked. Farryn had made me wonder and I was curious.

What exactly did that mean? Was there a ritual? Did I have to do anything? I didn't know any of the Fae Folk customs.

Suddenly, I felt butterflies in my stomach.

"Mmmm, Holly?" He said softly.

"Yes?"

"Do you want to be my girlfriend?"

The butterflies in my stomach suddenly ramped up their flight, and a low-grade nausea took hold in my stomach.

"Uh..." I said.

I heard a chuckle from Chance.

I swung round to face him. "Well, it's just that... I don't know exactly what that means in the Fae Folk world," I said, my hands fluttering. "Does it mean we..." I blushed.

"No. No, it doesn't mean anything, really," Chance said softly. "There are no conditions, Holly. It's just…"

He stepped closer to me.

I looked up at him.

He's gorgeous.

"Now that you're fifteen," Chance said quietly. "Some people might ask you…"

He seemed at a loss for words.

"What happens because I'm fifteen?" I asked.

"Some of the older traditions," he began again. "Well, it's customary for a young lady, Fae Folk, to become betrothed…"

BETROTHED?

Does he mean ENGAGED?

I took a step back and put my hands up.

"Look, Chance, I am extremely fond of you, you know that…," I started.

He grinned. "I know. You're not ready to commit to one person, right?"

"Uh, that's right. I'm still a kid…"

"You're not a kid," he said softly.

"YES, I am. I still feel the same as I did yesterday. I still like to climb trees and chew bubble gum and eat suckers…," I sputtered.

"Relax, Holly," he smiled. "I'm joking."

"You're joking?" I felt confused.

"Yes," he stepped closer to me. "I understand you still feel like a kid. And I understand you like me, but don't want to get serious. I understand that."

"Good." I folded my arms in front of me. "Uh, good. I mean... why does anything have to change?"

He shook his head. "Nothing has to change. We're still friends."

I blinked.

"Just... 'friends'?" I asked.

He nodded. "Well, friends who've kissed." He grinned.

"More than once," I smiled.

"More than once. More than twice," he chuckled.

"And now that I'm fifteen and starting second year, I'm going to have my hands full learning new things," I said.

"New classes," he nodded.

"And we don't have to get serious or anything," I murmured, staring at Chance's lips.

They were so full and so dark, in this moonlight...

He was nodding in agreement. "Don't need anything to be serious..." He said slowly.

Serious ...

I stepped closer to him.

The night breeze, heady with the strong scent of the blooming honeysuckle, the moonlight glinting off the lighter strands of Chance's hair... he was so handsome...

I leaned forward.

He stayed where he was, but I could tell he was looking at my lips, too...

His breathing became deeper...

My face felt warm...

I took a step toward him... leaned forward...

His hands came up to either side of my waist...

... our lips came together...

"Hey, you two!" Liesl's cheerful voice cut through the fog in my head.

We sprang apart.

Did our lips even get to touch?

Yes, I decided. Our lips had touched for a fraction of a second before...

"Whoa! Look at that moon!" Liesl bounced out onto the balcony.

I looked down at my feet, then up at Chance.

He'd taken a step back, and looked down as well. His lips were parted, a moist dew drop quivering on his lower lip.

"Hey, Ó Baoghill's invited us to go see her office tonight, before the craziness of tomorrow's morning classes, start of term, and all that." Liesl's eyes were sparkling in excitement. "What do ya say? Want to come?"

"Sure, Liesl, that sounds great," Chance said with forced enthusiasm.

"Sure," I agreed. "Let's go now."

Chapter Three

Midnight Foray and Late-Night Girl Talk

We all made our way down the center staircase from Professor Farryn's office. It was after midnight, and we'd had appetizers, and my head was swimming with the heady presence of Chance at my elbow.

"Watch your step," he whispered.

"I've only had two sips, didn't even finish my glass," I turned and whispered at him. He shrugged and smiled, still holding my elbow.

"Whoops!" Professor Ó Baoghill said as she caught herself. The old headmistress tottered on the step.

Jess and Brendan immediately hurried to either side of her, and hooked their arms onto her elbows.

We continued down the stairs.

I heard a loud hiccup from behind us, and turned in surprise.

Professor Farryn had his hand to his mouth, looking embarrassed. "Sorry."

Two flights of stone steps later, we had made it to the ground floor.

As a group, we tiptoed across the inner courtyard and into the hallway where the headmistress' office was located.

We gathered outside the outer door and waited as Professor Ó Baoghill fumbled with her keys.

Some minutes later, after some floundering with several keys, and muffled cursing, Professor Ó Baoghill declared that "they must have changed the locks."

Chance came forward then, to help and give constructive advice.

The moonlight was illuminating the short hallway from a nearby window, enough so I could watch Chance walk past me.

I caught my breath as he brushed my arm.

"Holly," Liesl whispered. "What's with you?"

"Nothing," I shushed her. "Nothing. I'm fine."

Renée snorted behind Liesl.

I turned and caught her eye with a questioning look.

Renée held up her hands in an "I don't have any idea what you're talking about" gesture.

I made a face and turned to face forward again.

In fact ...

I walked quietly forward to join the crowd at the door lock.

Chance was fiddling with his own key.

"Yes, they changed the lock, all right." he cursed under his breath, then looked at the headmistress. "When are they planning on meeting you tomorrow morning, Ma'am?"

"Seven o'clock sharp, Mr. Mac Craith," Ó Baoghill answered.

"Oh, good lord," said Professor Farryn in a louder voice. "It's already nearly two in the morning."

"That late?" Professor Ó Baoghill turned in surprise.

Farryn nodded vigorously.

Ó Baoghill turned and began heading back the way we'd come. "Back, everybody. Back to your beds. We need to sleep. It's very late. We'll do this tomorrow. Back. Back, I say!"

Liesl and I put our hands over our mouths to suppress our giggles as we walked back.

A half-hour later, Liesl and I were washed and in fresh pajamas, and in beds. We faced each other; our hands folded under our heads.

Aspen and Tundra snored next to my bed. They'd been happy to see me again, and their barks had been deafening in the quiet dorm.

"Shush, you two!" I'd had to stage-whisper.

Now, in bed, my mind raced.

"Holly," Liesl whispered. "You asleep yet?"

"No," I whispered back.

She grinned in the moonlight.

"What were you and Chance talking about on Professor Farryn's balcony?"

"Oh, that. Well, Farryn had asked me if Chance and I were committed."

"What? You're kidding."

"It was the weirdest thing," I said. "Farryn asked if we were..." I tried to remember. "He used the words, 'mated,' 'committed,' and 'dating.' "

Liesl sat up in bed. "Farryn asked that?"

I nodded, sitting up myself.

Aspen raised her head, looked around, then lay back down and was soon snoring again.

"And then Chance came, and I asked him about it, and he was all weird."

"Weird in what way?" asked Liesl.

"Well, he asked me if I wanted to be his girlfriend, and said some people might ask if I'm 'betrothed,' now that I'm fifteen. ... It was weird." I rolled my eyes.

"Whoa," Liesl murmured.

"Then we talked about how I'm too young to commit, and I said that I was still a kid, and he said that no, I wasn't then, ..." I stopped. thinking of the kiss that wasn't.

"Then what happened?" Liesl finally asked, after a minute.

"Nothing."

"Really?"

"Well..., we were talking, and then I just couldn't stop staring at his lips..." I stopped again, remembering.

"Oh, Holly, please tell me I didn't interrupt a kiss." Liesl sounded horrified.

"No comment."

"OH GOD!" Liesl thumped back down and buried her face in her pillow.

I laughed. "No, seriously, it's okay. There'll be other times..."

She looked up at me. "I can't believe this."

"Never mind. Like I said, there'll be other times." I thought for a minute. "Liesl," I started again.

"Huh?"

"You know I'm still learning," I said.

She nodded; I could see her head in the dim light from the window.

"Well, I just turned fifteen, right?" I said.

Liesl nodded and waited.

"Well, what did Professor Farryn mean? Like I told Chance, I still feel like a kid, I mean... I mean, I don't feel fully grown up yet." I floundered, unable to come up with the right words.

"Okay, what you have to understand is this: Professor Farryn is, like, a thousand years old," Liesl said.

"He is not that old," I answered.

"Well, it's close, trust me. He's OLD. Right?"

I nodded.

"So, for his generation, when a Fae Folk girl, I mean, young lady, turned fifteen..., sometimes... she would become betrothed — that's the old word ... um ..."

"Okay." I held up my hands. "Stop right there. I am *not* going to get engaged to Chance, certainly not right now." I lifted my hands in the air, palms up. "I mean, I'm barely out of childhood."

Liesl nodded.

"These aren't biblical times, after all. It's the twenty-first century," I continued. "I should have at least another ten years of dating and exploring in front of me, right?"

"Yeahhhhhh, I guess," said Liesl.

"What?" I put my hands in my lap and waited.

"Well, it's just that..." she stopped and looked worried.

"Liesl: what?"

"Holly, yes, you are young, heck, I'm the same age: *We're* young. And Chance and you just started seeing each other, and we're all in this group of friends, so everything's casual, right?"

I nodded.

"Okay, so yeah, it's way too early and you're too young to be committed, right?" Liesl said.

"Yeah."

"So."

"So what?"

So, if you don't want to be girlfriend/boyfriend with Chance, that's fine. Keeping your options open is great. But..." She stopped.

"But what?"

"Well," Liesl continued, "that means *he* doesn't have to be exclusive with *you*, either."

What?

I thought about that for a few minutes, a growing feeling of discomfort rising in my chest. I felt a red haze descend into my face. I was staring off into the distance, as Liesl watched.

My breathing became heavy, and I felt... I wasn't sure.

"Yeah, Holly?" said Liesl.

I looked up at her.

"That feeling you're having?" she continued.

I waited.

"It's called jealousy and possessiveness."

I blinked.

Liesl put her hand up. "Don't worry. It's not as bad as it sounds."

"It's not? Because it sounds pretty bad."

What was my body feeling? Was I okay with this?

"Look, Chance is your first crush. I've been crushing on various boys since I was eleven," Liesl said with a smirk.

I stared at her.

"All it means is that you like him."

"Oh, I think..." I started.

"No, I don't mean 'like him' — I mean you REALLY LIKE HIM. Like, Holly, he's captured your heart. You're crushing on him, and you don't want anyone else to have him."

"I..." I felt so confused.

"You've kissed, and held hands, right?"

I nodded.

"And he's captured the heat of your heart, right?"

"The... the what? I guess so," I answered uncertainly.

Liesl sighed. "Holly, do you dream of him?"

"Sometimes... I don't know. I also dream of all my friends, what's that supposed to..."

Liesl cut me off. "No, I mean romantically."

"Oh. I don't know."

"Well, my advice is just to take it slow and easy," said Liesl. "Don't rush into anything. You haven't..." she looked at me pointedly.

"Haven't what?" I asked, feeling clueless.

Liesl sighed. "You are hopeless. Let's just go to bed."

"Okay," I answered.

We layback in our beds.

I lay there, staring at the stone ceiling above my head, thinking.

How do I feel about Chance?

I wanted to kiss him, out on the balcony, sure.

But what else?

Part of me didn't know, but another part of me wanted to put my hands inside his clothes and touch him everywhere.

Ravish him.

Everywhere?

I blushed in the dark room.

I felt so warm it started snowing above me.

The next morning, I yawned as I dressed.

"God, I only got a few hours' sleep," I said sleepily to Liesl as she hunted for her shoes under her bed.

"Snowbear? Did you take my cross trainers?" Liesl's muffled voice could be heard from the far side of the blankets.

The snowy ermine, who normally slept next to Liesl's head, beside her on the pillow, trilled from the windowsill.

"Well, help me find them, will you?" said Liesl.

Snowbear chirruped and leaped down to the floor and ran under the bed. A minute later Liesl emerged, shoes in hand, snowy ermine on her shoulder.

"Thank you, love," she kissed her familiar and plopped down on the blankets, and proceeded to put on her shoes.

I shook my head, smiling and yawning.

"I think I need to wake up," I said.

"Yeah, me, too," my roommate replied.

Five minutes later, we headed downstairs and into the dining hall for breakfast.

Chapter Four
Emissary

Liesl and I were the first to arrive, and as we sat with our breakfasts, we chatted.

"What do you think Ó Baoghill will find when she finally gets back into her office?" I asked between mouthfuls of scrambled eggs and toast.

"Not sure," Liesl munched on bacon and looked off into the distance as she thought. "So Merryweather was in the office until... when?"

"I think Chance said he bugged out when the castle was attacked last term," I said.

"Ah, yes. The 'spray my school with water until everything is saved' night? I remember it well," Liesl laughed.

I chuckled. "Yeah, I was determined." I took a sip of grape juice, thinking.

"So if he's been gone over the summer, I wonder why the Academic Council kept the office locked all this time," Liesl said.

"I'm not sure. Maybe to fumigate?" I laughed, then choked a little.

"Hey, hey, hey, you okay there?" Chance ran up and started pounding me on the back.

I sputtered.

He pounded.

I finally found my breath.

"Here," Liesl said, handing me my juice. "Drink."

"Good morning, everyone." Renée walked up with a huge omelet on a plate, and a glass of orange juice. "Did you all hear what the headmistress found?"

Chance looked up. "I heard who she found, though I didn't see them."

"What, what?" I asked.

Renée sat down and leaned over. "Professor Ó Baoghill sent a missive to the council overnight."

"Overnight?" Liesl asked.

Renée nodded. "Demanding her office be opened immediately. Demanding, no less." She sat back.

We waited.

Finally, I asked, "So...? What happened."

"Well," Renée said, "She got in! Right after dawn."

"How did you find out about this, when I didn't?" Chance asked.

"Probably because *you* went to bed." Renée looked smug. "I mean, I did, too, but I was up a few hours later. The headmistress sent for me; she wanted to know which council members would be awake. Remember I told you last year? My uncle got elected to the council after the flood year before last, when several members drowned?"

Huh?

I looked back and forth at Chance and Renée, a quizzical expression on my face.

"Long story," Chance muttered. "Tell you sometime." He turned back to Renée. "So you saw this all unfold in real time?"

Renée nodded, then yawned. "The headmistress is in her office right now. Oh! I almost forgot. She wants to see you right away, Chance."

He rolled his eyes and got up. "Now you tell me," he muttered as he jogged away.

I turned back to Renée. "So your uncle is on the Academic Council?"

She nodded, chewing her breakfast.

"That's not such a big thingie." Liesl shrugged. "My grandfather was on it for a decade, before he died." She screwed up her face thinking. "This was in... oh... at least fifty years ago."

"Your grandfather was on the council fifty years ago?" I asked.

"Oh, yeah. At least fifty years ago." Liesl nodded. "May have been longer than that. I forget."

I shook my head and took another bite of bacon.

Renée leaned over. "Holly, Liesl's family is of Sylph heritage. They live hundreds of years."

Ahhh.

"Must be nice," I grinned.

Liesl chuckled.

"Oh, look, they're bringing in fresh scones," Renée hopped up and hurried over.

"Oh, I love scones," Liesl got up. She glanced back. "I'll bring you one, don't worry," she said before hurrying off.

I looked down at my plate and shrugged. I still had some scrambled eggs and bacon, and half a glass of grape juice. I munched on a piece of bacon as I watched the two girls descend on the hot plates where the chef was setting the newly baked scones.

They were back in a few minutes, triumphant.

"Here you go. A nice warm raisin scone, split with butter," Liesl announced, setting a plate next to me before sitting down with her own scone.

I looked at the pasty. It was a golden brown, and dotted with dark plump raisins poking out of it. Warm melted butter dripped from a slice going through it flatwise.

I inhaled.

Mmmmm. It smelled delicious.

I took a bite and confirmed: delicious.

We chatted for a few more minutes and finished our food, then began our walk out to the center inside courtyard.

As we passed through the dining hall door, I could see Chance sprinting toward us from the direction of the headmistress's office.

"Holly, you have to come, quick." Chance panted, catching his breath. "The Oak King Faction has... they've..." He bent his head and tried again.

"Chance, calm down," I said. "Why are you so upset?"

He started explaining again. "The Oak King Faction has filed a formal protest with the Elfen Ministry!"

"The what?" Renée, Liesl, and I all exclaimed at the same time.

A student pushed from behind, trying to get out of the dining hall.

Renée nudged us off to the side, "Let's get out of the way." She turned back to Chance. "Now, explain everything," she demanded.

"I don't know everything. But I know that the formal protest they filed is demanding that Holly be returned to Elfen lands. They are demanding she be reassigned to the Elfen Academy there."

"WHAT?" My voice rose. I could feel heat flood my face.

"Yes, and there's an emissary from the Elfen Court in Ó Baoghill's office right now. The headmistress wants you to come right now."

I put my head down.

"Will these fools never stop?" I heard Renée mutter.

"Holly, you can't leave. You just can't," whispered Liesl.

I looked up at Chance. "So I have to skip the first classes of the semester and go now to the headmistresss' office and meet this... this emissary?"

He nodded.

My face must be bright red with how hot it feels.

I balled my hands into fists. My father was the Holly King, his realm was the Fae Folk lands. I belonged here, at Titania Academy. Period.

"Well, fine. I will meet this emissary. I'll just tell them that I'm not leaving this Academy, not for any reason."

Fuming, I started walking.

My mind raced as I walked, with Liesl, Renée, and Chance trailing behind.

I will not let them remove me from Titania Academy. I have my classes to attend, I have private lessons from both Professor Farryn and Chance to attend. This is my home.

My father has dumped a buttload of money into this school to ensure I will have a place here for years to come.

"Can they make her leave?" Liesl whispered behind me.

Chance answered quietly, and I did not hear what he said.

I stopped and swung around.

"What?" I said in an angry voice.

Chance said, "Nothing. Let's just go see what's going on."

"I am *not* leaving Titania Academy," I practically yelled. "Not for any reason. Do you hear me?"

Chance nodded.

"Does everyone understand me?" I swung around, yelling at the large courtyard as a whole.

Students paused as they hurried here and there, some raised a power fist and nodded.

They were on my side.

Good.

Because this fight the Oak King Faction was waging against me was getting really old.

"I refuse to leave Fae Folk lands, too." I yelled out. "And no one can force me out. My father is the friggin' king!"

I fumed, fists clenched at my side, face red.

My ears burned.

My friends just stared at me. I looked from one face to the other.

Renée, the big-sister friend who I looked up to.

Chance, gorgeous boyfriend I was extremely fond of.

Well, I guess I do think of him as my boyfriend, huh?

Then there was Liesl, my friend from the very first hour. As I looked at her, I noticed her stricken look. She looked ready to cry.

I rushed forward, and she caught me in a hug, and we held on to each other for dear life.

For a long time.

Long enough so that the sounds of the school morning slowly returned to my ears, and the students started moving again, going to class.

Going to class.

This was the first day of my second year.

I'd been looking forward to Second Year classes for forever.

I opened my eyes, still in Liesl's embrace. I saw Chance next to us, his hand slowly rubbing circles on my back.

Renée was on my other side, a sympathetic look on her face as she patted my shoulder.

Everything was going to be okay.

Everything had *to be okay.*

I drew away from Liesl and wiped my eyes.

"Shoot, maybe now would be a good time for Father to appear and save the day, huh?" I chuckled, trying to stop the tears from coming.

My father was The Holly King. He ruled over Fae Folk land for half the year. He'd conceived me, with my mother, who was of Elfen Folk. It was weird. But I was okay with being weird. Heck, I was just getting used to being this extra weird.

The half of the year that my father was in a magical slumber, his brother, The Oak King, ruled. The followers of The Oak King were a tight group of power-hungry Fae Folk who wanted more than anything to overthrow The Holly King and keep their king in power for the entire year. They were called the Oak King Faction, and it sometimes seemed like they acted all by themselves. The Oak King himself wasn't with them, so it wasn't clear whether they were renegades acting in his name, or whether he was orchestrating everything behind the scenes.

But what was crystal-clear was that they hated me. There were even Oak King Faction students, undercover and acting on the Faction's political goals, right here at the school. They'd made my first year at Titania Academy a living hell. Especially the first semester.

I had hoped things would calm down here during Second Year. I was hoping they'd leave me alone.

I guess that was too much to hope for.

I looked down the hall at the outer entrance to the headmistress's office.

My feet didn't want to budge.

I swallowed.

Suddenly, Chance stood in front of me.

I looked in his eyes.

"Did you see the emissary, Chance? Did you see them? What do they look like? Was that them who arrived yesterday, in the cloudy streak of white?" I was talking so fast Chance couldn't get a word in edgewise.

He slowly shook his head. "I didn't get a look at them. I haven't even been inside Ó Baoghill's office." He took a shuddering breath. "The headmistress met me in the lobby of her office. She was talking with her secretary when I arrived. Holly, the look on the headmistress's face, it was... I don't know. She looked shocked."

Fresh tears flowed down my face.

"So it's serious?" I asked. "I was hoping I could take a stand. You know, refuse to leave?"

I heard Renée mumble something under her breath, and swung around to look at her. "What did you say, Renée?"

"I said, that didn't work out very well last spring, though, Holly." She looked sympathetic.

I stared at her, unbelieving.

"I just don't want you to get hurt," Renée said.

"Oh, God...," Liesl moaned.

Chance placed his palms gently on either side of my face. He looked deeply into my eyes.

Not saying a word, he lowered his full lips to mine, closing his eyes.

I closed mine as I felt his lips touch mine.

The kiss was gentle and warm. He kissed me with soft passion, and then broke off and touched his cheek to mine.

As his face was against mine, he whispered softly.

"Holly, please, fight this. Don't leave Titania Academy. Please." He withdrew and backed up a foot, still looking deeply into my eyes. "I don't want you to get hurt either, but please try hard to fight this, as I will fight on your behalf."

I nodded, my heart warm and my cheeks flush from the kiss and his touch.

"Can we wake my father, to come fight for me as well?" I whispered.

"The Holly King is under the earth spell for another two months at least, since he was awakened early already once this year, to do so again would bring him immense harm, or worse, I fear," Chance whispered.

Oh, God...

"Okay, okay, well," I straightened my uniform and looked down at my feet, then up again. "I'm fifteen now. I am stronger than I was last spring, and stronger still than I was last year. I can handle this problem without him."

I felt determined.

I turned toward the headmistress' office and started walking again.

I breathed deeply, feeling strong.

Nothing on earth could keep me from staying at my school, at Titania Academy. Nothing could tear me from my home.

I walked through the first door, my friends following me.

The secretary was expecting me.

"Miss Ó Cuilinn, go right on in; they're expecting you." She gestured to the inner door.

Chance, Renée, and Liesl must've looked at her expectantly as well, because she waved again. "Sure, go on in, the headmistress didn't say you were not allowed."

We filed in.

Professor Ó Baoghill was at her desk, a cup of tea in her hands, talking to her visitor, who was seated with their back to the door we'd just entered.

She looked up at our arrival.

"Oh, good, you're here, Miss Ó Cuilinn. I'd like you to meet the Elfen Chancellor Executor, Lord Amynn Umeqirelle. Lord Umeqirelle, may I present Miss Holly Ó Cuilinn."

I took a deep breath.

I would tell this Elfen whatever to go back to his lands, that I would not be coming there, that I would not be recognizing his authority over me, and that he was not welcome here at my school.

I watched as the figure sitting before the headmistress slowly rose and turned to greet me.

The breath left my lungs, I gasped so abruptly.

The Elfen emissary was tall and platinum blond, and he was the spitting image of Legolas from the *Lord of the Rings* movies my aunt had snuck me into.

He was gorgeous.

Chapter Five
Lord Umegirelle

The tall Elfen emissary came around the chairs and walked up to me, and bowed deeply, from the waist down. He bowed so low his long, platinum-blond hair touched the floor next to him.

He slowly rose back to his full height, then leaned forward and extended his hand.

I was mesmerized.

I wasn't sure what to do.

Is he trying to shake my hand in greeting?

I assumed he was, so I place my small hand in his outstretched one.

He slowly bent and kissed the top of my hand, murmuring, "Greetings, Princess Holly."

PRINCESS?

We all proceeded to sit, at the headmistress' request. There were only three chairs, and I sat in the one to the far right, my friends gathered behind me. Chance, Liesl, and Renée all stood tall in a semicircle around the back of my chair, in silent support.

But I wasn't sure I needed support.

This was feeling less and less like an attack and a forceful ejection from Titania Academy and the Fae Folk lands, and more and more like a respectful and jovial greeting from my mother's people.

The headmistress spoke a lot about how the Lord Emissary from the Elfen Lands was an honored guest here at Titania Academy, and practically gushed over him, extending an invitation for an overnight stay, and a tour of the castle and grounds.

Nothing was said of any demands that I leave school, and nothing was mentioned about the Oak King Faction.

It was bewildering.

Also, I kept finding it hard to concentrate.

Lord Umeqirelle was extremely subdued, quiet in voice with a deep brown thrum to his tone. He was very respectful and deferential to the headmistress, who was utterly charmed.

As for me? Well, this Elfen Folk man was the first I had ever met.

I had never even set eyes on any Elfen Folk, ever.

I found him incredible.

I could not take my eyes off him.

Whenever he spoke, my heart felt strangely pulled to his voice. I felt a warmth in my body and felt very drawn to this incredible person, who was the first of my mother's people I had met.

I found myself staring at his face, at his hands folded in his lap, at his entire presence. His posture, his radiance, the way he sat in his chair, the manner in which he kept referring back to me with a deferential nod of his head. He was acting extremely respectful, and it made me want to soak him up.

Every bit of him.

I inhaled slowly, savoring the scent of him.

He was enchanting.

He was looking at me.

My attention was pulled back to the conversation.

"Miss Ó Cuilinn? Miss Ó Cuilinn?" the voice of the headmistress finally penetrated my thoughts when Liesl gently tapped my shoulder and whispered, "Holly."

I blinked.

"Yes? Sorry? Can you repeat that?" I said.

"Certainly, dear," Professor Ó Baoghill said with a smile. "I was asking you if you'd like to accept Lord Umeqirelle's invitation to visit the Elfen lands?"

What?

I felt confused. When had they spoke of my mother's lands?

A few moments of silence ticked by. No one spoke. The Lord Emissary was looking at me, a polite smile on his face, expecting an answer. The headmistress was looking at me, a strained smile on her face, looking like she wanted me to say something.

Anything.

The silence stretched on.

Finally, Chance cleared his throat.

"Er, if I may, headmistress? Lord Umeqirelle?" he said.

The headmistress looked relieved *someone* was breaking the uncomfortable silence. "Ah, Lord Umeqirelle, if I may introduce Mr. Mac Craith, Scholar of the Lost Fae, Seeker of Foundlings, appointed by the Academic Council to serve Titania Academy."

Lord Umeqirelle rose to his feet and bowed, shaking Chance's hand.

I blinked in surprise. I had no idea Chance had such a long, official title.

Chance seemed appreciative of the respect Lord Umeqirelle gave him.

"Please, sir, have a seat," Chance said.

The Lord Emissary sat back down and waited expectantly for Chance to speak.

Chance cleared his throat again. "Headmistress," he nodded at Professor Ó Baoghill, "Lord Umeqirelle," he gave a short bow to the Lord Emissary. "If I may explain. This is the start of Holly's second year at Titania Academy. Classes started this morning, in fact, we are missing them as I speak. Holly also has special lessons in the coming weeks with both myself," he placed his hand on his chest, "and Professor Farryn, our Master of Sciences," Chance explained. "I am not sure Holly can be spared to leave school right now."

I watched Lord Umeqirelle blush a bright pink.

WHOA.

The Lord Emissary rose from his seat, rising half way up while he spoke. "Madam Headmistress, I had no idea Holly was missing classes to meet with us. Please, I propose that Holly immediately attend all her classes this week, and if I may alter the invitation to her," he turned in deference to me. "Princess, would you like to visit the lands of your mother's family ... perhaps ... on the occasion of the weekend?" He bowed his head as he sat back down.

I felt a buzzing in my head.

I was able to get one thought through to my brain before being towed under by the Elfen man's charms once again.

He is *so* formal.

And then I was gone once more. Staring at his eyes as he looked at me. My eyes wandering over his beautiful face, down his chest, to his hands, folded in his lap once again.

I finally noticed his uniform, if it could be called that.

He was dressed in ornate gold brocade, his outfit a broad, formal coat that extended down to his knees, and gave way to matching ornate trousers, and finally, ivory boots, tastefully decorated with what looked like yellow and white diamonds.

He is a fine, fine dresser. A gorgeous man.

Liesl was nudging me again.

I looked over at her.

"Say 'yes,' Holly," she was muttering out of the corner of her mouth.

I blinked at her.

She gave me an insistent look. "Say 'yes.'. 'YES.' SAY IT."

I blinked again, then turned to regard the Lord Emissary and the headmistress. Both were, once again, looking at me, waiting for me to respond.

To what?

I had once again lost track of the conversation.

Why does this keep happening to me?

Liesl nudged me again.

"Er," I cleared my throat. "Um, yes. Yes, that will be fine."

What am I agreeing to? Oh, wait. I remember now.

I put my finger up. "Um, although ...," I said, a tiny bit louder than before."

Everyone looked back at me, and I continued. "I would like to bring a companion along. It's not ... right ... that I go alone to a strange place without ... a friend."

I finished and sat back.

I felt Chance stir at my side.

Before my boyfriend could say a word, the Lord Emissary spoke.

"We agree. You may bring one female companion with you, er... to retain propriety, Princess." He smiled at me, then turned to the headmistress with raised eyebrows.

"Yes, that sounds fine. Miss Ó Cuilinn. You and Miss Becker will attend all your classes this week," the headmistress fixed Liesl and me with a pointed look. "And keep up with all your studies, and you may travel Friday afternoon. You must return by Monday morning classes. If this is agreeable to Lord Umeqirelle?" She looked to our visitor for approval.

The Lord Emissary nodded and rose from his chair. "Of course, anything the Princess agrees to is fine with us." He turned to face Liesl. "And this is agreeable to the Princess' companion?"

Liesl nodded. "Of course." she smiled at the Elfen man.

Why isn't Liesl affected by his presence? Can't she see he's absolutely gorgeous?

But they were talking again, and everyone was standing up.

I rose from my chair.

"Wait," I said. They all looked at men expectantly. I closed my eyes and took a deep breath, trying to clear my head. "Chance said the Oak King faction had filed some kind of protest with the Ministry?"

The headmistress nodded her head, "This is true, Miss Ó Cuilinn. We got the notice this morning. In fact, Lord Umeqirelle arrived shortly after I was informed of the complaint."

The Lord Emissary stood. "This is actually why I came, Miss Ó Cuilinn. Our own Elfen Council sent me. But do not worry: Nothing has been decided, and you are not being forced to leave Fae Folk lands or Titania Academy."

I let out an audible breath of relief.

Lord Umeqirelle continued. "We are just inquiring, investigating, if you will, the question of which school, and which Faerie lands, Miss Ó Cuilinn should be assigned to."

I felt indignant. "I should go where I want to go! It's not fair that my future be decided by other people. *I* should decide."

The Lord Emissary put his hands up in defense and closed his eyes for a moment. "Calm down, Princess. Please sit back down. Let's all take a deep breath, shall we?" He waited until I sat back down. "Now, imagine, just imagine, if you had been approached by an Elfen student finder, and invited to the Elfen Academy, and had moved there, instead of to Fae Folk lands. You would very likely had made Elfen friends there, and loved your experience. You see? It's all a matter of perspective. That is why I think a short visit is a good idea: you can have a taste of different possibilities. You can see what options you have. You can make an informed decision, Princess."

"But my mother didn't have ties to the Elfen lands," I protested. "She lived as a human, and was probably only half Elfen, I'm told. She did not live in Elfen lands, why should I?"

He held his hands up again. "Just visit. These are your mother's people: You never know, you might fit in better in our land. After all, I'm told your experience at Titania Academy has not been entirely positive for you, hmmm?"

I looked from him to the headmistress, who made a face that said she was not the one who told the Elfen lord about my being bullied.

Then who told him? How did he find out? And what exactly is going on?

I thought about my mother as I looked at this tall, gorgeous Elfen man. The people in the Elfen lands were my mother's people. Or were they?

Thinking about my mother led me to think about Aunt Clare, and what she had told me about my mother.

And ... wait just a minute. I had two parents. And my father was my guardian, no one else. My living father.

I felt my head filling with fogginess again.

What is that?

"Wait," I said. I shook my head, trying to clear the fog I felt. "Should I have my father notified? Um, his liaison? Or, whoever is in charge of communicating with him? He's my only parent, after all." I looked up at the grownups who were, in my mind, supposed to be acting responsibly.

The Elfen Lord Emissary raised his hand. "It's only a few days' visit, over the weekend. Not a lot of time, Princess. You'll be back by Monday morning, after all. I don't think there's any need to involve the king."

Hmmm.

I looked at the headmistress, who was blinking her eyes rapidly. "Oh, no, no," she repeated the Lord Emissary's words. "No need to involve the king."

Chance shifted uneasily next to me, but didn't say a word.

After a minute, the headmistress spoke again. "Very well, Miss Ó Cuilinn, Miss Becker, Mr. Mac Craith, Miss Page, you should all hurry to join your respective classes in session. I will send word to your professors on why you are tardy." She turned back to the Lord Emissary. "Well, then Lord Umeqirelle, I can give you that tour of the castle and grounds, if you'd like? We have accommodations for your stay with us..."

We were escorted out of the headmistress' office by the secretary, who seemed to have appeared out of nowhere. As we exited the inner doors, I realized with a start that the Elfen Lord had come with a guard.

Two Elfen footmen stood at attention on either side of the inner door; they had been facing us the entire time, watching us as we conducted what I had thought was a private conversation.

They were platinum-haired, and dressed in uniform, although their attire in no way matched the opulence of the ornate costume worn by Lord Umeqirelle. They stared straight ahead and held ceremonial spears, and did not seem to notice our passage at all.

Although if we moved to harm the Lord Emissary, something tells me they'd notice.

We passed through the outer door, the secretary holding it open for us, and shutting it firmly behind us.

I felt almost hurried out.

The fogginess in my head was slowly lifting as I walked along.

"Come on. First class has already passed. We have nearly half an hour before the next one starts," said Renée.

I shook my head as I walked, trying to clear the last bits of... whatever it was I felt.

"Come on, let's get an energy drink," Chance suggested. "Holly was way more affected than anyone else." He took my hand and led me back toward the dining hall, my friends following.

Chance led me to a table, and pointed. "Sit. We have to talk." Then walked off to get the drinks.

Renée and Liesl took seats next to me.

"Do you know what he's on about?" I asked the taller upperclassman.

"Yes, I think I do," Renée answered. "It's actually not good news."

A chill went up my back.

Chance was back with four tall, icy cans, and distributed them all around, then sat across from me.

We popped the tops and took sips, and I watched Chance over the rim of my drink, waiting for him to speak.

The fizzy orange coolness of the energy drink sizzled down my throat.

Ahhhh, that's so good.

I took another swallow, then another.

I began to calm down.

Stress is a killer.

I wasn't sure what was stressing me more, Chance or the fact that I left the headmistresses' office and been parted from the most gorgeous man I had ever laid eyes on.

I sighed and closed my eyes, then opened them again.

Chance was watching me.

I waited.

He stared at me a few minutes while he drained the contents of his can, then crushed it in his fist and threw it into a nearby trash can.

He turned back to me.

"Okay," he said. "The first thing you need to know is that, Mr. Lord Whatever-his-name-is? Was trolling you."

"What?" I felt confused as I set my can on the table.

"He was in full, full on power glamour. That's why you were swooning and couldn't concentrate worth crap." Chance sat back, his arms folded over his chest.

I blinked.

What?

Renée put her hand on my arm. "He's right, Holly. I think it affected you more powerfully because you're half Elfen. But even the headmistress was affected. Hell, I could feel it coming off him like a heat. It blew me back a bit at first."

I glanced at Liesl. "And you? Could you feel it, too?"

Liesl nodded slowly. "I'm less susceptible to Elfen magic, being of sylph heritage, but yeah. I noticed. How could anyone *not* notice?"

"Holly," said Renée. "There's another thing, too."

"What," I asked, feeling grouchy.

"Well," Renée continued, glancing uneasily at Liesl and Chance. "How do I put this...? It's... it's rather rude to do what he did. For an adult man to power glamour a young girl..."

"Hey, I just turned fifteen!" I protested.

"He's probably several hundred years old, Holly," Liesl murmured.

"...a young girl," Renée repeated, "it's considered... creepy. Rude. Unacceptable. Unethical, even." She sat back.

I blinked.

The phrase "dirty old man" came to mind.

Suddenly, I remembered something. "Chance, when I first met you, you said you kept your glamour on, so you'd blend in..."

"That's a normal appearance glamour, Hols. Mister Elfen Dude had on a bright power glamour, something totally different. Even you have on a slight appearance glamour, right now."

"We all do," Liesl said.

I took a deep breath.

"Okay, so the beautiful man who looks like he's straight out of a Tolkien movie was being rude and creepy? Is that what you're saying?" I asked.

They all nodded.

"Then why didn't the headmistress say something? Hmmm? Why didn't the secretary?" I asked, my eyebrows raised.

"I'm not sure," Chance said slowly. "But it's something that should be discussed with her, absolutely."

"She might have been affected herself," Renée ventured. "She seemed overly charmed when we first came into the room."

"True dat," said Liesl. "It was weird."

I thought of something that had been bothering me. "Chance, it seemed rather odd that the two adults in the room were against telling my father about this visit to faraway lands. I thought that was weird. And not very responsible."

Chance nodded slowly. "Yeah, that was way weird," he said. "I mean, on the one hand, the king is deep in hibernation, so it's kind of hard to inform him or get his permission. On the other hand, you were absolutely right in wondering if the king's liaison shouldn't be told, in case of an emergency."

"Who's the king's liaison?" Asked Liesl.

"Welllllll... Brendan and I are, but the Elfen Lord didn't know that," said Chance.

"Professor Ó Baoghill must know that, though," said Renée.

Chance turned to her with a smile. "Actually, no, she doesn't. The king's liaison is a secret, and changes periodically. She knows how to send a message, but that message goes to a second person, then a third, then to the liaison, and thence to the king."

"Sounds like a lot of chances for a mix-up," Renée murmured.

"The people trusted to relay messages to the king are ironclad," Chance said. "I should know, I'm one of them." He grinned.

"Is that why you didn't speak up when the headmistress and Lord Emissary were saying not to bother the king?" I asked. "Because you're the liaison?"

"Exactly. They didn't want to bother the king, but *I* know what's happening, and so I can use my judgement and 'bother the king' if I need to."

I thought for a minute. "I guess I feel better about things now. Still... I wish you were going with me, Chance." I turned to Liesl, "No offense."

My roommate shrugged, "Hey, I wish Chance was going, too." She winked at my boyfriend.

"It *was* a little creepy how the Elfen lord seemed to want to make sure your companion was a girl, Holly," Renée added. "Be careful with that, okay?"

I nodded. I would be careful.

I wasn't leaving until the end of the week, which seemed a long time from now.

Before that, I had classes, and private lessons, a full five days' worth.

A long time.

Chance looked at his phone. "It's nearly time for the next class. We need to go." He got up from his chair. "But Holly, you need to be more skeptical."

"Yeah, don't fall for a pretty face so readily," Renée said, hefting her book bag onto her shoulder.

"Come on, Holly, let's go. I'll explain it more on the way," Liesl pulled at my arm.

We left for class.

As we walked, Liesl bent toward my ear and asked, "And why did he keep calling you 'princess'?"

I shrugged and kept walking.

I had taken it as an older man's affectionate way to talk to me.

Nothing more.

Chapter Six
Friday is Here

The week went by very quickly, probably because I was so nervous.

"I'm not sure I want to go," I confided in Liesl on Thursday night.

Our bedtime chats were a destressing ritual I looked forward to, and as we lay on our sides, facing each other in our respective beds, the window let in just enough light to hold back the shadows so we could see each other as we talked.

"But Holly, aren't you curious?" Liesl said. "This is the land your mother's family came from."

"Really, Aunt Clare didn't mention anything about Mama even being nonhuman, let alone from another land," I said quietly. "I'm not sure how much I believe."

"Do you think your father was wrong? Isn't he the one who told you your mother was Elfen Folk?" asked Liesl.

I pondered this for a long time. Finally, I answered. "I don't think Father was wrong. I mean, he's the king, after all. I don't think he would tell me something that wasn't true."

I hesitated.

"What?" Liesl asked.

"Well," I said softly. "I never got the idea that Mother was someone of great importance in the Elfen world." I sat up. "You know how the Lord Emissary was calling me 'Princess' and how he came all this way to see me and arrange the visit and all? Why would he do that if my mother was just a regular, common, poor girl from the Elfen countryside? Father never mentioned she was an individual of royalty or political importance."

"That's true. It was kind of weird how he kept calling you 'Princess', I think," said Liesl. "He never explained it. I think if he had come to visit a royal Elfen princess he would have said you were royal."

"Yeah, exactly. I took it as him just being sweet, calling me 'Princess' and everything. But it kind of contradicts why he would make the trip for a nobody."

"Maybe the Elfen Folk want all the Elfen in Elfen land?" Liesl wondered. "Even half Elfen Folk?"

"I don't know," I said. "I wish I knew more."

The next morning was Friday, and we had classes and the last day of private training.

Since we'd be gone the entire weekend, I decided to pack early. I was up at dawn, too excited to sleep.

I packed a small bag Chance had loaned me. I put in clothes, underwear, my extra shoes, and, after thinking a minute, a few more things, to help me through the stress. I brought out the birthday necklace Chance had given me last summer, before I even got to the Academy. It had been a present from my father, and Chance had delivered it for him.

I stared at the green-leaf-and-red-holly-berry design on the charm, the gold winking in the sunlight peeking through the window.

The necklace was precious to me, and I had felt its magic coming through during times of trial.

I slipped it over my head, affixing the clasp securely behind my neck. I patted it where it lay on my collarbone.

Normally, I kept it in a lockbox safe in my room, but it felt better to wear it on this trip.

Next, I brought the rose forward. The magic rose that had grown from the ground where my tears had spilled onto Jacob Miller's grave in old, decrepit Saint Raymond's Cemetery near the Throgg's Neck burrow in New York City last spring.

The rose had granted me safe passage, kept the portal open so I could pass through from the Realm of the Dead, where I'd unknowingly ventured, back to the modern world I belonged.

The old ghost of a medieval knight named Markus had helped me, and I had felt the magic from the rose, now long dried out, still emanating from it.

I kissed the dried petals.

"Just in case," I whispered, before tucking it in the side of my bag, where it would be held securely by a book I was also bringing.

"Old Roads and Finding Your Way Back," by Provost, was a treatise on time travel using the old roads that crisscrossed the lands, many following the old ley lines. It was said to be helpful in bringing travelers safely home. Professor Farryn had recommended it.

I stood up and sighed.

Liesl sat up in bed. "I had the weirdest dream, Holly."

A chill ran up my spine. "Was it about this weekend?"

"No, it was about Jack and me," she said. "We were playing soccer together, but there was no one else on the teams, and we were playing in the clouds."

"What?" I asked, bewildered.

"Then he kicked the ball, and it went sideways, and I ran for it," she said. "But it fell over the side of the cloud and fell to earth." She looked at me and giggled. "It was the most random, ridiculous dream."

I threw a balled-up sock at her.

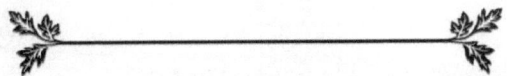

Later that day, I was just finishing up my second private lesson. Classes had gone smoothly, and the lessons with Professor Farryn on Concealment were going really well.

"You're a natural, Miss Ó Cuilinn," said Professor Farryn.

I grinned. I had successfully mastered Concealment, sliding through walls and doors, and fading, after only five days' practice.

"It's almost as if you're part ghost, Holly," laughed Liesl. "Seriously spooky."

"But not surprising at all, considering Miss Ó Cuilinn's heritage," said Professor Farryn.

I turned my head sharply. "What?"

Professor Farryn was famous for picking up information and storing it in his mind, and then dribbling it out here and there to the younger Fae Folk. Being several hundred years old, this probably came naturally to him.

He looked at me, a small smile on his face. "Miss Ó Cuilinn, ask the king about his own Tylwyth Teg heritage sometime." He winked at me.

Oh, lordie...

Several hours later, I faced Chance in the dying light of late afternoon. I crouched, my magical staff in my hands, balancing easily on the balls of my feet.

Chance approached me again, slowly walking sideways and looking off to the left.

But I knew his stance was a ruse. I gripped my staff and brought the tip up, and closed my eyes.

I could sense Chance approaching closer.

My energy surged, and I brought the staff down hard.

WHAM! The base of the staff thumped against the ground and let out a huge thud. A wave of power flowed out from the point of impact, rolling out rapidly more than fifty feet.

Chance was flipped over backward.

Off on the steps, safely out of range, Liesl clapped her hands from where she sat. I heard her let out a WHOOP!

Grinning, I stepped forward and stretched out a hand to help Chance up, which he gladly took.

"That was the best one of all," he said, brushing grass clippings off his legs.

I felt gratified I had learned Chance's lessons so quickly.

"Now, remember. Carry the staff with you when you travel," he said. "You've practiced fading with it?"

I nodded. "Sure have. Works great every time." To demonstrate, I concentrated and vanished, the staff disappearing with me. A few seconds later, I reappeared.

"Excellent," said Chance. "I almost feel sorry for anyone bothering you."

Liesl ran up to us. "Holly, you ready?"

"Nearly. I just need to shower and change." I was sweaty after the hours of private lessons from Professor Farryn and Chance.

"Okay, hurry though," Liesl said. "I think the Lord Emissary might already be waiting in the headmistress' office."

"Well then, he can wait," I said. "I stink."

Liesl laughed.

Chance nodded, "Yes."

I grinned, and hurried up to my dorm room, staff in hand.

Ten minutes later, I came down the steps, freshly washed, staff clean, bag slung over my shoulder.

Liesl was already waiting in the center inner courtyard, her own bag at her feet.

Chance and Renée waited next to her.

I hugged them both tightly.

"Listen, keep in touch, okay?" Renée whispered in my ear. "And let us know if you need help." She pulled back and looked into my eyes, her hands still grasping my shoulders. She held my gaze for a minute.

I nodded.

Renée nodded back, then stepped to the side to give Chance a turn at goodbyes.

I stepped up to him.

He embraced me, laying his warm cheek against mine. He smelled of the freshly mowed grass he had tumbled over, and... something else. He held me a long time, not saying anything.

My arms were around him, and I closed my eyes, feeling warmth growing in my chest.

Oh, Chance.

He pulled back slightly and brought forward something that had been in his bag.

"Here," he said, placing a small book in my hands. "I've been working on this for a while now. Rushed and finished it last night, so I could give it to you."

I took it.

It was a small book, hand-bound. It smelled of leather and parchment.

"It's a book of poems I wrote for you, I've been writing them since I met you," he said. "I wrote the first one back in New York City, in that bakery we got you those rainbow bagels." He smiled.

"Oh, Chance..." I smiled and felt tears form in the corners of my eyes. Then I chuckled. "I remember that shop. Those bagels were delicious." I looked down at the book, then hugged it to my chest. "Thank you," I whispered, raising my lips to his.

He kissed me gently. He smelled of spearmint toothpaste.

I leaned against him, savoring his kiss and his warmth more than ever.

I wish Chance was going with us.

The sound of a cleared voice filled my ears, and I opened my eyes reluctantly.

"Princess, friend of Princess, are you ready?" The voice of Lord Umeqirelle came from the side.

I turned and saw him standing there, his two guards behind him. The headmistress, Professor Ó Baoghill, was there as well. They waited expectantly.

I pulled back from my friends and straightened my traveling tunic.

"Hello again," I said. I glanced at Liesl and nodded, taking her hand. "We're ready."

"Very good, Princess," the Lord Emissary said. "We shall depart immediately." He turned to the headmistress. "Madam, thank you for your hospitality. The week has been... most enlightening." He bowed.

Professor Ó Baoghill blushed.

"Wait!" Professor Farryn came running down the stairs as fast as a three-and-a-half-foot-tall mountain dwarf could run, holding an envelope. He trotted up to me.

"Miss Ó Cuilinn..." He stopped, bending over slightly and breathing hard, then straightened. "Thank goodness I caught you. Here." He handed me the thick envelope. "Here," he said again. "This is... to open after you're settled in your guest quarters in the Elfen lands." He nodded and took a step back. Looking deeply into my eyes, he nodded again.

"Have a safe weekend." He glanced at Liesl. "Both of you." He smiled and took another step back, then stepped to the side to stand beside the headmistress.

I looked down at the envelope he'd handed me, wondering what was inside. The envelope's contents were clearly important. "Thanks, Professor." I tucked it into a side slot in my bag, then lowered the bag's flap over it, and patted it.

Safe and sound.

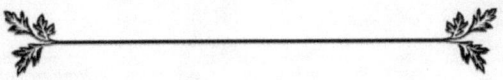

Chapter Seven
In the Elfen Realm

That evening, Liesl and I found ourselves in a huge Elfen courtyard, surrounded by a ring of massive, ancient trees. Beyond the trees, we could see city lights all around us. Tall white spires rose above ancient architecture, stretching out before us in a city to rival that of any land.

Our host, Lord Umeqirelle, led us to a tower on the outskirts of the city. This is where we would be staying during our visit.

Whereas most of the buildings in the Fae Lands had been built with dark, natural stone, accentuated with wood, the Elfen buildings had been fashioned from white stone. When I asked later, I was told it was a combination of white marble and white quartz.

The architecture was tall and thin, drawing the eye naturally upward, toward the sky.

We weren't staying at the Academy, which was some distance outside the city. I wanted to see the school, but I was also relieved. Maybe they weren't going to force me to attend there, after all. Besides, our suite was very nice. And, like the rest of the city, very .... white: walls, floor, and ceiling. We had a small living room, a larger bedroom with two beds, and a bathroom.

We set our things down and sat on the pristine white covers of our respective beds.

"Not unlike our dorm room," Liesl remarked.

I just stared.

The walls were so white, the effect was almost blinding.

After a moment, I got up and walked over to the large bay window. I could see the countryside and other buildings from my vantage point.

I drew the white drape across the window, leaving just a few inches open.

The rooms were instantly slightly dimmer. Much more manageable for my eyes.

"Oh, that's way better," said Liesl. "Wow, it was intense."

"Wasn't it? I said.

We explored the rooms and found them to be clean and bright.

"Lord Umeqirelle said to meet him downstairs in a half hour for dinner," said Liesl. "Ready to go?"

I got my brush out of my bag and stood in front of a mirror, studying myself critically. "Almost."

Liesl came to stand next to me. "Need help?"

I hesitated.

"I want to look good, but I also need your help with our host," I said in a small voice.

"So you want to look good for Lord Elfen GorgeousDude, but you don't want him to overwhelm you," said Liesl, instantly summing up the situation. "Gotcha."

I exhaled. "You always understand me," I smiled and began drawing the hairbrush through my thick locks.

"Want me to braid your hair?" Liesl asked.

"Maybe tomorrow. We don't have enough time tonight," I finished and studied myself critically in the mirror.

"You look fine, Holly," said Liesl. "Really."

"You think so?" I tried to flatten my bushy platinum hair so it would look tamed. "Let me try wetting the hairbrush." I walked into the bathroom.

"It'll just dry later," Liesl called.

"Yeah, but it will definitely help, at least a little," I called back as I brushed the wet bristles through my tresses. The bushiness went down, and I felt satisfied.

I walked out.

"How do I look?" I asked.

Liesl rolled her eyes. "Like a wet-headed geek."

I grinned.

"Come on, I'm starving," she said. "I hope they have yummy food."

We went down to the ground floor, where Lord Umeqirelle was sitting patiently in a chair, waiting.

He rose to his feet and smiled upon seeing us.

"This way, ladies," he murmured politely, and led the way into the side dining room.

An hour later, Liesl and I sat, feeling happy, at the table.

Our meal had been several exotic salads, complete with some vegetables I'd never seen or tasted before. But it had all been delicious.

"Dessert," said Lord Umeqirelle. "You're going to enjoy this, Princess."

The waiter brought a large tray of about a dozen delicacies, different fruits from all over the world.

"Ohhh," I said as I bit into a kiwi. "This is delicious!"

"Those are from Australia," Liesl said. "We spent a week there two summers ago, right before I started at Titania Academy."

Lord Umeqirelle looked at Liesl sharply. "Oh? You've done a bit of traveling, then?"

She nodded as she selected several Mediterranean fruits. "Yes, my mother is a liaison for the queen, and frequently travels for her job."

"Interesting," he murmured.

"Lord Emissary, do you think we could see the countryside tomorrow?" I asked.

He smiled. "Yes, indeed. In fact, I can arrange for a tour of the nearby Elfen land, if that is to your liking."

"That would actually be really nice," said Liesl.

I nodded in agreement.

A new Elfen page appeared and tucked a note discretely next to the Lord Emissary's plate, then backed away out of sight.

Nibbling on the fruit, I watched him. I'd found myself feeling insanely curious since I arrived in the Elfen Lands, not only about the land and the city, but about the surrounding forest.

Liesl leaned over to whisper in my ear, "I think something's up."

The Lord Emissary was reading the note, and his brow was furrowed.

I cleared my throat.

He did not notice at all, didn't look up, didn't seem to hear.

Liesl gave me a look.

"Everything okay?" I asked.

No response at all.

It was my turn to give Liesl a look.

I shrugged, and mouthed "let's wait" — to give the Lord Emissary time to take care of his business.

Liesl and I helped ourselves to more of the exotic fruit. It was really delicious. I tried some kind of grape. It was round and purple on the outside, but when I bit into it, I found the inner flesh was yellow.

Weird.

Liesl giggled.

I gave her a look that said "what?" and she just shook her head and giggled more.

I glanced at the Lord Emissary. He seemed upset about something.

"Ladies, will you excuse me for a minute?" he asked. He waved over the waiter. "Last course, Frib."

The Elfen waiter nodded and left the room, then returned shortly with small dishes of what looked like ice cream. He set them before us.

Lord Umeqirelle nodded and rose from his chair. "I will return in a few minutes. Enjoy your aperitif while I am gone."

Liesl and I nodded, and we both dug into the ice cream with the small, delicate spoons the waiter had provided.

"Ohhh, Holly, this is sooo good," Liesl moaned.

"Mmfff," I answered, my mouth full.

It was indeed good. In fact, it was exquisite. Smooth and delicious, with a flavor I had never tasted.

I leaned over to ask Liesl, "What flavor is this?"

"I think it's lavender cream. But I'm not sure," she said, licking her spoon.

"It is indeed lavender cream," said Lord Umeqirelle walking back into the room. "Ladies, I have some bad news."

We both looked up.

The Elfen Lord looked very serious as he took his seat again.

Liesl and I remained silent for a minute. Then, "Everything okay?" I asked.

He was lost in thought. He looked up, a worried expression on his face. "Not really. Where we are now, we are near Mount Storm. Quite near, in fact."

Liesl inhaled sharply and looked stricken.

"What?" I whispered.

She looked at me. "I've heard of that mountain. It was in the news recently, and the High Council was trying to decide if..." She fell silent and looked down at her now-empty ice cream dish.

Lord Umeqirelle shifted in his seat. "Yes, mmm, well, Miss Becker, the Fae Folk High Council decided not to lend aid, so the Elfen world is on its own in this regard."

"I'm sorry, Sir. I wish they had sent help," Liesl said in a small voice.

I looked from one to the other.

"This sounds serious." I shifted uncomfortably in my seat. "What exactly is the issue? Did you say 'Mount Storm'?"

"I'm sorry, Miss Ó Cuilinn. I forget you are new to the Faerie lands. We are situated to the north of Ireland, in a land not visible to the human world. In fact, Scotland has a land mass three times the size the humans think it is, and it extends to the north and west. These are the Elfen lands. Our land covers an area roughly half the size of the Fae Folk territory, and to the north of the Fae Folk lands. At the northernmost reach of Elfen land is Mount Storm."

"Ah, okay," I said, feeling even more confused than before.

He continued. "Mount Storm is an active volcano. We had hoped the Fae Folk High Council might send aid, but, alas, they have declined." The proud man sounded both hurt and dismissive. "It is a loss, to be sure. The Fae Council has the magic to help; they could contain any blast and minimize the damage to our city. Elfen magic is a different kind of magic, and the best we can do is evacuate and hope the volcano doesn't destroy too much of the city." He cleared his throat and took a deep breath. "Unfortunately, news has just reached us that the volcano's readings have gone off the charts. Its eruption may be unavoidable."

"My gosh," I felt astonished. "What can we do? Are we in any danger here?"

Liesl shifted in her seat. I glanced at her. She was looking out the nearest window.

Ready to bolt to safety, no doubt. But where would we flee to?

"Don't worry, Princess. This building is far enough south so that the nearly the entire city would have to be enveloped before we'd be in danger here," Lord Umeqirelle said. "Besides, the volcano *will* likely erupt, but our scientists have surmised that it will probably be this winter or spring.

I felt slightly less tense, but still worried.

An entire city at risk. My God.

A thought occurred to me. "Why won't the Fae Folk High Council help? It could save lives."

Lord Umeqirelle gave a skeptical grunt. "Unfortunately, Elfen lives are considered not as important as Fae lives. We are the 'ugly ducklings' of the Faerie World. Not important enough to the Fae Folk High Council to send aid in an emergency such as this."

I felt so sad my chest hurt.

"I am so sorry," mumbled Liesl. "If it were up to us, we'd force them to send help."

"We definitely would," I echoed.

"Thank you, both of you. It is heartening to see the youth changing. Maybe someday, the old ways can be made new." He sounded sad.

I looked down at my empty dish.

Perhaps a change of subject.

"That ice cream sure was delicious." I looked up at him and grinned.

He smiled briefly. "It's one of my daughter's favorites. She requested it be provided at your meal, so you could get a taste of 'the best ice cream in the world.' " He chuckled.

"Oh, you have a daughter?" I asked.

Lord Umeqirelle nodded, and his face warmed. "She is my sweet princess. Perhaps you may meet her this weekend."

"You call her 'princess' too?" I asked.

He looked up. "Yes, Princess. It is a term of both reverence and endearment, it is a custom among the Elfen to call young ladies 'Princess.'"

Well, that explains that.

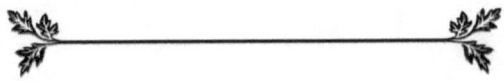

Chapter Eight
The Elfen Youth

The next morning, Liesl and I were up and dressed and waiting for our escort at an early hour. The hotel lobby was deserted, and we sat on a bench in the foyer, waiting and anticipating what we would see during the day.

"Do you think we'll see any other students today?" Liesl asked. "Or do you think they'll have already evacuated?"

"Lord Umeqirelle said they haven't evacuated the city yet," I answered.

"Yeah, but they might have," Liesl said. "You know, overnight or something."

"I think someone would have come to get us. We're in the city, too." I replied.

"But Lord U said we were farther out. I thought, if the school was farther north, they might have..." Her voice trailed off as several people entered the lobby.

Lord Umeqirelle was accompanied by two other Elfen Folk: an older man and a younger woman.

"Greetings, ladies, I trust you slept well?" Lord Umeqirelle said as he walked up. "Today we will tour the Elfen Academy, and I will show you both the surrounding forest gardens." He indicated his two companions. "This is Chancellor Xilmenor of the Elfen High Council."

The older man bowed deeply, his greeting in the Elfen language so rapid I couldn't really understand it, even though I'd been brushing up on familiar Elfen terms to prepare for our trip.

"And this is Miss Alasse Olovalur, she is the vice-headmistress to the Elfen Academy and will be conducting your tour."

The lady grinned and stepped forward.

"How are you two students doing?" She stuck out her hand eagerly.

Liesl and I looked at each other and shrugged. We stepped forward to shake the woman's hand.

She grabbed our hands, and shook them vigorously, up and down, in an exaggerated manner. "I am so happy to meet you! I spent a year in the human world, undercover of course, to better learn about them."

She turned to me, "And are you the transfer student I was told about?"

What?

"Uhh, erm ... We really have to be going, we are late for our appointments," Lord Umeqirelle rushed forward to grab the shoulders of the vice-headmistress and steer her toward the door. "Let's get going. The transport is waiting. Come now..., everyone..."

Weird.

We were hustled rapidly out the door, then rushed down the walkway and around the bend.

I glanced back and saw Lord Umeqirelle whispering urgently into Miss Olovalur's ear; she reacted to whatever he'd told her with an expression of shock.

"Holly!" Liesl squealed. "Look!"

I turned around and saw our "transport" was a massive, ornate carriage, drawn by four unicorns.

I blinked.

Unicorns?!

We slowly approached the beasts, our mouths open.

I glanced at Liesl, then whispered to her, "This is not a normal part of the Fae Folk world?"

She shook her head, her gaze transfixed by the palomino unicorn she was reaching up to pet. "No... I mean, I've heard they live in the northern reaches, but they're super-rare. I've certainly never seen one, not even in a zoo." She slowly touched the animal's neck, drawing her hand down its soft fur.

I reached to touch the unicorn, and placed my hand on its forehead. It dipped its head down, clamping its mouth on the white bit held there by the light leather bridle.

I glanced down at the bit. Every part of the bridle was white, even the fittings. The effect was gorgeous.

I touched the ring of white holding the straps to the unicorn's head.

"Lord Umeqirelle?" I asked over my shoulder.

The Elfen Lord Emissary came near.

"What is this made of?" I asked, holding the ring and straps in my fingers.

He glanced down and in a cursory tone, said, "Quartz, I believe. Carved by artisans." He walked away to consult further with the other Elfen.

I studied the bridle leather. The surface was intricately tooled in swirls and feathers; and was quite beautiful.

The unicorn gently jiggled its head, blowing air out its mouth.

I wonder if it's a girl or a boy?

I walked around Liesl, who was still entranced by the beast, and dipped my head down to look between its hind legs.

Okay, that's a boy, definitely.

"Come, come, everyone. Please enter the carriage. We have to go now," Lord Umeqirelle said in a loud voice, clapping his hands.

We all boarded and settled down into plush velvet seats the color of blood.

Liesl and I sat next to each other, running our hands over the soft cushions. I almost couldn't keep my hands off the material: It was so buttery soft, it felt like heaven under the palm of my hand.

We looked out the windows as the coachman kissed and clucked his tongue to the unicorns, and we started down the gravel road.

Everything around us that was handmade had been constructed in the color white. I imagined most of it was white quartz or white granite. The road was formed from small white stones held in place. The carriage ride was smooth, the wheels turning over effortlessly on the stone roadway.

It was all so different from the Fae Folk land that we couldn't stop staring at everything.

At one point, I glanced over at Miss Olovalur and caught her watching us and smiling broadly.

"I was the same way, when I visited the human world. Everything was just so different!" she said.

"Where did you go? What city?" I asked, curious.

"I was in a city called Los Angeles. It was near an ocean, and it was amazing. Museums, and amusement parks. So many human people! They traveled on immense roadways in cars and trucks. The roads were grey and black! Very few dirt roadways." She looked at me closely. "It must have taken some time for you to become accustomed to all the dirt roads when you moved to the Fae Folk lands, eh, Miss Ó Cuilinn?" she asked.

I blinked.

Was she looking down on the Fae Folk roadways?

I wasn't sure. I mentally shrugged and decided to overlook her tone.

"The dirt roads through the Fae Folk lands are through and around forests. It is entire appropriate for them to be dirt," I said. "And they are well maintained. Besides, they don't have all the traffic and smog you get with human roads."

Liesl spoke up then. "It would look ridiculous if the roads weren't dirt, they are in nature," she said. "We want them to blend in, not look out of place."

Miss Olovalur nodded. "Of course. That makes sense." She smiled and looked out the window.

We were passing along a plain hillside, approaching what appeared to be a forest. But it didn't look like any forest I had ever seen in the Fae Folk lands.

The trees were stunted and dying.

The Fae Folk forest surrounding Titania Academy was huge: Trees grew up several hundred feet, healthy and vigorous natural life.

The trees here were barely a few dozen feet tall, and they looked curled and stunted.

Our carriage was traveling on the road alongside this forest, bringing us quite close to the stunted trees.

I could see the tree bark was covered with some kind of dark coating.

Miss Olovalur remarked, "The trees have been sprayed with the fertilizing coating for the bottom ten feet of their trunks, to help them grow healthy and retard insect attacks. They have been struggling for years, now."

I felt sad. The trees looked like they were losing the battle against whatever was attacking the forest.

I couldn't tell whether it was insects, a fungus, or pollution that was killing the forest.

It almost seemed like the trees were dying because they had failed to thrive.

Glancing at the sky, I saw the horizon was a dull, pale yellow.

"Is that air pollution?" I asked.

"It is from the volcano," Lord Umeqirelle said. "We'll be drawing closer to the mountain in the next ten minutes."

We rode on in silence, and my eyes scanned the sky as we went. The color grew deeper as we drew closer to the mountain.

After another few minutes, my eyes began to sting slightly.

It's almost as if I'm back in New York city. The sky looks polluted with smog.

After ten minutes, the mountain came into view on our left.

It was massive, almost completely obscured by dark roiling clouds of smoke that billowed forth from the top.

"Yep, that's a volcano, for sure," Liesl said grimly. "It looks like an angry volcano at that."

I nodded.

This does not look good.

"We are drawing close to the Elfen Academy," said Lord Umeqirelle.

The carriage turned down another road, and a few miles later the school came into view.

Tall white spires reaching up to the sky; it looked almost like a church.

Impressive.

Ten minutes later we were all disembarking onto the white gravel path in from of the Elfen Academy.

We spent the next three hours touring the Academy.

It was indeed like a church inside as well as out.

White interiors made it nearly blinding, and I had to shield my eyes in places where the sun came through the windows.

We were introduced to the Elfen students.

This school started earlier than Titania Academy, and the students were as young as ten years old.

They lined up in the hallways in an almost militaristic fashion.

The younger students seemed almost alien: Their skin was nearly translucent.

I mentioned it to Liesl in a whisper. "They look almost ethereal."

She nodded.

Thin and slight, almost airy, it seemed like they could blow away in a strong wind.

I said as much to Miss Olovalur.

She nodded. "I remember when I visited the human world. Our children are much different than the human children, or even the Fae Folk children, I think." She looked pointedly at Liesl, who blushed.

"Are they all like this?" I asked. "Are these healthy children?"

Miss Olovalur nodded. "Absolutely." She stopped before a queued line of children. "This is how all Elfen children look."

We all stopped to look.

Lord Umeqirelle stood in the back.

I stared at the children, then looked at him and Chancellor Xilmenor.

Something looks off.

"If I may ask, how old are you all?" I was curious.

Lord Umeqirelle smiled. "I am two-hundred and fifty-seven. In my prime." He glanced at the Chancellor. He asked the older man a question, in the Elfen language.

The old man rumbled a sentence back to him, nodding and smiling.

"The Chancellor is seven-hundred and three," Lord Umeqirelle said. "He is considered older middle-aged, but not close to retirement."

"I am ninety-four," Miss Olovalur said with a grin.

I blinked.

Weird.

"The average lifespan on the Elfen Kind is over a thousand years, Princess," said the Lord Emissary. "Were you not told this?"

I ducked my head in embarrassment. "I did not realize."

I looked back at the children, still lined up.

"Are they lined up for some activity?" I asked.

"Yes," Miss Olovalur said. "Their mornings include an hour of vigorous sport."

I felt surprised.

"Can we watch?" Liesl asked.

We glanced at each other. We had to see what these ethereal, fragile looking children were going to do.

They stayed behind, still lined up behind the doors, as we made our way out to the side yard, which was in sections, green grass surrounded by white stone fencing.

Elfen adults held several balls; the adults all had whistles in their mouths.

We were directed to seating on one side, where we made ourselves comfortable and waited.

Then the doors opened, and the students walked placidly out. But as soon as their feet hit the grass, they all began running and yelling out a fierce roar, until they had all emerged from the building and were out on the grass, running to the far wall.

When they got to the wall, each one turned and leapt up, running along the side for maybe ten feet, their momentum keeping them on their feet, before leaping down again and hitting the grass at a run.

Their ethereal bodies clearly masked a strength humans did not possess.

Liesl and I watched them, open-mouthed.

They ran around the large field, over and over, and each time they came to the wall, they ran up and laterally across it for several strides, before descending to continue sprinting on the grass.

I could never do that.

"That is nuts," Liesl murmured. I glanced at her.

"I'm glad you agree," I said, looking back at the students. "Crazy."

"These kids are definitely not fragile," Liesl whispered in my ear.

I shook my head.

No, they are not.

The display of athleticism lasted nearly an hour.

When it was over, the students ran back to the school doors and lined up at the edge of the grass. Not one of them seemed out of breath or sweaty.

I just stared.

It was a cool day, but really, they should have been sweating at least a little.

It's like they're aliens.

Liesl whispered in my ear as the students filed back in through the school doors. "Holly, they are a different species of Faery Kind. That's why they seem so different."

I nodded, still amazed.

As we rose to leave our seats, a student came back out of the Academy; this one looked a bit older — taller and slightly heavier than the other students.

The boy ran up to the vice-headmistress, Miss Olovalur, and handed her a sealed note, then bowed as she took it, and ran back inside.

We waited on the grass as she opened and read the note.

"Oh, no," she said softly.

"What is it?" asked Lord Umeqirelle.

"It's the grandson of the headmaster," Miss Olovalur looked up at us. "He's run away again," she said in a resigned tone.

"Again?" I asked.

She nodded. "The headmaster lives with his family in their quarters on the school grounds." She indicated the rear of the school with a wave of her hand. "This boy is quite young. Too young to attend school yet, but he has run away before. He very precocious."

She folded the note and put it in a pocket. "I must leave you for a time, and coordinate a search for the boy. I am sorry." She looked sad.

"Let us help in the search," Lord Umeqirelle said. "The forest is quite dangerous for a child that young."

Miss Olovalur nodded. "Come with me, everyone." She turned and hurried around the back of the massive Academy, leading the way to the headmaster's family quarters.

A half-hour later, we had dispersed into the forest, in groups of three, searching for the child.

Liesl and I were paired with the boy's older sister, who was fifteen and a student at the Elfen Academy.

I stared at her as we picked our way through the rough foliage and into the dark forest.

The trees were just as curled and dark as they looked from the road.

"Watch out for the bark," I whispered to Liesl. "It looks wet."

She nodded to me, glancing over at the older sister.

She'd been introduced to us with a long Elfen name. I hadn't remembered it.

She led the way silently through the trees. She seemed angry.

I glanced at Liesl.

"Wait up, there," I called. The older sister was nearly out of sight.

She stopped and turned, an angry looked on her face.

"Are you okay?" I asked as Liesl and I caught up to her. She was at least a head taller than we were, even though we were the same age.

I stopped in front of her. "What was your name again?" I asked.

She glanced into the trees, then back at us.

"I'm Filaurel Ellarian Fazorwyn, but please, call me Laura," she said in a thick accent.

"I'm Holly," I said, "and this is Liesl. We really want to help find your little brother."

Laura looked gratified. "I'm thankful for the help." She looked at her feet, then into the forest. "If I seem angry or ungrateful, it's not directed at you."

I had wondered. I was glad to hear she was not upset with us, but I wondered what she was upset at.

Liesl and I waited silently for an explanation. Laura seemed to be thinking to herself.

She glanced at us. "Can you two keep a secret?"

We both nodded.

"Don't tell the adults," Laura said. "We'd be in bad trouble if you did."

Chapter Nine
Lost Elfen Boy

I was insanely curious.

Liesl and I stepped closer to Laura, shielding her from the forest.

She spoke in a low voice. "It's not as wonderful as it seems here."

She looked scared. She glanced over our shoulders in several directions, then motioned for us to follow her deeper into the forest.

We picked our way carefully through the heavy brambles, and passed at least twenty diseased trees as we went.

The trees and bushes got worse the deeper into the forest we went.

"Laura," I asked quietly as we hiked, "Miss Olovalur told us that the trees are in poor health because of the volcanic activity. And that the dark substance had been sprayed onto the trunks to help the trees. Is that the truth?"

Laura turned and snorted over her shoulders as she hiked. "No," she said shortly. "I'll tell you in a little while."

We searched for her brother as we hiked, but our primary goal seemed to be to get away from the school so we could talk.

Laura led the way, and finally, we stopped by the side of a hill. The trees were growing close to the rock face, near a small half-cave.

Laura stopped and stood with her back to the rocky outcropping.

"The trees are dying because of the chemicals poisoning the forest," Laura said quietly. "It has nothing to do with the volcano, except maybe the volcano is active because of the chemicals injected into the ground."

What?

"Are you serious?" Liesl asked in a loud voice.

"Shhhh!" Laura held her hands out, palms down. "We must be quiet."

Liesl held her hand to her mouth, and whispered, "Sorry."

Laura waited several minutes before she continued.

"The factories are out of sight, farther north. They dump chemicals into the rivers, and the widest, deepest river flows into this forest," she whispered. "It's been going on for a very long time."

I looked at the trees around me. They looked very sick, even the older ones.

"The trees and bushes have been affected for at least the last hundred years," whispered Laura.

This was so sad.

"What can we do to help?" Liesl asked.

Laura shook her head. "You can't do anything. The adults won't listen. All they care about is their white shining cities."

"What about your brother?" I asked. "At least let's find him."

"He ran away because our family is so strict," said Laura. "They don't allow him to run and play; they say he's too young."

Huh?

"But we saw the students at the school running all over the place," Liesl said.

Laura nodded. "In formation, right? Yeah. We aren't allowed to run and play until we enroll at the school. For the first ten years of our lives, we're kept indoors and not allowed outside at all, except for primary school outings," she said grimly. "That's why they're so freaked about Tam running away."

"Tam's your brother?" I asked.

She nodded. "The reason the kids aren't allowed outdoors for the first ten years is because of the old traditions that have been around for almost a hundred years," Laura explained. "The Elfen Council enacted them because of the stolen children."

" 'Stolen children'?" Liesl asked.

"Yes. The legends say the goblins in the hills used to steal children and spirit them away to the human world, and exchange them for human children, who they took to work in the goblin mines," Laura said.

"Changelings?" I said. "I have read about such things in a library book. But I thought they were all just stories. Not real. Stories told to teach young children not to wander far from their mothers."

Laura shook her head. "Not just stories. This really happened." She huffed. "But the laws have gone too far. There's no reason Elfen children should be kept inside the home for the first ten years. It's ridiculous!"

"How do they get away with such a thing?" Liesl asked.

"It's the way things are, for the most part. The kids are used to being in the home," said Laura. "But when you see older siblings going outside, you start to question why you can't go outside too. At least, you do when you're precocious and intelligent, like Tam is."

I looked around the forest. "You say he's run away before?" I asked.

Laura nodded. "And I know his hiding place." She grinned. "Let's go." She turned and ran off in the direction of the volcano.

Uh oh.

We trotted after Laura, who ducked under trees' low branches and around gullies, on her way to her brother's hiding place.

Laura ran through the forest as if she knew it well. "This way," she said at one point, ducking behind a small waterfall.

We must have run for an hour.

"Laura," called Liesl, panting. "Stop, please can we stop?"

Laura looked over her shoulder and saw Liesl and I had stopped to catch our breath.

"We're not used to this much exercise," I said. My forehead was sweaty.

"Oh, I'm sorry," said Laura. "Let's rest a bit here." She sat down on the ground, and Liesl and I sat next to her.

"Anyone have any water?" I asked.

Laura brought forth a small canteen, and passed it around. Each of us got several swallows, and the water tasted cool and wonderful going down my throat.

"Ahhh," I said, handing it back to Laura. "That was good. Thank you."

She nodded, and put the canteen away in her bag.

"If I had known we were going on a long hike, I'd have prepared," said Liesl.

"Is it much farther ahead?" I asked.

Laura glanced over her shoulder. "A bit. He goes far away because he knows the searchers will track him if he stays closer."

"How close are we to the volcano," Liesl asked, her eyes looking up at the darkening sky.

"Closer, but it's still miles away," said Laura.

Laura smiled, remembering. "The first time he ran away was last year. Father thought he had been kidnapped." She chuckled.

"Sounds scary," I said.

"Wouldn't that be worse?" asked Liesl. "Kidnapped and held for ransom? He could be harmed or killed."

Laura shrugged. "Might be worse, or running into the forest might be worse. Who knows?"

I blinked.

This Elfen teen had a strangely cavalier attitude about her little brother being in danger.

Liesl looked around. "Laura, is the forest dangerous?"

Laura smiled. "Yes."

A shiver ran up my spine.

"There are wild animals that could maul you in the forest," Laura said. "But I think it's mostly dangerous at night."

It was still early afternoon.

I let out a breath of relief.

As if on cue, a low growl sounded through the trees.

I immediately tensed up.

"Is that...?" Liesl went quiet as we heard a second growl, and this one sounded closer than the first.

"Okay," Laura got to her feet. "Let's get a move on. That was a jaguar, and those can be a bother."

She nodded and turned to continue on.

A bother? A BOTHER?!

Laura started to trot through the forest.

Liesl and I hustled to catch up.

"She's going faster this time," Liesl puffed. "Come on, hurry!"

Liesl and I sprinted after Laura, ducking under and through the forest foliage, trying not to get the black coating from the trees onto us.

My shoes are getting filthy.

I had worn the new boots I had picked up at the end of summer. They were hiking boots, good for running through dirty forests, but they were still new, and I wanted to keep them that way for as long as I could.

We all ran through the forest for almost a mile before the jaguar growled again.

"Hey," I suddenly had a thought. "I though jaguars were found mostly near the equator," I asked as we ran.

Liesl ran beside me. "Maybe no one told the jaguar."

Laura stopped as a second growl from the jaguar sounded, quite close. This was more a scream than a growl.

"Crud," she said, turning on the path. "I was hoping to avoid this."

"What," Liesl asked as we came to a stop next to our guide.

Laura reached behind her and drew out a long sword from an invisible sheath.

"WHOA."

"Laura, that..."

Laura grinned at us.

We waited.

The jaguar screamed again, this time very close to us.

Laura bent her legs slightly.

"Where's it coming from?" I asked.

"In front of us, I think," answered Liesl.

"Nah, it's over there," Laura pointed to the side.

I turned my head just in time to see the jaguar walk into view. It was coal black and as big as a large pony, standing at least four feet tall at the shoulder.

"Good God Almighty!" exclaimed Liesl.

My heart started thudding loudly in my chest.

Neither of us had brought any kind of weapon. We had no idea the forest was filled with wild beasts.

"Stand back," murmured Laura. She took a step toward the massive jaguar, holding her sword in front of her.

I had no time to wonder how the sword in the scabbard at her side had been invisible.

Laura rushed forward, swiping at the beast, hitting it on its head.

The jaguar screamed and brought its paw up to strike at Laura, and I saw the wicked sharp claws extended.

Laura moved faster than I could follow, swinging her sword again and knocking the jaguar's paw to the side before it could get anywhere near her.

The jaguar screamed again; this time, I surmised it was in frustration. It crouched on the ground, flicking its tail back and forth.

Laura lunged again, this time aiming for the beast's back.

A thick red stripe of blood appeared on its shoulder.

It screamed in rage and pain.

It whirled and leapt back into the trees and climbed up one of the taller trunks. It sat on the branch, watching us, its tail twitching back and forth.

A moment later, we heard several more wildcat screams sounding in the forest.

"What's that?" I asked in a quiet voice.

"I was afraid of this," Laura murmured. "This cat has friends."

" 'Friends'? What do you mean?" Liesl whispered.

"More jaguars are coming," said Laura.

"I thought large wildcats were solitary hunters?" Liesl said.

"Well," I said quietly. "Like you said, maybe nobody told the jaguars." I closed my eyes and began surging up my Elemental Powers.

Looks like they might be needed here.

Liesl let out a breath. "Well, someone needs to educate these cats on what they are teaching in the schools."

The jaguar in the tree went silent.

Another jaguar screamed, very close now, and took a step out of a bush, coming into view about ten feet from us.

Oh, great.

Laura took a step back, crouching, balancing her sword in front of her, an easy smile on her face.

"The trick," she said, "is to keep your cool. Don't let them see they've rattled you."

Suddenly, the jaguar in the tree launched itself at Laura, and the jaguar emerging from the bushes ran toward Liesl.

Liesl brought her hands up in front of her face to defend herself.

Laura jumped sideways and brought her sword around in a lightning-quick arc and hit the leaping jaguar across its foreleg. It dropped to the ground, snarling and angrier than ever.

I jumped in front of Liesl. My friend had no defense against the other jaguar. I brought my hands up and called forth my Elemental Power. I imagined the jungle was icy cold and freezing. Flames shot from my hands like dual flamethrowers, reaching the advancing jaguar and enveloping it in heat. It screamed in pain and surprise.

The jaguar Laura had dropped in mid-flight was hit with heat, too: It reared back and sideways, jumping in surprise... toward Laura.

Fortunately, she was ready. She struck quickly with her razor-sharp sword and buried the blade into the midsection of her jaguar.

The beast screamed in pain as blood appeared on the side of its ribcage.

Laura leaped toward Liesl and me, and faced the injured jaguar.

More screams sounded from the trees.

"How many of these things are in this forest?" I asked, feeling mildly panicked.

"Not many," replied Laura. "Although last spring several of them had large litters." She lunged at the injured cat again and pierced its side with the tip of her sword.

The jaguar struggled weakly. It let out one last scream and then fell silent, closing its eyes and dropping.

Laura straightened. "I don't think it will be bothering us again." She walked up to it. "Pity. I didn't want to kill it."

I straightened as well. The jaguar I had targeted was now a black mound of charred kitty.

The flames were dying out on the corpse but had spread to the surrounding bushes. Half a dozen small fires flickered near me.

I brought my hands up again, closed my eyes, and imagined it was a scorching hot day.

Water...

Twin streams of water flew out from my fingertips, and I pointed them at the flickering baby wildfires. They went out with a hiss, and smoke poured from the scorched plants.

I walked over to the burnt-to-a-crisp mound that used to be a jaguar.

"Yeah," I said. "Too bad I had to crisp this one." I glanced around us. "Think the others will bother us?"

Laura came to look at the burnt jaguar and the soaked ground. "Nice trick," she grinned. "Is that some kind of magic? Or science?"

"Both," I grinned at her. "I just found out what my Fae Folk Power is: It's power over the elements. I'm still learning how to focus it. My teacher back home, Professor Farryn, is giving me private lessons. They're really helping."

"I'm impressed," Laura said.

"This was unexpected," I said. "Giant jaguars in an Elfen forest."

I brushed off my hands, wiping the last of the soot from my fingertips. I realized I had been holding my breath and exhaled loudly.

Liesl made an exuberant WHOOP! and smiled. "Laura! Holly! You're both so bad ass! WAY TO GO! WOOT!"

I laughed in relief and patted our host's shoulder as she bent over her sword and wiped the blade a few times.

"Thanks, you were awesome, Laura," I said.

"Well, you were unbelievable," Laura said. "That magic stuff is... incredible."

Liesl laughed.

It was infectious. She soon had us chuckling.

Laura grinned. "Sheesh, you guys, that was nothing. At least there were just two of them, so I didn't have to do aerial acrobatics."

I laughed in surprise.

Liesl was doing a Happy Dance.

"Cool it, Li," I laughed. "Calm yerself."

She stopped dancing and grinned from ear to ear, clapping. "Soooo happy you're with us, Laura. That was soooo cool!"

"I guess there aren't too many wild beasts in the Fae Folk forests?" she asked, still smiling.

"Pffttt. Not that size," said Liesl. "What was that? That must have been five times the size of a normal jaguar."

"Those are Elfen land jaguars," Laura said. "They're pretty rare in the wild woods."

"Well, I'm just glad you can handle yourself." I patted her shoulder again.

"Right back at ya, Holly," Laura said, giving her sword a final wipe and carefully sliding it back into the invisible scabbard at her side. Once it slid all the way in, even the pommel disappeared from view.

"That's a neat trick," I said. "Any way I could pick one of those up before I leave the Elfen lands?"

Laura stood up straighter. "Huh? You're leaving?"

"Well, yeah. We just came for the weekend. A visit, you know. To see the land of my mother's people," I said.

Laura blinked in surprise. "I was told you were here for good."

WHAT?

Chapter Ten

Misunderstanding?

We hiked through the forest to a little hunter's house in the woods, finally arriving about fifteen minutes after the jaguar incident.

"Tam," Laura called. "Come out." She walked up to the door and turned the knob.

There was no answer.

"Come on, Tam." Laura opened the door and took a few steps in. We walked in after her.

I had a million questions.

Like, why was Laura told we would be staying?

Who'd told her that?

Was it just a mistake?

Or were we not going to be allowed to leave?

"Don't worry," Liesl whispered. "They can't hold us against our will," she patted my shoulder and stepped into the shack behind me.

Ohhh, I'm not so sure about that ...

The little house appeared empty. Laura banged around and opened all the doors and cupboards, calling for her brother.

"Come on, Tam, come out. I've got two Fae Folk visitors with me, come say 'hello' to them," Laura called.

There was a noise from under the bed in the back room.

A small boy came crawling out from under the bed; he was covered with cobwebs and filthy. He looked small and thin. His skin was very translucent. He looked even more waif-like than the students at the school we'd seen earlier.

He walked up to us.

"You're filthy," his sister said.

He ignored her. His eyes were on Liesl and me.

"Hello," I said softly, kneeling down to his level. "Are you okay?"

He nodded.

"Are you thirsty or hungry?" Liesl asked.

He shook his head no.

I glanced at Laura. "Can he talk?"

She snorted. "Of course, he can talk. Sometimes he won't shut up!"

I looked back to the little waif. "Tam? Are you all right?"

He seemed to hesitate.

"He's fine," said Laura. "Come on, Tam, let's get back. I want to return home before the sun sets. Come on."

She reached for her brother's hand.

He looked down as she took it, yanking it harshly.

"Hey, hey, take it easy there," I protested. "He's so thin, he's gonna break."

"Oh, he's fine," Laura stepped forward and grabbed him bodily. She swung him over her shoulder in a fireman's carry, grasping both his wrists in one hand, and hooking her arm over his ankles.

Tam giggled.

Oh, brother.

I peeked at Tam's face, and he tried to hide his eyes, but I saw his grin.

"He's shy," Liesl said.

Laura sighed. "Yes. It's because he doesn't see many strangers." She turned to the door. "Come on, let's get back."

"You gonna be okay carrying him back like that?" I asked, following her out of the little house.

"Yeah, I'll be okay," Laura said. "He hardly weighs anything, and I'm stronger than I look."

We all traveled back to the school grounds at a run.

Halfway there, Laura let Tam back onto the ground, after he protested mightily.

"Don't like being bounced all over the place, huh, kiddo?" Laura asked.

She grabbed his wrist tightly and wouldn't let go.

"No way, you'll just run off again," she said. "Tam, you have to stop doing that, Mother was really scared this time. That stupid volcano is about to erupt, remember?"

She ran and dragged him along. He took leaps and bounds to keep up with his sister.

Liesl and I trotted after them, careful to keep them within view.

"We would be in trouble if we lost sight of them, come on," I said.

"Hey, Holly, Lord what's-his-name has a lot of explaining to do, huh?" said Liesl.

"He sure does," I said. "I'm actually kind of upset."

Liesl snorted. "I would be, too, in your place. Besides, I'm here, too, and I want to get back and see Jack."

I chuckled.

We got back to the school fast, if not tired out.

Laura ran ahead with Tam, and I heard a cry of happiness and saw his mother grab him up in a hug.

Lord Umeqirelle and Miss Olovalur handed us both water, and we stood there at the edge of the crowd, gulping down the cool liquid.

Laura walked to a man we hadn't seen before, gave him a hug, and whispered in his ear. He nodded and looked over at us, then came to say hello.

"Thank you for helping find my son. I am eternally grateful," he shook both our hands, a smile on his face.

"We were just happy to help."

"Just glad he's okay, Sir."

"I am Tam and Laura's father. I understand you are new students to the Academy?" he said.

"Yeahhhhhno," I said loudly, turning to look at Lord Umeqirelle. "There's been a mistake, Sir." I looked back at him once I saw I'd caught Lord Umeqirelle's eye. "Liesl and I are just visiting for the weekend. We return to Fae Folk lands early Monday Morning."

Lord Umeqirelle walked up to our little group. "Yes, um, yes. Miss Ó Cuilinn and Miss Becker are just here for a visit. They wish to return after the weekend," he looked pointedly at the other man.

I stared at the tall Elfen Lord Emissary. "You *will* be returning us home Monday morning, won't you?" I asked him pointedly.

He looked at me hesitantly.

I took a step toward him. "Because there will be trouble if we don't return home. I hope you understand that."

For some reason, I no longer felt under the Elfen Lord's spell. I think it had been wearing off for a while, and it was gone now, totally gone.

Lord Umeqirelle looked the same as he had when I first saw him in the headmistress's office at Titania Academy, and at the very same time, he looked different.

I stared at his face, his platinum hair with not a strand out of place, even though he'd supposedly been in the forest searching for the lost Elfen boy, as we had been.

I studied his face: It looked just as smooth and young and handsome as I remembered it had, a week ago, when it had reminded me of the Lord of the Rings movies and Legolas the Elf, only somehow it looked different.

Less... *hmmm* I couldn't put my finger on it, but he looked less appealing. Much less appealing.

I stared at him.

He stared back.

Then, he grinned and spoke, "Of course you're returning early Monday morning, whatever gave you the idea that you weren't, Princess?" His voice was smooth and suave and... creepy.

It was somehow creepy now.

Not handsome.

Not appealing.

Just creepy.

I nodded.

"I guess there was just a misunderstanding," I said slowly.

Miss Olovalur stepped up then, and squeezed in between Lord Umeqirelle and me, and I shook my head. The spell was broken.

Sort of.

I would remember this moment for a long time.

"Hey," said Miss Olovalur in a falsely cheerful tone. "Miss Ó Cuilinn! You and Miss Becker didn't even get to finish your tour of my school. We still have the classrooms to peek in on. Hurry! Come on: Classes are still in session for another hour. We can catch them if we hurry."

I sighed.

"Of course," it had been the whole reason for my visit, after all. "Okay, lead on, vice-headmistress."

We all hurried back inside the castle and resumed the school tour.

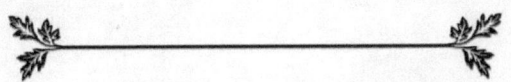

Chapter Eleven
The Study of Powers

We sat in on three different classes, in the back. Miss Olovalur, Lord Umeqirelle, Chancellor Xilmenor, Liesl and I. The classes were... interesting.

We were told Elfen classes were held seven days a week, without pause.

Strict.

Elfen classes seemed to concentrate on history, and pageantry, politics, and power. They were extremely different than the Fae Folk classes at Titania Academy I was so used to.

"Let's gather after this last one, here in the professor's dining hall, for our evening meal?" Lord Umeqirelle suggested.

"Good idea, sir," Miss Olovalur remarked.

Ten minutes later, we were seated in a small yet opulent dining room, off the third-floor wing that housed the professors.

White marble tables were set with white cloth napkins, white carved dinnerware and plates, and crystal glasses filled with cold water.

We were again thirsty, after the end of the tour and the rush to sit in on classes.

Liesl and I drank deeply from goblets full of cool water, after which nearby waiters came around and silently refilled.

"Well," said Lord Umeqirelle, "I must say Miss Olovalur, that was a grand save from the day's interruption. What a wonderful tour! Don't you agree, Chancellor?" He turned to ask Chancellor Xilmenor on his other side.

The old man responded with a completely unintelligible sentence.

Miss Olovalur smiled and bowed her head. "Thank you, sirs, thank you. We're very proud of our Academy."

I glanced at Liesl and raised my eyebrows.

The first course was set before us.

It was a wonderful salad, with exotic fruits and deep green leafy vegetables.

We spent the next few minutes eating, and while I was unable to speak with my mouth full, I was deep in thought about the classes I had observed.

As I put my salad fork aside, I cleared my throat.

"Miss Olovalur, I had a question about the classes here at your Academy," I said.

The vice-headmistress looked up with interest.

"Well, I cannot help but compare your classes with the classes we have back home," I said.

Miss Olovalur had provided Liesl and me with a list of first- and second-year classes at the Elfen Academy.

I looked down at the list now, studying it again.

"I do not see..." I cleared my throat again, think on how I wanted to phrase my question. I thought for a few seconds and then started again. "Do you teach Powers at this school?"

Liesl smiled, I think she had been wondering the same thing.

"Powers, Miss Ó Cuilinn?" asked Lord Umeqirelle.

I glanced at him and then back to Miss Olovalur, waiting for her answer.

"I don't understand exactly what you mean by a class on Powers, Miss Ó Cuilinn," the vice headmistress finally answered.

How do I phrase this?

Liesl cleared her throat. "Do you have classes on magic?" she asked.

"Magic?" asked Miss Olovalur.

"Magic and the Powers each Faerie Folk has," I clarified.

I thought of my own Elemental Powers and how in my second year, I was starting to learn how to hone them, so I could use them with more precision.

Lord Umeqirelle, Miss Olovalur, and Chancellor Xilmenor all looked puzzled.

"For instance," I decided to just jump in and reveal my gifts. "I, in particular, am gifted with the Power of the Elements."

The three adults looked surprised.

"And I am gifted with the Power of Purifying the Air," Liesl said.

The three adults said nothing.

I tried again. "I'm in my second year of classes at Titania Academy," I said. "If I were to move here, how would I continue to learn about my Elemental Power?"

The three shifted uncomfortably in their chairs.

I looked point-blank at the vice-headmistress. This was her school. She should be able to give me a straight answer.

"Miss Olovalur?" I asked.

She sighed.

"Miss Ó Cuilinn, we do teach magic, but in private classes," she said. "Magical abilities are very rare in the Elfen land."

I blinked.

Well, this explains why my mother fared so badly.

"Wait," Liesl said. "Are you telling me that Elfen Kind aren't magical? That the thing that sets us apart from the humans, as Faeries, isn't abundant here?"

Lord Umeqirelle sighed. "It is and it isn't." He stared at me. "Miss Ó Cuilinn, Princess, you must understand, not everyone has magical abilities here. And not everyone has the resources to develop any they might have."

Aha.

"So only a select few have the... 'resources' to develop their magical abilities?" Liesl said in a small voice.

Resources?! I'd been born into this world with nothing and spent most of my life on the streets. I knew what it meant not to have those "resources." I'd even felt guilty asking for my father's help with tuition at Titania Academy. I was feeling even more guilty now that they kept calling me "Princess" and talking about their own people being unable to... afford?!... to learn about their own magical gifts. It all seemed incredibly unfair.

I held up my hand.

"I don't mean to change the subject, but please. Lord Emissary, stop calling me 'princess' — I'm not a little girl," I said.

"But you are of royal blood," rumbled Chancellor Xilmenor.

I stared at him, my mouth dropping open.

"I thought you couldn't speak Fae Folk language? Er, I mean... English, to my ears?" I said.

"I can speak any language I want, Princess," Chancellor Xilmenor said with a wink.

He'd been putting us on. Holy Hell.

I took a deep breath and tried to gather my thoughts.

"Okay, I know I'm of royal blood, my father is The Holly King..." I started.

"That's not the only royalty in you, Princess," said Chancellor Xilmenor.

"Stop with the 'Princess' thing!" I said in a loud voice.

The room hushed, and they all stared at me.

I started again. "My name is Holly. All of you may call me Holly," I said in a quieter voice.

"Holly," Chancellor Xilmenor began, "your mother was the offspring of our Crown Prince. You are of royal blood on your Elfen side, as well."

What?

"Explain this, please." I said.

"Gladly. Your grandfather was an Elfen Crown Prince. He lay with a human, while on sabbatical to the human world," said Chancellor Xilmenor. "Your mother was born here, in the Elfen lands. The Crown Prince brought your human grandmother here, and she gave birth in his castle."

The Lord Emissary snorted. "During a revolution."

"WHAT?" Liesl asked sharply.

The Chancellor Xilmenor sighed. "There was a small, albeit violent revolution, and Holly's mother, Noelle, was born here, in Elfen lands. But the revolution put her at risk, so she was taken back to the human world. The Crown Prince was killed in the process, I'm sorry to say. But that doesn't mean Noelle was not half-Elfen. And of royal blood." He sat back, satisfied, and apparently tired out from the long explanation.

I was speechless. I had learned more about my mother in the last few minutes than I had learned from Aunt Clare.

Well, mostly.

"Excuse me, I have to go vomit," I stood up.

"What's the matter, Princess?" Lord Umeqirelle asked.

"DON'T CALL ME THAT," I screamed. "MY MOTHER DIED HOMELESS, IN POVERTY. IF YOU AND YOUR STUPID CROWN PRINCE'S FAMILY

HAD HELPED HER, SHE'D PROBABLY STILL BE ALIVE." I turned and ran from the room.

Liesl followed me.

So did Chancellor Xilmenor.

I ran out of the room and to the adjoining room, and stopped there.

I was stuck. I had no place to go. "RRRRR!" I growled in frustration.

"Holly." Liesl ran up to me. "Are you okay?"

"No, I'm not okay!" I sat down on the bench that was beside the door. "I am not okay, and I don't plan on being okay for a very long time!"

Chancellor Xilmenor walked up to us and sat on the nearby chair.

Liesl sat next to me.

We both stared at this wrinkled old man.

He stared back at us.

Finally, he spoke.

"I don't blame you one bit," he said.

Surprise deflated my anger a tiny bit. I waited for him to say more.

"Noelle was my cousin. My father was the brother of the Crown Prince. I would like to have known your mother, Holly. I really wish I could have grown up with her. She seemed like a brave person, from what little I know."

I huffed out a breath. I was still plenty angry.

Chancellor Xilmenor fell silent for a few minutes. The other adults were staying in the dining room.

Probably giving this old man a chance to calm us down.

"You know what?" Chancellor Xilmenor whispered. "To be perfectly honest, I don't think you should move here, especially after hearing about your Elemental Power, Holly."

I raised my eyebrows in spite of myself.

"Why not?" I whispered back.

"Because they just want you to live here as a royal," he whispered, glancing to see the other two adults were not nearby. "Nowadays, the royals are purely decorative. They have no power. If you moved to Elfen lands, you would be an ornamental figure within the Elfen society. You would never be trained to use your elemental magic. That is for families with members on the Elfen High Council. Those who hold the real power, politically speaking."

I stared at him, my eyes wide. I was speechless. I was just... speechless.

The chancellor was proving to be a friend, after all, instead of just an old man.

I looked at the ground.

I didn't know what to do.

Liesl put her hand on my shoulder.

"Holly," she whispered. "At least you have the truth now."

I nodded.

"Your friend is right," said Chancellor Xilmenor. "It is better to be well informed than to be in the dark."

I looked up at him. "So, you're my cousin? My cousin twice removed?"

He chuckled. "Something like that." He grinned at me.

I sighed.

"Holly, why don't we just return home now?" whispered Liesl. "I mean, do you even feel like staying?"

I didn't know. I felt so confused and conflicted.

"I did want to see the Elfen lands, I won't lie," I started.

I felt so disappointed I felt like crying.

I looked up at Chancellor Xilmenor.

"Do females or royals ever even have a strong place in Elfen society?" I asked. "Are they ever trained as warriors, for instance?"

He lowered his head in defeat. "No."

A cold chill filled me.

"So why does Lord Umeqirelle want me to move to the Elfen lands so badly?" I whispered, pleading to understand the inexplicable.

He shook his head, then looked at me. "I don't know, Holly. I just don't know."

"Miss Ó Cuilinn, Miss Becker! There you are!" Lord Umeqirelle walked out of the dining hall with Miss Olovalur. Smiling, they both walked over to us.

"Ladies," said Lord Umeqirelle. "Please, I want to turn the day around. It was going to be a surprise, but I must let you in on the secret now."

He beamed with happiness and glanced at Miss Olovalur, who nodded with a grin.

Lord Umeqirelle turned back to us. "There is to be a grand ball in your honor, an absolute extravaganza. Tonight. You are going to love this so much! Now, dressmakers are heading to your hotel quarters as we speak. They will outfit you both in beautiful dresses so that you can enjoy this Welcome Ball in your honor. It will be an evening you will never forget!" He beamed at us both.

I stared at him.

It did sound fun. I had never been to such an event.

I rose to my feet, Liesl beside me. I did not trust myself to speak, so I just nodded to the tall Elfen Lord.

He seemed so happy.

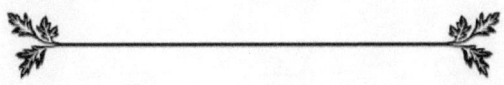

Chapter Twelve
The Grand Ball

We retired to our room to shower and calm down. I wasn't sure I wanted to go to any gathering, the way I was feeling.

"I can't believe they don't use magic here," said Liesl.

"I don't think they have much of it at all," I said dryly. "Especially for females or royals. I mean, what kind of land is this? Does no one have much magic? Or do they just not allow it?" I ranted.

"I don't think you could ever be just ornamental, Holly," Liesl said. "You'd be bored out of your skull."

"Agreed! Can you even believe they want me to do that?" I paced rapidly back and forth in a huff, my arms folded over my chest, fuming.

"Then don't do it," Liesl said.

I stopped. I had been striding back and forth, my hands in the air, gesticulating.

I looked over at Liesl, she was sitting on the edge of her bed, an amused look on her face.

I grinned. "Sorry."

"Holly, no matter what happens, no matter how these Elfen run their lands, no matter what, really: You are Fae Born. You are the daughter of The Holly King, and you have enormous natural abilities. They can't stop the magic in you."

"Pffttt. They seem to want to try," I said.

"What do you mean?" Liesl looked concerned.

I stared at her.

Was I overreaching? Overanalyzing? Was I?

I put up my hand and ticked off fingers as I made my points. "One, they want me to move here, to live here. Two, they say I'm considered a royal. Three, they say their royals are just ornamental, and do not have any power. So I'd just be like a floral arrangement on a side table. Four, they don't seem to stress or even have much magic in their land, or in their school. That sucks."

I stood there, hands on my hips, looking at the ceiling in exasperation.

"I mean, I've just started my training with Professor Farryn. My Elemental Power is still very wild. I need training to hone and focus it."

Liesl mumbled, looking away.

"What?" I walked over to her and stood in front of her. She turned to look at me.

"What did you say?" I asked.

Liesl took a deep breath. "I said, you didn't seem to have much problem out in the forest with that jaguar."

I sighed, feeling exasperated. "That was instinct. I need to be able to really focus. I know I could hone my abilities into something better. You know Professor Farryn. He wouldn't give me private lessons if he didn't think my powers needed them."

"True." Liesl got up and walked to the window, looking out. "Oh, Holly. Come look at this."

I walked over to see what she was looking at.

"Oh. OH," I exclaimed.

Out the window we could see the volcano. It was nearing sunset, and the sky was orange and pink, but close to the volcano, the smoke had covered nearly everything.

"How far away did Lord Umeqirelle say that thing was?" I asked.

"I've completely forgotten, but I won't lie: I'll be happy to leave the Elfen lands *and* that volcano," Liesl murmured, mesmerized by the sight. "They *may* say it's not going to erupt for months, but have they informed the volcano of this?"

"Maybe we should find out more about it," I whispered.

"Sounds like a good idea." Liesl turned and walked to the bathroom. "If we're going to be asking him about the volcano, we should get dressed and go. I'm going to hop in the shower, if that's all right?"

"Sure," I said, distracted. I pulled myself away from the window and turned to the room.

Didn't he say he'd had clothes sent up?

As if on cue, there was a knock at the door.

Two hours later, I couldn't stand it anymore.

"Holly, you look divine," Liesl said, grinning.

"Oh, shut up," I replied.

The seamstresses had descended on us, showing us several different styles of Elfen formal attire. I had rejected them all.

Liesl had chosen a deep midnight blue outfit that look part Cinderella gown, part Ninja warrior.

I had gone full Ninja, opting for a black-and-red outfit that accentuated my movements, and blended well with my magical staff, which I'd finally decided to carry.

"Wish I'd taken this with me into the forest," I murmured, gripping the heavy staff. "Might have come in handy."

"I think I need to acquire one of those," Liesl said. "I need to carry some kind of weapon."

I glanced at her and grinned.

The Elfen seamstresses had been happy to coordinate our outfits, and once they understood we weren't the ball-gown and fancy-hairdo kind of girls, they got to work.

I was especially happy with my new boots, and kept glancing at them in the mirror.

"You should ask if you can take those back with you," Liesl said. "They look fabulous."

I glanced over at her footwear. "Yours are great, too. You should ask to take them home as well."

Liesl's boots were a midnight blue with black leather cutouts. The effect was striking without being obvious. I almost wished I had a pair.

There was a knock at the door.

"Princesses?" A strange voice called from the hallway. "Are you ready?"

"It must be the escort," Liesl said.

We were driven by carriage again, back to the Elfen Academy, and around to the side where the ball was being held.

The sun had set, and someone had gone to town decorating. Tens of thousands of twinkle lights were strung along the road, and the castle itself was festooned with the beautiful lights.

I stared at them as the carriage trundled around the castle.

"They almost look like they're moving," I murmured.

"I think they are, Hols," said Liesl. "Those are pixies."

I blinked.

"Those are... what?" I asked.

"Pixies." Liesl looked at me and giggled. "What, did you think they were? Christmas lights?"

I was glad for the low light. I could feel my face getting hot. "Something like that," I mumbled.

I looked out at the decorations again.

Makes sense that they're pixies. How would strung lights be plugged in along the road?

The carriage rolled to a stop at the edge of a lit pathway that led from the ballroom doorways. It extended several dozen feet out to the roadway.

A footman reached and opened the carriage doors, and Liesl and I disembarked.

I stared at the decorative lights up close.

"Oh, my goodness," I whispered, bringing my hand up to the tiny creatures. They looked like fireflies, except they were bigger and had lit-up fluttering pink wings in addition to the lights on their...

"Their pixie butts are lit up," I said. "Oh my God."

Liesl giggled. "We have these, too, in the Fae Folk land. They're just kind of rare." She held a finger up to one pixie, and the delicate creature approached and alighted on her fingertip.

It rested there a minute, its wings slowly flexing.

It looked, now that I could observe one at rest, almost exactly like a miniature dragonfly. They were about a centimeter long. Their double wings were fluorescent. Their bodies extended backward, just like a dragonfly, each ending in a bulbous tail that was lit on the end.

Different pixies tails winked in different colors.

In some cases, the lights on their wings matched the color of those on their tails; in other cases, the lights of different colors could be found on the same pixie.

Purple, pink, blue, yellow, and white lights blinked on and off, all along the road and trail.

We finally started walking on the pathway to the door. More footmen in ornate uniforms lined the path, and at the end, two of them stood ready to open the doors for us.

I turned to Liesl and took a deep breath. "Ready for this?"

She nodded, a grin on her face.

I think she's going to have more fun tonight than I am.

I glanced at the doors. Faint music was leaking out and drifting on the night air.

I took another deep breath and grimly whispered to my friend, "Remember, watch out for me. I have a feeling Lord Fancy Pants is going to be at it again tonight."

Liesl nodded.

I turned to the two footmen and nodded.

They nodded back and opened the double doors, and we stepped through.

It was an incredible cacophony of light and sound. Brilliant Elfen Folk in outrageous attire drifted here and there, and the dance floor in the middle was thick with people. They swayed back and forth, two by two, seemingly hypnotized by the loud, olde-fashioned music being performed by the...

"Live orchestra!" Liesl practically squealed.

Lord Umeqirelle was waiting near the door for us, and came forward immediately. He was dressed in his fancy ornate uniform again, and also wore a massive hat with a huge ostrich feather flowing from the side, which defied gravity and reached up into the air at least two feet.

It was bright pink.

The room was huge and warm.

Lord Umeqirelle came directly up to me and bowed.

I felt a huge wave of dizziness, much stronger than the time I first met this Elfen man, back in the headmistress' office at Titania Academy.

I swayed.

Lord Umeqirelle took my hand and kissed the top of it. "Princess," he said in a low, seductive voice, "So glad to see you here. You look wonderful. Welcome to your ball."

I blinked.

Why does this guy do this?

"Holly?" Liesl whispered in my ear. "You okay?"

I didn't answer.

I couldn't take my eyes off Lord Umeqirelle. To me, there and then, he looked like the most exquisite vision of a man I had ever seen. He looked like Legolas in those movies, sooooo gorgeous, sooooo handsome, soooo ...

"OUCH" I said, closing my eyes and grabbing my arm.

Liesl had given me a hard pinch on my upper arm.

"Snap out of it," she whispered fiercely.

I looked down.

Lord Umeqirelle had a hold of my hand. He hadn't let go after grabbing it and kissing it. His grasp on my fingers was tight.

Liesl, on the other hand, had her arm hooked around mine, and was pulling me the other way.

My foot was stepping toward Lord Umeqirelle. He had hypnotized me again, stronger than ever.

I looked down at my feet.

"Do not look into his face," Liesl whispered. "That seems to make it much stronger."

I nodded, still facing down.

"Amrynn, you old codger, are you monopolizing the honored guest's time?" The new voice was loud and raucous, and I felt a new hand on my other arm, pulling me to the side.

I glanced up and saw the newcomer was another Elfen male, dressed just as ornately as Lord Umeqirelle, except this fellow looked even more handsome.

But... something was off.

The ears, the platinum hair... *way* off.

"Holly, he's a..." Liesl's voice in my ear was suddenly cut off.

"We don't need you putting ideas in the Princess' head, companion." The new man was pushing Liesl away.

I looked at him sharply.

He smirked down at me, very sure of himself, and I saw what Liesl was trying to tell me.

The new fellow was not Elfen, as I had originally thought. He wore fake Elfen ears, and the platinum wig he sported looked very obviously fake.

"Who are you?" I asked, deeply suspicious. He did not look like anyone I was familiar with, and did not look like any Elfen or Fae Folk I had ever set eyes on.

"Listen, man," Lord Umeqirelle stepped forward and knocked the new fellow back with his chest. "Stay back from the princess. No one wants the likes of *you* here, Blackjack." He grabbed my left arm back from the wigged man, who just stared in shock at the Elfen Lord's actions.

I was steered away by Lord Umeqirelle, and walked a few paces to the right.

Where was Liesl?

I dug my heels in and stopped, my head still very foggy. Glancing back, I searched the crowd.

"What is it, Princess?" the smooth voice of Lord Umeqirelle was close to my ear.

Oh, yuck, did he whisper in my ear?

"WehrrsLisl?" my garbled words were low, and no one heard me.

"What?" Lord Umeqirelle asked.

I took a deep breath.

"WHERE IS LIESL?" I said louder.

A fumbling ensued, then, Lord Umeqirelle's smooth as silk voice, in my ear once again, "She's right here, Princess."

A fumbling sound again.

"Get off me!" Liesl's voice sounded angry. Then, she was there, at my elbow again.

"Here's your friend, Princess," thrummed Lord Umeqirelle's warm, cajoling voice. "Why don't you both come to the dance floor?"

"NO. Holly, look up," Liesl demanded.

One thing my drug-fogged brain knew to do was obey my friend. My head came up, and my eyes opened wide. I looked around.

To my left, the wigged man was about five feet away, trying to talk to me, but I couldn't hear what he was saying. Even though he was close, it was as if his voice had been muted. His lips moved, but no sound reached my ears.

Directly in front of me stood Lord Umeqirelle, very close. His hands were on my left arm and hand, and he was trying to pull me away from the man on my left, the one I could not hear.

To my right stood Liesl, looking furious. Her hair had been messed up, and several strands were pulled the wrong way.

We'd both had our hair done before embarking on the carriage trip to the ball, so she looked like she'd been in some kind of struggle.

"Holly. HOLLY," she said, pinching me again.

"OUCH." Liesl had my attention.

I blinked and looked directly at her, and waited.

She bent her head forward and whispered. "He's doing it again. They all are."

"Doing what?" I whispered back.

"GLAMOURING," she said in a loud whisper.

Lord Umeqirelle now began to softly deny this, protesting while he pulled on my left arm.

Liesl stood firm, her arm hooked through mine, leaning to the right.

"Okay, okay," I said loudly. "OKAY. THAT'S ENOUGH." I grimaced up at Lord Umeqirelle.

He stared back, shocked.

"LET GO," I demanded of him, baring my teeth.

Liesl was breathing as if she'd just finished a marathon.

Lord Umeqirelle let go of my arm.

The new man on the left, the one who was posing as an Elfen but was clearly not, strode forward.

I put my arm out, hand raised in a "stop" gesture.

"GET BACK, YOU!" I said in a loud voice.

He stopped immediately, one foot still in the air.

"Now, both of you, AND ANYONE ELSE: Just leave us be. Give us space. I MEAN IT!" I growled out at the crowd near me.

I was breathing hard.

The foggy spell had left my head for the time being. I looked from Lord Umeqirelle to Fake Elfen Dude and back again.

My hand was still up.

I nodded and backed away slowly, and allowed Liesl to pull me.

We walked to the right about fifteen feet.

There was a punch bowl and a table of sandwiches and snacks.

"That was magnificent, really," a voice said.

Could that be ...?

Laura stood off to the side, a few feet away, grinning at me.

"I have never seen anyone put an Elfen Lord in his place so fast," she said. "Well done."

"Oh, thank God," murmured Liesl, turning to Laura. "Where can we go to rest?" she whispered to the Elfen girl.

"This way," Laura led us to the back of the large room, past tables laden with food and drink — "Don't touch any of that. It can't be trusted" — and to several tables where students and teachers were sitting.

We sat at the very end, behind half the professors.

Miss Olovalur was seated nearby, a plate of vegetables in front of her. She spotted us as we sat down and smiled. "How are you doing?" she mouthed.

I smiled and made a "so-so" gesture.

Her mouth briefly formed an "oh no" expression.

I shrugged and smiled again, then sat down facing Liesl and Laura, and facing away from Miss Olovalur.

She'll get the picture. "Do not disturb."

Liesl and Laura sat and glanced over in the direction we'd just come from.

I couldn't see where the Emissary or Mister Fake Elfen had gone.

"Where's they go?" I whispered.

"Not sure. I can't see them now, but we need to keep an eye on their whereabouts," Liesl whispered. "I have never seen anything like that in my life."

"Holly, you realize they're both trying to persuade you, right?" Laura murmured, leaning forward so only Liesl and I could hear her.

The room and the table were rather loud with laughter and conversation, so I felt we were somewhat safe communicating like this.

"What is with those two?" I asked. "Are all the men in the Elfen lands like this?"

Laura shook her head. "That other dude was not Elfen. Can't you tell?"

"Uh, der," said Liesl. "Tell me something I don't know."

Laura smirked, "All right. Well, he's not only not Elfen, he's a spy."

My eyebrows went up. "A spy? For whom?"

"For the Oak King Faction," Laura replied.

Chapter Thirteen

Spies and Subterfuge

"Please tell me you're kidding," Liesl said in a low voice.

Laura shook her head. "That's why I finagled my way into attending this event. Father was talking about it after you left, telling Tam and me, and Mother, all about it. Telling Tam that this is why he can't run away again, not until this stuff is over with, if it ever stops," she said in a dry, low voice.

"I can't believe they're in Elfen lands, spreading their crap," I said in a low voice.

Liesl looked at me and nodded.

A waiter came by.

"Madams, can I bring you anything?" he asked.

"No, nothing. Leave us," Laura snapped, shooing the man away before we could say anything.

She turned back to us. "Do not eat anything offered to you at this event."

We both stared at her.

"You don't understand what's going on, just trust me," Laura said.

"Pffttt. I think you're the only person here that *we* do trust," I said.

Liesl nodded.

Laura pulled her bag up and dipped her hand inside, bringing out two sealed bottles of water.

"Here." She handed one to each of us. "Drink these to stay hydrated. It's hot in here."

We took the water gratefully.

I unscrewed the top on mine and took a low swig.

"Now, one thing I hope you already know: Elfen men have the ability to glamour a woman, especially an Elfen woman, or someone with Elfen blood." She looked at me pointedly. "It's a way for them to persuade you to do anything. And I mean anything. You'll think it was your own idea. You've got to be on the lookout and guard against it."

"How do you guard against it?" Liesl whispered. "Because this is getting ridiculous."

Laura pulled out two flowers, and handed one to each of us. "These are Snowdrops. Stick them on your person somewhere, preferably near your face."

I took the little flower and brought it close to my nose. I had a thing for smelling flowers.

The stem was about five inches long, and the flower was a white dropping cup, very simple, very sweet.

I looked down and saw a buttonhole near my collarbone. I pulled the stem through that, and secured it in place, then looked back up, smiling.

Liesl had tucked her flower into her neckline.

Laura nodded. "You should be okay now."

She looked out onto the dance floor.

Lord Umeqirelle was now there, on the outer edge, scanning the room.

Probably looking for us.

I turned to Laura. "Do you think we should hide from them the whole night? Because I think I'm expected to interact with them..."

"The flower should protect you," Laura said. "It shields the wearer from most magical influence."

"Do you want me to come with you, Hols?" Liesl sounded concerned.

I kept my eye on Lord Umeqirelle; he was looking gorgeous. Still scanning the room.

He'll see me in a minute.

"I'll probably be okay." I thought for a few moments, then turned to Laura. "Does Lord Umeqirelle have a wife and children? I remember he said something earlier."

"Yes, he's got a whole family," Laura answered.

"You'd think that would keep him from flirting," I said quietly.

"Unless he was under some influence himself," said Laura.

I looked at her. I hadn't thought of that.

"You mean, he might be compelled against *his* wishes? To seduce me?" *That would be ridiculous, wouldn't it?*

"You never know. Elfen political intrigue can be exhausting," Laura nodded.

I looked back over to Lord Umeqirelle. He met my eyes and began to make his way over to our table.

Oh, lord...

"Oh, boy," Liesl said. "We've been spotted."

"Yeah, I noticed," I mumbled. "Here comes Lord Umeqirelle now."

"That's not who I meant," Liesl indicated the other side of the room. I looked.

The fake Elfen dude was staring straight at us, and talking in a sneaky manner with several other men. From this distance, I couldn't tell if they were also in disguise.

Will this never end?

"Princess," Lord Umeqirelle said smoothly, having traveled to our table and sat down across from us. "I trust you have calmed down and are feeling better?"

That was insulting.

I took a deep breath, patted the snowdrop flower in my buttonhole, and stood up. "Lord Emissary, how are you? Feeling less like glamouring young coeds and more like acting the proper host now?" I smiled sweetly at him.

He stood as well and held out his hand. "Of course, and please forgive me for my earlier mistake, I was completely besotted with you and your companion's evening attire." His smile was so cheesy I ducked my head and laughed.

"Holly, that spy guy is getting closer." Liesl had stood up and was whispering in my ear.

Oh, God...

"Princess, would you like to dance?" Lord Umeqirelle was still holding out his hand.

I hesitated only a moment, then took his hand and slowly stepped around the others and out onto the dance floor.

I glanced back once.

Liesl looked strained and worried.

Laura grinned and nodded and placed her finger on the side of her nose, then moved it to her upper chest.

Where the snowdrop was held on my own person.

I brought my other hand up to make sure the flower was still there.

It was.

The band was playing a slow waltz, and the gentle tones were soft and sweet. I loved olde-fashioned music, and so I glided effortlessly into Lord Umeqirelle's arms, careful to maintain at least six inches between us — which wasn't easy — and we began to dance.

The Elfen Lord Emissary was the picture of chastity itself as he guided me along, slow and easy, across the dance floor. We danced through the other couples, the entire ensemble coordinating beautiful together without any direct communication.

After a few minutes, while we glided along, he spoke.

"Princess, you are looking quite beautiful this evening. Thank you for making such an effort."

I nodded. "And thank you for being understanding and not insisting that Liesl and I wear ballgowns. The seamstresses told us you had instructed them to dress us any way we liked."

He nodded. "Of course. You are entirely in command in this situation, Princess."

We danced on for many minutes, the Lord Emissary was polite and very respectful, and if he enhanced his glamour, trying to fog my brain again, I wasn't aware of it.

The flower was working.

After at least fifteen minutes of dancing, I was somewhat exhausted.

I should suggest to Chance that we do this. It's a wonderful exercise.

"Would you like to take a break?" Lord Umeqirelle suggested quietly.

I must be looking tired.

"Uh, sure. A short rest will be fine," I said. He guided our slow waltz to the side of the room, and stopped near the edge.

"Come, we can spend a few minutes on the patio," he said softly. "The ballroom can get warm at times. Especially in late summer." He indicated the doors with a questioning look.

I smiled and nodded. He was right, it *was* warm, and I was actually thirsty.

Remember not to eat or drink anything they offer you. I guess the magical flower doesn't work to keep from being poisoned.

Lord Umeqirelle opened the outside doors and led me out to the cooler night air.

I touched my chest, to reassure myself the Snowdrop flower was still there. It was, but it was hanging, half dropped out. I quickly pulled it back through the buttonhole and back into place.

Can't lose you, little magic flower. You're my saving charm.

Lord Umeqirelle led me to a bench on the patio near some bushes; dozens of pixies hovered above.

I sat and stared at them. "They're so beautiful," I said. "Back home, they're said to be very rare, I'm told."

"Yes," the Lord Emissary agreed. "I believe they are more plentiful in the cooler climates." He fanned himself with his hand and looked around. "Although this summer heatwave is making things much warmer than they normally are."

"Has the volcano contributed to the unseasonable warmth?" I asked politely.

He nodded and smiled. "Yes, it has. In fact, that's most of the reason right there." He studied me for a minute. "You're a very beautiful young lady, Princess."

I shifted uncomfortably.

Lord Umeqirelle scooted closer on the bench we shared.

I grimaced. "You know I have a boyfriend back home? At Titania Academy."

Lord Umeqirelle began to fan himself again. "Yes, was it that young man who was with you in the headmistress' office that first day?"

"It sure was," I confirmed. "Chance has my heart, and," I added, looking directly at the tall Elfen man, "he has the blessings of my father. You know, to date me." I smiled, showing my teeth.

Lord Umeqirelle chuckled. "I'll bet he has. And your father, the, er... The Holly King, correct?"

I nodded.

"He is... very protective of you?" Lord Umeqirelle asked.

"He sure is," I replied.

"Well," the Lord Emissary nodded. "I can certainly understand a father's protectiveness over a beloved daughter." He grimaced and then coughed a few times.

Lord Umeqirelle turned to me and smiled. The moon was full behind the Lord Emissary, and it made him look as if he had a halo around his head. His long, platinum hair was braided several times on the side, but most of it hung loose about his shoulders and down his back.

His eyes were dark and brooding.

He looked even more delicious than Legolas in those Lord of the Rings movies Aunt Clare had snuck us in to see.

I gulped, my fingers still on the snowdrop flower stuck in the buttonhole of my top.

We were separated by only about three feet.

"Do you like the night air?" he asked softly.

I blinked, and the spell was broken.

"Y...yes." I gulped. "It's very nice."

I closed my eyes.

Get hold of yourself, Holly. Seriously.

The gorgeous Elfen Lord stayed three feet back from me.

So he's not trying to seduce you anymore. Right? So get your head on straight.

I closed my eyes and shook my head, trying to clear it.

"You don't like the cool breeze?" He sounded mildly distressed.

My eyes sprang open. "No, no. It's not that." I looked around us, searching for an excuse. "Do... do you think we could take a walk?"

His smile deepened. "Certainly, Princess." He held out his hand, and I took it.

The second our flesh touched, I felt an electric shock that made me jump.

"Easy there, take it one step at a time," he said smoothly. He turned and led me off the patio and onto the walkway that wound between the Academy's buildings.

We strolled for a few minutes.

"Do you miss your friends at your old school?" he asked.

My eyebrows furrowed. "Titania Academy is *not* my *old* school," I said crossly. "I was just there yesterday morning!"

"Forgive me, Princess. I meant no disrespect," he said softly. "I only meant to ask if you missed your friends?"

I took a deep breath and closed my eyes briefly, trying to calm down.

"I fear we got off on the wrong foot, Princess," Lord Umeqirelle said. "I am interested in your experiences only. Think of me as a father figure." He smiled down at me.

I nodded. "Okay. Well, as a matter of fact, yes. I do miss Chance and Renée," I said. "Especially Chance."

"You are quite fond of the Seeker, yes?" He asked.

"Yes, uh... yes." I had never thought of Chance as a "Seeker" before, but I guess that's what he did for the school. "I miss him very much."

"He is a good friend," the Lord Emissary said.

"He is," I agreed, remembering. "In fact, he's saved my life on more than one occasion. Him and my friends, all of them. I wouldn't know what to do if I didn't have them." I looked up at the tall Elfen Lord.

He looked back earnestly, nodding softly. "Friends make life worth living," he said softly.

I nodded.

"It's very good Liesl came with you on this trip, Princess. I'm betting you would have been quite lonely without her," Lord Umeqirelle said.

"I would have been lost," I agreed.

I thought of how I would have fared without Liesl on this trip.

The journey here, the hotel room, the carriage rides, the tour of the school, the foray into the forest. All of it would have been completely different and utterly worse without Liesl.

I sighed.

I would be nothing without my friends.

Nothing.

I looked over at the Lord Emissary. He was studying me closely, an indecipherable look on his face. Almost a longing.

I inhaled deeply and let out a long, loud breath.

The cool air felt wonderful after the stuffy interior of the ballroom.

I glanced back the way we'd come, wondering how long we'd been out here.

"Uh..." Lord Umeqirelle started to say something, then stopped.

I looked at him.

He smiled at me, and it was his turn to glance at our surroundings.

Something caught his eye and he took a deep breath.

"See the berry bushes?" He pointed to the row of thick, lush plants running along the side of the ballroom building.

I nodded, unable to find my voice. The feel of his soft, warm hand on mine was distracting. He applied just enough pressure to keep hold of my fingers and guide me.

"They were planted nearly a hundred years ago, and save for the first few years they spent growing, they've been producing berries every summer since." He slowed and stopped at the last berry bush, and we stood there looking at it in the moonlight.

He bent and plucked a sprig from the plant, and brought it up to us.

"These are rare and very hard to find outside the Academy grounds," he said in a deep voice.

I swallowed. That voice, it was so... so compelling.

I brought my fingers up to the snowdrop flower again. It was still there.

He lifted the sprig of berries to my face. "The smell is said to be magical."

I bent politely and inhaled the heady, fruity scent of ripe berries.

They looked dark red in the moonlight.

"The taste is said to be somewhere in between that of the blueberry and the blackberry," he whispered. "Would you like to taste it?"

I swallowed.

"Is... is it safe?" I asked.

"Of course. These berries are used in parfaits for the students. Perfectly safe," he brought the sprig to his own mouth, and nibbled off one berry with his full, soft lips.

I stared at this action, and my breathing quickened.

He brought the sprig of berries to my mouth.

I closed my eyes and opened my mouth.

Lord Umeqirelle moved the berry sprig to rest on my lips, and I began to nibble at them.

A massive berry flavor flooded my mouth. I reached for more, my lips eager. Juice flowed down my throat in exquisite drips of dark berry essence.

I ate the last berry and opened my eyes.

The Elfen Lord had stepped closer, and his ornate brocade-clad chest was less than an inch from mine.

The snowdrop flower quivered between us, still in place in my buttonhole.

Lord Umeqirelle was so close I could smell him.

His scent was that of pine, and deep, dark man scent.

What? What the heck is that?

The voice in my head, my conscience, sounded far away, and I could dismiss it easier than I normally could.

"Princess..." The Elfen Lord's deep brown voice murmured softly.

I looked up.

His eyes were warm and inviting. His lips were full and moist. I stared at them. He leaned closer.

He was soooo handsome.

I wanted to kiss him.

I thought of nothing else.

Not our age difference, not that we had just met, not that he was an Elfen Lord and I was just a... a...

A homeless girl recently... adopted... into Fae Folk Society...

Lost...

I leaned toward him...

Our lips were a centimeter apart...

I could feel his warm breath on my mouth...

What am I doing?

I stopped, as my lips were about to touch Lord Umeqirelle's lips...

Chance's face flashed into my mind. *"Don't leave..."* he'd said.

Chance. My true love.

I turned my head away at the last moment.

Lord Umeqirelle's lips landed on my cheek.

WHAT DID I ALMOST DO?

A deep hurt filled my heart at my own stupidity.

GREAT. NEARLY SEDUCED BY A LEGOLAS LOOKALIKE.

I closed my eyes, my face still turned sideways and now downward.

HOLLY Ó CUILINN, YOU SUCK.

Looking down, I could see my feet, and Lord Umeqirelle's boots as well.

I said nothing, but kept facing down at the ground.

After a few minutes, he turned and walked away without saying a word.

I sat down on the trail, the berry bushes next to me.

The stones that made up the winding walkway were cool on my backside. After a minute, cold, even.

I sat, freezing my rear off, brooding.

I deserve to freeze.

"HOLLY," Liesl's sharp voice broke the spell, and I opened my eyes.

I looked up. Liesl was slowly walking toward me from the patio. She sat down next to me on the walkway, not saying a word.

After a few minutes, Liesl finally spoke. "That guy sure is handsome."

I nodded. "But a lot of guys are handsome."

"True," said Liesl. "Life is more than just a pretty face."

I nodded.

We fell silent.

After another few minutes, Liesl spoke again. "Doesn't he have a wife and kid?"

"He does. He does indeed," I said.

"Kinda lets you know what kind of man he really is," said Liesl.

"I don't even know why he went after me," I murmured. "Liesl, you're far prettier than I am."

She blushed and lowered her head.

"You know it's true," I said.

"Well," Liesl said quietly, "The man is a troll for going after either one of us. A goon. A complete goon."

"Not a good man at all," I said.

"Deeply agree," said Liesl.

We fell silent again, and listened to the crickets for a few minutes.

I thought about everything, then smiled. "You know the man who keeps proving how great he is?" I glanced at her.

"Chance?" She asked.

I nodded. "Chance."

"Chance is pretty special," said Liesl. "He's always been there for you."

I nodded.

"He was your first kiss," Liesl said.

"My only kiss," I corrected.

She nodded happily. "I wasn't sure."

"Yeah, well: be sure. Chance is the only boy who's ever kissed me."

She nodded and smiled, falling silent.

Then, "Chance is very special," said Liesl. "We don't even know everything about him, but we know he works closely with the king, and he's protected you many times."

"Many," I agreed, nodding my head and smiling.

"And he's gorgeous," Liesl noted. "I myself had a crush on him first semester."

"Many girls did," I reminded her.

She nodded. "But he chose you, Holly."

My face felt hot.

"He picked you to be his girlfriend," Liesl repeated.

"I heard you," I said, blushing even more.

"Okay, well, just so you know. If I had to give up hope of having Chance, if all the other girls had to give up hope, don't you screw it up, okay?" Liesl whispered.

"I know, Li. I know." I sighed.

We stayed sitting in silence for a while.

After ten minutes, Liesl wiggled her legs. "My butt is freezing," she said, standing up. She turned and reached out toward me with both hands.

"I deserve to have a frozen butt," I murmured.

"You deserve to be able to walk, and a frozen butt will keep that from happening," she said.

She has a point.

I reached up and grasped her hands, and she pulled me to my feet.

"Besides," Liesl said. "There may be a reason you let that go so far."

"Really?" I looked at her.

"Yeah, Laura's father joined us after you left, and he mentioned that some of the higher, more powerful Elfen were immune to the protective power of snowdrops." She nodded toward the flower still in my buttonhole.

I glanced down at the drooping flower. "You're kidding."

"I am not," she put her arm around my shoulders. "Come on, let's go talk to Laura about it."

We slowly walked back to the patio.

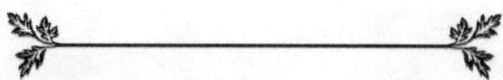

Chapter Fourteen

Explanations

Laura was just coming out the door, followed by her father.

"Holly has just escaped the clutches of a dirty old man," said Liesl.

I blushed.

"Oh, no. He didn't...," Laura looked stricken.

"No, no no," I held up my hands, shaking my head. "Noooooo."

Laura let out a loud sigh of relief.

"I am glad, Miss... er...," Laura's father, standing next to his daughter, said.

"Ó Cuilinn," said Liesl.

I smiled at her.

"Miss Ó Cuilinn," Laura's father smiled.

I grinned.

"What I don't understand is, why?" the man continued.

"Why what, Sir?" Liesl asked.

"I don't understand why Amrynn would try to seduce a student," the older man said.

" 'Amrynn'?" Liesl asked. "Is that Lord Umeqirelle's first name?"

"Yes," Laura's father answered. "Anyway, he's not only a family man, he's in a position of power on the council. Why would he jeopardize that?"

Liesl and I shrugged.

"I wonder if it has something to do with those Oak King Faction spies in there?" Laura wondered softly.

Her father nodded. "You may have hit the nail on the head, dear." He glanced at me. "Anyway, Miss Ó Cuilinn, you can toss that snowdrop flower. Those haven't worked for a long time," he gestured toward the flower in my buttonhole.

I looked down.

Guess not...

I picked it out of my top and held it in my fingers, looking at it thoughtfully.

"Might have worked a few hundred years ago," Laura's father said thoughtfully. "Or a few thousand... who knows?"

"Now that I know, I feel awful," Laura said, looking at me. "I'm sorry, Holly. I let you down. I feel very foolish."

"This is why you need to study up on your history, my dear," her father said. "That has never been your forté."

"I hated that class," Laura laughed. "Guess I should make it my specialty, from now on."

Her father nodded in agreement.

I took a deep breath, and looked down the path.

"Did he just flee for good?" I wondered out loud.

"I hope not," said Liesl. "I have questions for him, and for those Oak King Faction spies in there," she nodded back at the doors to the ballroom.

"Which one should we go after first?" I asked.

"The spies are closer," Liesl suggested.

"Very true," I stepped toward the door, and pulled it half open, then glanced back at the others. Liesl, Laura, and her father looked back at me curiously.

"Well," I said. "You all coming?"

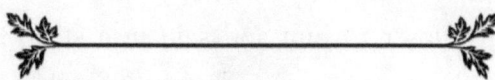

We walked into the ballroom, and the heat and the sound of the music hit us full force, like a physical thing.

"Boy, it's hot in here," Liesl mumbled at my shoulder.

I scanned the room, and my eyes fell on the group of fake Elfen at the far corner of the room. I made my way over to them, winding between tables and chairs, making a path through the mass of people milling about.

I kept my eye on them.

I was angry.

They were talking among themselves and didn't see us approach.

I walked right up to them.

There were four of them in all. I could see clearly through their disguises.

"Hello there, gentlemen," I said.

They turned to me, looking surprised.

The first to recover his composure took a small step toward me, a smile on his face.

I could tell he was trying to be menacing, but the band was playing "Some Enchanted Evening" and his effort fell flat.

I leaned closer to him and said in a steely voice, "I know exactly who you are, and who sent you."

The man's face blanched white.

To his own credit, he recovered almost instantly.

His face still pale, he purred, "Whatever do you mean, Princess?"

"Don't call me that. You have no right," I practically growled. "What did you threaten the Lord Emissary with?" I got right to the point. I had a feeling these goons were behind everything, and I wanted to get to the bottom of it.

His smile vanished in an instant.

"You don't belong at Titania Academy, girl," he snarled.

AHA. He let me see his hand.

I beamed at him. "So *that's* what this is all about. You're trying to get me away from my people before you make war on us."

His face got beet-red, and his lips contorted into a grimace. He raised his hand to grab my neck. "Rrrrrrr!"

He never got the chance.

The other three men in his group, which I had now dubbed "the fake Oak King Faction goons badly disguised as Elfen Folk" grabbed him from behind and pulled him away.

He protested, but they dragged him all the way out the front door, all the while making excuses and mumbling about "our drunk friend" and how he had "embarrassed himself" and they'd "had a lovely time!"

We watched them go.

I grabbed a glass of water from a passing waiter's tray, and raised it to salute them as they departed.

Liesl laughed and imitated my action.

"To friendship," she said heartily.

Some in the crowd heard her and cheered, raising their glasses.

"To friendship!" over a dozen people echoed, laughing.

And the party continued.

"Hey." I turned to Laura and her father. "Do you guys know of a place we can get some food? Food that we can trust?"

"Yes," Laura father said. "My house."

Laura grinned and nodded.

We made our way out of the ballroom, and down the curving pathway that led around to the back of the school.

Laura's father led the way through the moonlight, because, "I know the path best of all."

"Father, I *am* a student here at this school," Laura protested good naturedly.

"Ah." Her father put his finger in the air. "But have you gone on hundreds of late-night walks through the campus, as I have?"

Laura shook her head, smiling. "No, father. I have not. Lead the way."

As we walked, I asked Laura is a quiet voice, "Does your father go on these walks because he is restless?"

She grinned, "No. He is the head of security at the Academy. He walks the grounds at night himself, I guess, because he wants to make sure everything is secure and safe."

"Ah." I nodded.

The moon lit the way for us, but after a short while, Laura's father turned onto the outer path that ringed the school, and I saw that the stones edging this path were luminous. A faint blue light guided us now, and it was a pleasant evening stroll in the cool night air.

As we rounded the last corner on our way behind the school, I heard urgent whispers up ahead.

Laura's father put his hand out to stop us from walking any farther, his finger raised to his lips in a silent plea for quiet.

We waited behind him, and tried to locate the source of the slight commotion.

It was some men behind a large bush by the path, arguing in loud whispers.

Laura's father turned to us and mimed that we should wait here while he went ahead to investigate.

We nodded and waited, watching as he crept closer to the men.

We could tell from the sound of their voices that there were three men in all, and their arguing was getting louder. I watched from afar and could see that one of the men was threatening one of the others, while the third one stood behind the aggressive one.

Laura's father walked up to the three and confronted them.

He looked every bit the part of the head of security: a large man who could look intimidating if he wanted to.

Like now.

I was amazed at how his attitude changed when he confronted these men.

Laura glanced back at Liesl and me and nodded, as if to say, "See? He can do his job well."

We watched as Laura's father had words with the three men, and the aggressive man and his buddy eventually skulked off.

Laura's father was returning with the lone man who'd been threatened. As they approached, I was amazed to see it was Lord Umeqirelle.

"Okay, why don't we all continue to the house?" Laura's father said. "I've invited The Lord Emissary to join us."

I glanced at Lord Umeqirelle, who had been so different just a short while ago.

He looked contrite as his gaze fell to his feet. He remained silent as Laura's father glanced at him, but I thought I detected a slight nod of his head.

We all turned and continued following Laura's father as he led us on the path, his hand on Lord Umeqirelle's arm.

Probably wants to make sure that dude doesn't pull any more of his glamouring on me.

We all walked to Laura's house in a far more solemn procession than before.

When we got to the large house I'd seen earlier in the day after the hunt for Tam, Laura's father led us all inside.

"Father! You're back early!" Tam's voice could be heard.

We filed in, and the boy fell silent.

Lord Umeqirelle was an imposing figure, known to the community as an important official. But Laura's father seemed unimpressed. He guided the tall Elfen Lord to a chair, then sat down next to him.

Laura's mother came forward and whispered in her husband's ear; he turned and whispered back. She nodded and disappeared into another room, returning after a brief absence.

It seemed we were to investigate what was going on, before we were to eat.

Laura's mother quietly brought a box to her husband. It was black and red, adorned with ornate markings.

He took it from her, and said, "Thank you, dear," and he smiled gently at the kind woman, who retreated again.

The box was about fifteen inches long, five inches wide, and two inches thick.

We all looked at it expectantly.

Laura's father carefully lifted the lid and pulled it aside, so we could see the contents.

Inside, a thick golden cord lay curled up on a satin cloth.

Upon seeing it, Lord Umeqirelle bolted from his chair and made a run for the door.

"Get him!" Laura's father exclaimed.

We all jumped up, but Laura's brother was fastest. He leapt in front of the door, blocking the Lord Emissary's path out.

Laura's mother joined the blockade, standing next to her son, her arms folded in from of her, a steely look on her face.

From a back room, another man came forward. He was massive, and his face was set in a stern expression. He looked like a younger version of Laura's father.

"My uncle," whispered Laura in my ear.

I nodded.

"Sit down, Amrynn," Laura's uncle commanded, pointing to the chair in which the Elfen Lord had been seated. "The time has come for honesty."

Lord Umeqirelle looked from Laura's father to her uncle, who now stood next to his nephew at the door. He looked all around the room.

Then he slowly sat back down, a resigned expression on his tired face,

Laura's father also sat down, and the look on his face was frightening. He was very angry.

We all sat down to listen.

Laura's uncle came to stand behind Lord Umeqirelle. He put his hands on the Lord's shoulders and just stayed there, a silent monolith.

Laura's father turned his attention to the contents of the box again. He withdrew the golden rope from where it lay on the silk, and lifted it into the air reverently.

Slowly he stood, lifting the rope high into the air. It floated with a power of its own, and I marveled at the obviously magical object.

Laura's father turned to Lord Umeqirelle and the magical rope was gently placed over the Elfen Lord's head and shoulders, and pulled tight.

Lord Umeqirelle's eyes went blank as the rope tightened, and the stress drained out of his face.

"You are compelled," Laura's father murmured as he sat back down.

Lord Umeqirelle nodded slowly.

Laura whispered to Liesl and I, "No we'll get answers. Finally." She nodded and looked back toward her father.

Laura's father started immediately.

"What business do you have with those men?" he asked. "Why did you seduce our honored guest from the Fae Folk lands? Why were those Oak King Faction men in disguise at the ball? Why were they even there?" Laura's father demanded answers.

I wanted to hear Lord Umeqirelle's explanations as well.

The Elfen Lord that looked so handsome and so much like Legolas, the Lord Emissary who I had been so enamored of so recently, dissolved into agonized tears.

Chapter Fifteen
Deception and Deceit

I could not believe my eyes.

Smooth, suave, charming Lord Umeqirelle, Elfen Emissary who had been seductively enchanting Titania Academy's headmistress Professor Ó Baoghill less than a week before, the man whose charismatic magical glamour earlier had me completely bamboozled, was a complete mess.

His face was in his hands, and he was sobbing.

We all stayed quiet, waiting. Laura's father, the head of security at this Elfen Academy, was running this show.

So we waited.

Lord Umeqirelle's shoulders shook. Minutes passed.

I was starting to feel sorry for him.

Then I began to feel angry.

No matter what his reasons had been, it was very creepy that he'd tried to seduce me.

Laura's father tried again.

"Amrynn, this is the time to confess and explain yourself," the head of security said. "It would be best of you spoke."

Lord Umeqirelle pulled his hands down from his wet face and nodded.

Laura's father sat up tall and tried again. "What business did you have with those Oak King Faction men?"

The Elfen Lord took a deep breath and began to talk.

"You people have no right to hold me here," he began. "No right at all."

"Answer the questions," Laura's father said in a low voice.

"No," Lord Umeqirelle flashed him a look filled with hatred. "I will not."

Laura's father stood up and adjusted the golden rope around Lord Umeqirelle's shoulders.

"What's that supposed to do?" I asked.

"Compel him to tell the truth," Laura whispered.

I glanced over at the Elfen Lord. He looked angry. Angry and obstinate and extremely upset.

"Let me try," I said softly.

Laura's father looked at me. "Really, Holly, you don't have to, I know it must be difficult..." His voice trailed off.

I rose from my seat. "Switch seats with me," I asked him.

He shrugged and came over and I went and sat where he'd been sitting: right next to Lord Umeqirelle.

I turned to this Elfen Lord, and leaned over until I was close to him.

Our eyes met.

He looked slightly worried, slightly confused, and very embarrassed.

"Hi," I said softly, smiling. Our faces were perhaps a foot and a half apart. As close as I could get and still focus on his eyes.

I waited for a response.

After a minute, he said, "Hi," in a quiet voice.

"What is your name?" I asked.

He blinked and didn't answer.

I turned to Laura's father. "I thought this magical rope was supposed to compel him to tell the truth?"

The other man shrugged. "It's supposed to. I don't know why it's not working."

I turned back to the Elfen Lord Emissary and studied his face.

He looked defensive.

I don't want him to think I'm the enemy, because I'm not. I just want to know what's going on with him and those Oak King Faction goons masquerading as Elfen men.

Think, Hols, think.

I took a deep breath and tried again.

"Lord Umeqirelle?" I said softly. "You seem upset."

He blinked. After a minute he nodded slowly.

"Why are you upset, Sir?" I used the most soothing voice I could muster.

He struggled against the rope.

I glanced back at Laura's father. "Is the thing binding him? It doesn't look that tight."

"It's not. It's a pretty thick rope, so it's nearly impossible to tie it tightly," he answered back.

I turned again to the Elfen Lord.

"Sir, I don't know why you glamoured me back at my school. Heck, you glamoured anyone who you could, didn't you? My headmistress, too. Right?"

He blinked again and looked down.

I rapped my knuckles on the table in front of us. "Hey, hey..."

He looked back up at me.

"Listen, the Oak King Faction has made numerous attempts on my life," I began, trying a new tack. "I have done nothing to harm them. Nothing at all."

I felt a tap on my shoulder, and glanced over.

Liesl was whispering in my ear. "Holly, you did pop Jessica pretty hard on your first day."

"So?" I whispered.

"So, she's part of the Oak King Faction now, right?" Liesl whispered, her hand cupped on her mouth, trying to keep her words private.

"Yeah, but I don't think she was back then," I whispered back.

"Do you know for sure?" Liesl murmured.

Oh, God ...

I turned back to Lord Umeqirelle and smiled. "They've made numerous attempts on my life, Sir. Numerous." I stared at him for a minute. "Sir? I'm an innocent fourteen..."

"Fifteen," Liesl whispered in my ear.

I turned and nodded to her, "Thank you, Liesl," I whispered. I turned back to Lord Umeqirelle. "... fifteen-year-old girl, and this... this political group... is actively trying to harm me."

He stared at me. Unblinking. Unmoved.

Think, Holly.

I turned to Laura's father. "May we have some water, please?" I asked in a quiet voice.

I had to do something to buy time while I thought this out.

Stream of consciousness.

I closed my eyes.

I could hear Laura's father get up and fumble around in the other room.

Probably the kitchen.

I sighed.

I rubbed my nose.

Think. Think. Think.

I took a deep breath.

I heard a faint sound and opened my eyes.

A cup of water had been placed in front of me, and another in front of Lord Umeqirelle.

I took a sip.

What was this Elfen Lord thinking? What had he been doing? And why won't he talk to me?

What is most important to him?

I had it.

"Lord Emissary," I said. "How is your family? Your wife? Your child? Didn't you say you had a daughter?" I didn't take my eyes off his face.

His breathing quickened, and tears came to his eyes. He opened his mouth to speak but couldn't get any words out.

Aha.

He stared at me, his jaw moving but no sound issuing forth.

"Lord Umeqirelle," I began again. Then I paused and reached forward, taking his hand in mine. "Lord Umeqirelle," I said in a quiet voice, "what have they done with your wife and daughter?"

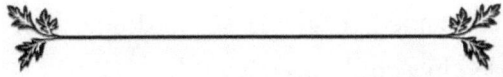

We spent an hour more in Laura's house, and the information the Elfen Lord had spilled had been incredible.

"They sent me a message last week," Lord Umeqirelle told us. "They said I had to stay away from my house, and do what they asked, or they would kill my wife and daughter."

Lord Almighty, what a mess.

"Well, first things first," I said. "We take out those who are watching you."

"They're watching everyone," he whispered.

"Are they watching us now?" I asked.

He nodded.

I told everyone to stay put, and motioned to Liesl to join me outside, ostensibly to chat about Chance. We stayed there, about twenty-five feet from Laura's house, giggling as we pretended to have a lighthearted conversation. Then we put our heads together and whispered. "I see two of them, on the far side of the house, behind those trees."

Liesl pretended to giggle so hard she doubled over, and whirled in a circle, acting giddy.

People will believe the oddest things about schoolgirls.

She came to a stop, dizzy from twirling, grinning like a lovable idiot, then touched her forehead to mine and nodded, her lips pressed together.

"Come on," I laughed, and we'd chased each other back into the house. "That's enough fresh air!"

We let the others know where to find the spies, and Laura's father and uncle snuck out. A few minutes later, the two Oak King Faction men were tied up in the garden shed, and the authorities had been alerted to come pick them up.

The same thing had happened near the school. We bagged four of the goons, and stuffed them in the Astronomy Class, which had a door directly leading outside.

Very convenient.

Having taken care of the spies, we made way to Lord Umeqirelle's house and started looking for clues.

It was near midnight by the time we got there. All of us, including both of Laura's parents, her little brother, and her uncle, were with us, hoping to find out where the Oak King Faction kidnappers had taken Lord Umeqirelle's wife and daughter — where they were holding them hostage.

"Amrynn, hurry up," I said.

We had all agreed to drop the formalities. Since we were all together on this, it just made sense to be on a first-name basis.

We entered Amrynn's home, leaving the lights off and trying to be quiet.

"Amrynn, hurry up," I whispered as we passed from room to room, looking for anything that might tell us where his family had been taken.

He had stopped at a photo of them all during happier times. I grabbed it and pulled his arm along. "Here, take it, but come on," I whispered.

I wondered if we would find any clues about what had happened here.

Aha!

In the far room, toward the back of the house, Laura's father and uncle had found signs of a struggle.

Amrynn dropped to his knees when he saw the scene, and slowly picked up a piece of clothing off the floor.

"My... my wife was wearing this blouse... the morning I said last saw her." He sniffled. Someone shushed him. He lifted the blouse to me. "She was wearing this the day before I arrived at Titania Academy," he whispered.

I took the blouse and shone my tiny flashlight on it.

The material was yellow and silver, with dark stains.

"Is that blood?" whispered Liesl, coming up behind me.

I looked closer, then brought the material up to my face to smell it.

"No," I whispered, "I don't think so. It smells of blueberries."

"Blueberries? Why would there be stains of blueberries on it?" Laura on my other side whispered.

Amrynn stood up again, wiping his eyes. "We grow blueberries in our garden out back," he said. "Through the back door, there." He pointed to a side door out of this back room I hadn't noticed.

Laura's father and uncle finished searching the room, and we all went out back.

Moonlight flooded the area as I stood on the edge of the garden, searching for clues.

Everyone looked. It wasn't easy; the garden was overgrown.

The plot was about twenty feet square, and a number of trellises supported berry plants along the outer edge of the square.

We bent, feeling our way through, trying hard not to disturb any clues we might find.

It would have far easier to search during the daylight hours, but sunrise was still more than five hours away, and time was of the essence.

The confrontation we had witnessed between Lord Umeqirelle and the Oak King Faction men had revealed their frustration with the Lord Emissary and how he was proceeding with the seduction of one Titania Academy student.

Me.

He'd been tasked with seducing me, luring me from the Fae Folk school, from my friends, from my support system.

From my home.

I suspected it had all been in preparation for some kind of attack on Titania Academy, and that they couldn't risk carrying out their plans while I was there. My Elemental Powers were just too strong. They'd seen what I could do last semester, and they knew I would jeopardize their plans.

Their plans to destroy the Academy once and for all.

I wonder why they just didn't kidnap me? There. Problem solved.

I stopped and closed my eyes, putting my finger to the bridge of my nose in chagrin.

I felt annoyed with myself.

It's a good thing the Oak King Faction can't see inside my head.

I grinned to myself and resumed my search.

"Hey," Amrynn whispered. "I've found some trampled berry bushes. I think the intruders got the juice when they accidentally smashed berries on themselves, then tracked them into the house and got them on my wife during the struggle."

I tiptoed over to where he was crouched.

Yep.

A lot of berries had been trampled underfoot there.

Enough for several pies. Damn.

"Keep looking," I whispered to him. "We need some clue as to where they might have gone."

He nodded and resumed his search.

I found a berry and popped it into my mouth.

Ripe. Mmmmm.

I rolled my eyes.

Concentrate, Holly!

I moved a few feet over and bent to search the ground again.

It was surreal that the hot guy who'd been trying to get me to kiss him less than six hours before was now amiable and friendly, and that I was helping him find his kidnapped wife and kid.

All of us had studied the message that had been sent to the Lord Emissary.

Umeqirelle, we are tired of discussing our objectives with you. To hasten your implementation of our plans, we have taken your wife and daughter and they will be staying at an undisclosed location, to better help you focus on the objective. See that you do not go back home. We will be watching.

Evil. Pure evil. It was one thing to fight one against the other, but to take hostages, that was above and beyond.

This is war.

I knew things were getting bad. The Oak King Faction was getting bolder and stranger, and we didn't know what they would do next.

I wondered when and if open hostilities would begin. The physical attack on the school last term had been a good indication that they wanted to force a full-scale war. Whether or not they had the resources, and the foot soldiers, was another matter entirely.

"Found something," Laura's uncle whispered faintly from the other side of the garden.

I looked up and saw everyone headed over.

I was the farthest away, and I took my time making my way over to them.

I kept my eyes and ears peeled for anyone who might be watching.

I thought I saw movement off in the trees to the left, but when I glanced over, everything was still.

I stopped and held my breath for the count of ten, listening for any sound, but all was silent.

Silent as a graveyard.

When I finally got to where the others were gathered, I look to see what they'd found.

Oh my.

It was a shoe, encrusted with distinctive looking yellow mud. There wasn't any soil like that in the garden.

"That's from the old estuary," Laura's mother said, "Five miles yonder."

"It's got a leaf stuck to it," said Laura's little brother.

"That's from this garden," Laura said. "Wait. No, it's not."

"How can you tell?" asked Liesl.

"See here, and here," Laura said, pointing. "These are grape leaves. Huge. Not like berry plant leaves."

"There's an overgrown vineyard next to that estuary," Laura's uncle murmured. "And an abandoned farmer's shack right on the edge of it. I passed it t'other day. It had smoke coming out of t'chimney. I found that very odd."

"I'll bet those goons have taken up residence in that shack," Laura's father said, "and are there right now, all cozy and warm."

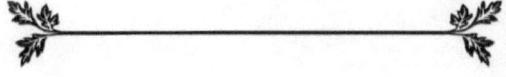

Chapter Sixteen
Rescue

It was a long ride out to the estuary. Since we couldn't go by carriage (the unicorns being all put to barn and the carriage being ungodly loud), we decided to go by bicycle.

Yes, that's right.

Bicycle.

Laura's uncle was a racer, and he had multiple bikes back at Laura's house, behind the storeroom. Two of them were tandem bicycles.

Laura's uncle was extremely enthusiastic and made it seem like a wonderful idea.

Even though Liesl and I had never ridden a bicycle, we all decided to give it a go.

We got about two miles before being caught.

"What are you all on about?" said a voice off the side of the road.

"Oh, my God, it's a family of halflings," groaned Liesl. *What?*

"Don't bother us now, Moronga, we're on a quest," Laura's father said quietly.

"Well, what if I want to come with you," said the halfling who had spoken first.

We had all stopped, and I peered in the moonlight to look at the smallish people who were just now emerging from the forest.

We'd been taking a shortcut ("this is the fastest shortcut I know, and faster even than the road," Laura's uncle had said), and the wide path through the forest had, happily, been smooth enough for our bicycles.

Liesl and I had been riding a tandem bike together, and after falling no fewer than half a dozen times, we'd finally gotten the hang of it. One thing that had become abundantly clear, though, was that the best way to keep tandem bikes from crashing was to maintain your forward momentum. When we stopped, we nearly fell off again.

232

"Feet out," I'd said, as we rolled to a stop. Liesl and I had narrowly avoided another crash by placing both pairs of legs out as we came to a stop. But it was wobbly, to be sure.

Laura's father was discussing whether the halflings should join us on our two-in-the-morning impromptu raid of the Oak King Faction hideout in the abandoned vineyard.

"Listen, you know I'd normally say 'yes,' but this is a special circumstance," Laura's uncle was saying.

They must be acquaintances.

"We want to go," a shorter halfling said from behind the first one. "This is our wood, you are passing through, therefore we have a right to join you on your quest."

There were about five of them; in the moonlight, I couldn't be sure. Some looked shorter than others, and some looked wider, but I wasn't acquainted with the inhabitants of the Elfen Lands, so I couldn't tell if any of them were children. I stared and listened and didn't interfere.

The argument went on for some minutes, and it was clear from the beginning that Laura's father was losing it.

I glanced around us. The forest had gone quiet.

"Laura," I whispered. She turned and stepped back to me. I continued. "Are these woods normally this quiet at night? Could the Oak King Faction men be near?"

"I don't know," she whispered. "We're still miles away from the estuary, and the vineyard is beyond that." She looked around us, then added, "It's almost like the creatures of the wood are listening in."

I frowned and stepped closer to the trees, trying to peer into the thick vegetation.

"Quite different from our own forests, huh?" Liesl whispered beside me.

I jumped in surprise, which set her off silently laughing.

"Don't do that, you nearly scared the wits out of me!" I quietly scolded. She just laughed harder, still silent, but now doubled over in mirth.

"Ohhh you," I murmured, walking back to our bike.

A very small halfling was standing next to our tandem bike, examining the handlebars.

"Hey," I said, grabbing the bike. "That's ours."

"You weren't here. It was alone. I saw it alone," the little halfling said quietly. I could not tell the little one's gender at all.

"Well, it's mine. My friend and I were riding it, just now, when your... uh... friend stepped out of the wood to speak to my... uh... my friends and me." My hand gripped the bit above the front wheel.

The halfling's hand gripped the left handlebar.

We both refused to let go.

I glanced over my shoulder to get help.

"Liesl," I called in a strained whisper. "LIESL."

"The jaguars will hear you," the halfling murmured, "You should just shush and let go. This is mine now."

"Like heck it is, halfling. Now let go!" I protested.

Liesl finally came over, walked to the other side of the bike, and nudged the halfling in the shoulder. "Oi. Let go of our bike, little one, or I'll steal your hat," and she reached out as if to grab the dark cap that was perched atop the halfling's head.

The little person's mouth went wide with surprise; the halfling let go of the handlebars in order to secure their hat with both hands, then ran off back to the others as fast as a halfling's legs could go.

"Phew," I whispered. "Thanks for that, I was getting a bit worried he... er... she... was going to steal our bike." I looked to where the halfling had run, wanting to be sure they had not circled back.

"She, I think," said Liesl. "We had one visiting my neighbor last summer. Unintentionally." She chuckled, then glanced at me. "I keep forgetting you didn't grow up among other magical folk."

"Tell me about it," I murmured, staring at the halflings, nearly all of whom were now involved with the "discussion" about accompanying us to the vineyard.

More like a debate than a discussion.

"Holly," Liesl bent and whispered in my ear. "I don't want to be overheard." She glanced at the halflings. "I've been told they have really good hearing. But listen: If you come across one of the foundling races, just say something to get them to grab something other than what they're trying to make off with. Do you understand?"

"I think so," I whispered back. "So, foundling races are those races that...?"

"Try to make off with things," she whispered nearly inaudibly, despite her mouth being so close to my ear that it tickled when it moved. She withdrew and looked into my eyes and nodded with a questioning look.

Ohhh.

I nodded back to her.

Good to know.

The heated yet whispered discussion Laura's father, uncle, and now mother were having with the family of halflings went on for a while.

I sat down, and Liesl and Laura joined me.

"How long do you think they'll keep at it?" I murmured. We still had to keep our voices low.

"Until my father, mother, and uncle figure out they're not going to get their way," said Laura. "No one ever does, not with halflings. They've been known to argue for days."

"Laura, where's your bike?" I asked, then spotted it. Laura's brother had hold of it. They'd ridden on the second tandem bike. The young boy was holding firmly to their two-seater as he watching his parents argue.

The discussion was amicable, and Laura was right.

An hour later, we were back on our way, us on our bikes and the halflings running after us, apparently effortlessly.

We came to a hill and stopped next to the crooked trees and looked down.

The estuary.

I had been wondering how we were going to get over the water, but now I could see: There was a small tree bridge. Wide, hanging roots had been trained to grow across, and the river, banked by large boulders, ran between them.

"Is the vineyard beyond the bridge?" Liesl asked.

"Yes," Laura's uncle answered.

"How do we get across without being seen?" I asked. "Don't we need the element of surprise?"

This stopped Laura's parents and uncle in their tracks, and led to another discussion with the halflings.

After a brief discussion, the little people assured us they would travel on ahead and make sure any lookouts were dispatched.

I wasn't sure of the strategy, but I was following adults who supposedly knew better than I, so I couldn't complain.

Amrynn had been silent this whole time, except for a few words he'd contributed here and there to the first discussion they'd had with the halflings, in the woods several miles back.

I turned to him. "Amrynn, have you ever been to this hideout of theirs?"

He shook his head. He looked miserable. "No, I haven't. I'm just so worried about my wife and daughter. I can't really think straight. I'm just following them." He indicated Laura's parents and uncle.

They did seem to be very sure of themselves. I was counting on that. I think Amrynn was, too.

By now it was after three in the morning.

Three of the halflings had taken off down to the bridge, and we watched them until we lost sight of them altogether.

"Can you see them?" I whispered.

"No," came several answers.

The halflings that had stayed behind — I assumed they were younger — turned and whispered, "We can see them just fine," and grinned.

Huh?

Laura whispered, "I'd be able to see them if I had night vision, too."

I rolled my eyes.

A half-hour later, they were back.

"The coast is clear," they beckoned. "Come."

We followed them down, walking our bikes the whole way... which went much, much slower and took another hour.

By the time we'd crossed the edge of the vineyard and found the shack — which was really just a cabin made of logs — it was nearing four-thirty in the blessed morning.

We were going to get caught, I was sure of it. Oh, Lord Almighty.

Laura's father and uncle crept up to scope the place out, then came back to let us know.

"Everyone except the sentry is asleep," said the burly uncle. "But I counted a dozen men in there."

"Did you see my wife and daughter?" Amrynn whispered, nearly sobbing with worry.

This is pathetic.

I tried to remain silent, and was barely successful.

If my family had been kidnapped and I was outside the place they were being held, I would not be no teary eye or worried, I'd be all like, IMMA STORM THIS PLACE AND THEY DEAD.

I did not understand these Elfen. I knew my mother was half-Elfen, but really, *how far do you take things into the realm of academics and culture, then have no courage or backbone to storm a castle when it needed to be stormed?*

Sheesh.

The adults were making plans and strategizing.

I thought of something and pulled Liesl and Laura back a bit to talk to them.

"Hey," I whispered. "What if we're outnumbered and this whole thing goes south?"

Liesl looked stricken. "How could this go wrong? We've got four adults, three students, and five or six halflings. We'll overpower them with sheer numbers."

Laura looked thoughtful. "We need a Plan B," she said.

I nodded; my eyebrows raised.

After a minute, Laura turned to her little brother. "Tam, you stay back. Watch the fight. If things look bad, I mean, if they overpower us and we get caught, take your bike and ride it like the wind and alert the council, okay? You'll be a real hero."

The boy grinned and nodded vigorously.

Laura gave her brother a nod.

We turned forward. The adults had come up with a plan.

"We're going to rush in, and then you littles rush in after us," said Laura's uncle. "Don't hold back. We need to free the woman and the girl, but we also need to capture the leaders." He nodded.

The halflings nodded back.

Laura and Liesl and I nodded as well, more slowly.

A dozen is a lot.

I hoped we'd be enough.

Laura's father and uncle were big men. Amrynn would help too, I hoped. He was tall but thin.

The halflings were small, but there were five of them.

And there was us.

I glanced at Liesl, and gave the cross-fingers gesture.

She looked at me like, *"What?"*

I grinned, and mouthed, *"Good luck."*

She nodded.

We were ready.

Laura's uncle gave his brother a pat and then mouthed, *"GO!"*

And we were off.

The three Elfen men banged down the door, yelling loudly.

Laura's mother went in after them.

The halflings crashed through a big window. Liesl, Laura and I went in after them.

The fight was a loud and jumbled mess of craziness.

"YA!" we screamed, and hit the Oak King Faction goons with whatever we'd brought.

I had my magical staff, Liesl had brought a cricket bat. Laura had a hockey stick.

The three Elfen men had brought clubs and brooms. Laura's mother had, believe it or not, a large frying pan. She'd carried it strapped to her back. It was heavy.

Every time she hit one of our enemies, it made a solid metal CLANGGGGG, and nearly toppled her over. But she knocked two men down before she lost the pan. Then she just fought with her fists.

I banged my staff against heads whenever I could. The close quarters made it too hard to use magic, but the staff was heavy and long, and I knocked several of them down before someone grabbed me from behind. I swung my staff behind me and thwacked the guy in the head and stunned him long enough the break free.

The fight went on a while.

We caught the Oak King Faction men — and there were only men in their party — by surprise. Which was a good thing. I think if we hadn't, the fight would have been over a lot sooner.

Amrynn, mister Elfen Lord Emissary Fancy Pants, was no help at all. He subdued one adversary, wrestling him to the ground, then tossing him into a corner and kicking him in the side. But then he ran into the back bedroom, found his wife and daughter, and fled out the back door with them.

Gone.

Speaking of back doors, I wondered why on earth we hadn't just snuck in through the back door and rescued the hostages, and tiptoed away? That might have actually worked.

Unlike what we'd actually tried to do. The only reason we were even mildly successful was because Amrynn got the hostages out, and because of the help we got from the halflings.

Laura's father and uncle were big and strong, and they fought valiantly. But when four or five Fae Folk men jump you at the same time, even if you're a big Elfen man, you'll go down.

Oh, and the "dozen men" Laura's uncle had counted turned out to be at least twenty.

Remind me to have a word with that man about counting properly and being sure of how many people we're up against before we get in another fight.

The halflings were fabulous. They attacked from the bottom up, hitting the Oak King Faction men with sticks and rocks they apparently carried in their travel bags for just such occasions. But even with their valiant fighting, screaming, and general enthusiasm, they were eventually subdued.

I'm just glad the bad guys didn't use magic in the fight. They must have been worried about hitting each other with the oversplash magic often takes.

In the end, we found ourselves in the back bedroom, tied up. Laura's father, Laura's uncle, Laura's mother ("Get your filthy hands off me, you rhinoceros piddle! You stink, you sweat from a baboon's balls!"), Laura, Liesl, myself, and five halflings.

Tied up.

With rope.

Thin rope, that made tight knots, not like that golden rope Laura's father had tried to use back at the house, the rope that had done absolutely no good, except for looking showy and impressive.

The halflings had already gotten started on trying to undo the knots. When our captors saw this, they tied triple knots on the halflings: They were trussed up so tightly the smallest one started to cry.

Great.

Laura's little brother, Tam? He hadn't even entered the shack. He'd obeyed his big sister, thank the Gods, and was, hopefully, halfway back to the Elfen Academy by now.

The Oak King Faction men crowded into the back bedroom, and there was barely enough room for all the bodies. They stared at us for a few minutes, trying to decide what to do with us.

They finally agreed to keep three men watching us, since "there's so many of them, we can't leave just one, right?" and the rest would go off and consult with their leader.

Whoever that was.

That was the question.

Who is directing the Oak King Faction forces? Is it the Oak King himself?

I felt a bitter cold feeling flow over my head, as if a bucket of ice water had been dropped onto the top of me. Serious, ice cold. My heart pounded. My breathing became labored.

"You okay?" Liesl asked from beside me.

We had decided ahead of time not to use names, because the Oak King Faction had targeted me. Who knew if these particular henchmen knew what I looked like? I didn't recognize any of them from before, at the ball.

I could be mistaken for an Elfen student.

My platinum-blonde hair certainly helped me blend in with the locals. And although my eyes were a dead giveaway, apparently these bad guys hadn't yet noticed the color.

I kept my eyes and face downcast, to hide them.

"You okay?" Liesl repeated out of the corner of her mouth.

I nodded slowly.

"I just really hate being tied up."

The Oak King Faction guys were still talking among themselves, and going in and out of the back bedroom, which was actually quite cramped with all of us.

I could hear some of what they were discussing.

"There's more than ten — eleven of them in there. What you gonna do with that many hostages?" One of them was raising his voice. Two others argued back and forth with him.

"Heck if I know. Go ask the boss. Tell him what happened, okay?"

"Well, who would we use them as leverage for? That Lord Emissary guy, he was here in the fight, but he's gone now, and so are the woman and girl!"

"I can see that, thanks. I don't know what to do any more than you do."

"Let's just wait for orders, okay?"

"FINE."

"Anyway, we're going to need more food."

"Yeah, and toilet paper. We were almost out yesterday."

"Oh, great. GREAT! This is turning into a DISASTER!"

"Hey, don't yell at me!"

"You two just stay here, I'll send the outside guy to the store."

"You can't just send him to the store, he's got to look like one of these Elfen."

"Well, where the heck's the makeup?"

It went on like this for over an hour.

I hoped Laura's little bother Tam would be back with the authorities fast.

Did the Faerie world even have police?

I whispered to Laura and asked.

She nodded, looking scared.

Then I remembered: Her father was head of campus security for the Elfen Academy.

And he was here.

Tied up alongside us.

Oh, no.

"What kind of police does the Elfen land have anyway?" I asked quietly. "I mean, besides campus security."

Laura's eyes were tearing up.

"You okay?" I asked. "I didn't mean anything, just wondered who would be coming later this morning to rescue us."

Laura shook her head and dropped her chin.

"Holly," Laura's father whispered across the four tied-up halflings between us.

I bent and looked over at him.

"The Elfen Council that rules over the Elfen lands," he said. "They send out assigned Elfen to carry out their rules."

"Yeah, okay," I whispered back. "But who responds in an emergency? Holding a council session takes times. We need to be rescued right away."

His response was the last thing I wanted to hear: "Each area is assigned to a different security force. This vineyard is under the Academy's jurisdiction. And I am the head of security for the Academy."

I blinked.

"So, what, do you have a second in command, Mister 'Head of Security'?" I asked, feeling desperate, which made me mouthy.

Laura's father looked at me with a strange expression, and a heartbeat later I found out why.

His brother, Laura's uncle, stuck out his head so he could see me; he had been tied up on the other side of Laura's father. He caught my eye, waved with a pained grin, and said in a stage whisper, "Second in command? That would be me."

Oh, great. Just wonderful.

Chapter Seventeen
Explosive Rescue

"Do you want to talk?" Liesl asked me.

I had been lying sideways, my shoulder on the floor, angry as hell.

We were still tied up, and the others gave me a wide berth — as wide a berth that they could, anyway.

I had spent the last hour and a half thinking about my family. My birth family.

My mother had died from neglect after giving birth to me, because she was homeless.

My father hadn't even known I existed, for nearly a decade and a half of my life. I'd first met him when I was fourteen years old. I loved him dearly, and he was my main connection to my Faerie life.

"I'm just angry about my mother being homeless and dying, when she could have been a princess in the Elfen Land," I said. "And I'm tired of things going wrong."

I had been thinking about this and seething quietly, until I had felt so bad I'd dropped over to lie on my side, tears falling freely. My face was red with anger, and everyone saw this.

Liesl began to rub my back slowly, trying in her own way to soothe her friend.

It didn't work.

Well, it didn't work much.

At first.

But I did finally fall asleep.

I awoke several hours later, when the guard came into the room and passed out water.

Stretching, I yawned and looked around. Aspen and Tundra lay next to me, snoring.

I smiled gratefully at the reassuring presence of my two arctic wolf familiars, and gently moved my hand down their fur for a few minutes.

Last night, both of them had tried to bite through the rope binding me, but they couldn't. The rope must have been made with magical properties or something.

I didn't know.

But I was glad they had tried, and glad they'd slept next to me.

Some of the halflings were just waking up, and Tam and Laura yawned and sat up as well.

"Liesl, did you sleep at all? I asked softly as I accepted a small paper cup of water being distributed.

"A bit. I woke up about a half-hour ago," she said.

I yawned again and watched as the guards finished passing out water and left the room.

"Today is Sunday," I said.

Liesl nodded.

"We're supposed to return home tomorrow morning," I said.

Liesl wriggled against her bonds. "Well then we're going to need to escape," she said.

The rope that tied my hands behind my back was really starting to hurt. "I've had enough of this."

As if on cue, there was a loud explosion from outside. *BOOM!*

"What was that?" I said, jerking my head toward the sound so fast, my neck hurt. "Owww," I said, rubbing my shoulder.

We heard the three Oak King Faction guards run outside.

"We need to get out of here," mumbled Laura's father.

I held my breath, straining to hear anything from outside the door.

This room is a prison.

We could hear *something* happening.

I struggled against my bonds, pulling my wrists against the rope so hard it began to really hurt. And still I struggled. Tears dripped down my face. I felt so frustrated I wanted to scream and rage against the people who'd tied me up.

"Holly, stop," Liesl said. "You're bleeding."

I stopped and turned my head. "What?"

"Your arms: The rope is making them bleed," Liesl said softly, looking behind my back.

I slumped on the floor, dejected.

The stinging pain was starting to get bad.

As I sat there, breathing hard, wrists hurting, I noticed everyone had gone still.

I listened again.

I could hear nothing, nothing at all. Whatever had happened outside, it was now quiet.

Then... I heard the door in the other room open loudly, banging against the wall as it flew wide and hit the doorstop.

Then I heard whispered admonishment.

A minute later, the door to the room opened. The room that was our prison. The room we'd sat in for half the night and half the morning. A good seven hours or so.

Seemed like longer.

A head appeared around the edge of the door.

A halfling head.

"Groble!" exclaimed one of the halflings who was tied up next to us. A long string of halfling language poured out of our companions' mouths.

The long and short of it was this: We'd been rescued by the rest of the halfling village.

I'd had no idea there were so many of them.

And Tam and Amrynn were with them.

Tam hurried and helped untie us. "You would not believe what happened," he said.

"Tell us!" Tam's father and uncle said at the same time.

It turned out that Amrynn had rushed his family to Laura's house, where he'd met up with Tam. The council was nowhere to be found.

"We think the Faction has them somewhere, but we're not sure," Amrynn told us. "Basically, they're missing."

"Where did you look? It was the early morning. Maybe they were still asleep," Laura's father suggested.

"Oh, right," said Amrynn.

I rolled my eyes.

Tam had ridden his bike back home, met up with the Lord Emissary, and then they'd gathered some weapons and started back to the vineyard. They'd met up with the halfling villagers on the way.

"Well, we're extremely..." Laura's uncle started.

"VERY HAPPY," Laura's father had interjected.

"... very" — Laura's uncle glanced at his brother — "very happy you rescued us."

"What was the explosion?" I asked.

"Oh, that was a firework I had left over from last summer," Tam said, laughing. "Father told me to dispose of it, but I knew it would come in handy, so I stuffed it in the back of my closet..."

His father tousled the boy's hair, smiling. "For once, I'm glad you disobeyed me."

Tam shrugged with a smile. "Well, it made a good diversion."

We were all finally untied and outside. The Oak King Faction guards had been tied up and left in the room where they'd imprisoned us. We'd let the authorities know about them, when we were safe and back to the school.

"We need to get back to the Academy," said Laura's mother. "Amrynn said he checked the Gathering Hall and found it empty — not surprising, since it was five in the morning. But we need to warn the vice-headmistress."

Amrynn looked down at his feet.

I patted his arm.

"Well, let's get back then," I agreed. I turned to Laura's parents and Amrynn: "I've been meaning to ask, why is the vice-headmistress the one we're reporting to?"

Laura's dad gave Amrynn a look. Amrynn turned to me. "Because the headmaster himself is already in control of the Oak King Faction."

Oh my God.

"We need to hurry," Laura's uncle said.

We ran up the hill and got our bikes, then hightailed it back to the Elfen Academy. It took several hours.

The halflings bade us goodbye when we passed their wood, shaking our hands vigorously, as they thanked us for "a wonderful adventure" and insisted, "We must do this again soon."

"Didn't they realize we were in quite a lot of danger?" I asked Laura's father after the halflings had disappeared into the trees.

"They love adventure, the more thrilling, the better," he said. "I'm not sure they ever think the danger they're in is quite as threatening as it really is." He smiled.

I couldn't help but like the halflings. They were fearless.

I doubt you'd ever see halflings crying, even in frustration.

In the light of the morning, I felt very foolish and weak about how upset I had been the night before. No one else had been anywhere near that distressed, and while I acknowledged to myself that I had a personal stake in things, I wished I had not cried quite so much.

I'm fifteen now. I need to act more mature.

Thinking about the night before helped me to pass the time, and I didn't even notice the hours going by while I pedaled behind Liesl, on the rear seat of our tandem bicycle. Still, I realized the toll those hours of pedaling had taken on my sleep-deprived body, when we finally rounded the last curve in the trail and the Elfen Academy came into view.

A couple of hours' sleep is definitely not enough.

We rode our bikes around the outside of the Academy and pulled up to Laura's house around back, and I dropped off my seat, my legs so wobbly they jiggled.

I was so tired, I dropped to a bench and sat there, bent over. My hand could barely hold my magic staff.

"Father!" Amrynn's daughter cried, running out of the house a step ahead of her mother and rushing up to greet her father.

I smiled at the reunion.

Watching them cuddle made me miss my familiars.

I had sent Aspen and Tundra back to their realm, to wait until I really needed them.

I'd been more selective in calling them to me in the months since the attack on Titania Academy. I was fifteen now, and I wanted to try and be more self-sufficient and resourceful. I think they'd come to sleep beside me because I'd been so upset. They usually acted on their own when tears were present.

I slumped on the bench, smiling.

"Here," Liesl reached out her hand, and helped me up.

"Sorry, where to now?" I said. I took a deep breath, trying to get my strength back.

"We wait here. Amrynn will go in to see if the council is here," Liesl said.

We watched as the Elfen Emissary bade his wife and child goodbye, and jogged away toward the school.

We all waited. I lay down on the grass outside Laura's house and chilled with Liesl and Laura. Tam brought out some sandwiches, and we all ate and rested.

They had really nice grass, with roses nearby.

I wonder why I didn't notice yesterday.

"Tam, have you started at the Elfen Academy yet?" I asked, stomach full and feeling sated.

"Two more years," he said. "I'm still attending the Primary School. It's dull, and I hate it."

"Liesl," I said.

"Mmmm?" she answered lazily.

"Did you go to a primary school when you were young?" I asked. I was curious what Fae Folk children did when they were young.

"Uh, no actually," Liesl replied. "Some do, but many are taught at home like me."

That sounds like something I would have liked.

"I guess you were, too, huh, Holly?" Liesl said.

"Sort of," I murmured. Aunt Clare had taught me a lot of things when I was younger, but since we'd been homeless, I doubted it had been anything like Liesl's childhood. "Tam?" I said.

Tam didn't answer.

Laura nudged her little brother, lying next to us on the grass, and he opened his eyes.

"Huh?" he said.

"Oh," I said. "I was just wondering what kind of things they do in your Primary School?"

"Oh," he said. "Well, there's Arts and History, of course. But my favorite part is the Explores. We have one every day. Last week, we went caving. It was an overgrown cavern as tall as a tree, with vines growing so long over the entrance you couldn't even see the opening at all. We had to push through so much ivy to get in, I got spiders in my hair." He glanced at his sister. "Laura, you would've hated it."

I looked over at Laura. "You don't like spiders?" I asked her.

"No, I actually don't mind spiders. But I've been trying to make my hair curl, and I just changed the color, so I'd have probably freaked out because of that," she chuckled.

I sat up and looked at her hair. It was gently curled, and the color was a light strawberry blond. It looked platinum in the sunlight, but with a golden-red tint in the shadows.

"That's cool," I said, lying back down in the grass.

The adults were milling about, going back and forth, in and out of the house, talking and going about their business.

I wondered at how everything seemed to have just gone back to normal so quickly.

In the human world, the police would have been called, and they would have come and taken our statements, and then gone to the vineyard shack and arrested the kidnappers.

Those Oak King Faction men who'd held us would've been in so much trouble: the kind of trouble where bail money is needed.

"I guess here in the Faerie Lands, there aren't any consequences for kidnapping?" I murmured aloud.

"Oh, there are consequences all right," Laura said. "It just happens so seldom that the authorities are slow to act."

"Well, then, they might get away," I said.

Chapter Eighteen

The Elfen Academy Council

"They're back," Laura's mother called.

We all looked over.

Amrynn had returned, and the vice-headmistress, Miss Olovalur, was with him.

We stood up, eager to hear what was going to happen.

I hope they throw those Oak King Faction kidnappers into prison. Or whatever passes for a prison in the Elfen lands.

My heart fell when I saw the expression on Amrynn's face as he drew near.

Oh, no.

Laura's father, mother, and uncle walked up to Amrynn and Miss Olovalur, and they all began to talk.

Laura didn't go with them, so we stayed with her, but after a few minutes, my curiosity got the best of me. I wanted to hear what they were saying, so I moved as quietly as I could over to where they were standing.

"How bad is it, Miss Olovalur?" Laura's father was asking the vice-headmistress.

"Bad, sir. Very bad," the lady replied, looking grim. "They're in session right now."

"Let's go," Amrynn replied. He turned to his wife and daughter. "Come," he said. "They ought to hear from you."

They all nodded and we rushed to attend the council meeting.

Liesl and Laura hurried to join me as I followed. Miss Olovalur led the way, and we were soon at the entrance to the Elfen Academy Council hall; a guard there held a finger to his mouth, signaling that we should enter quietly, as he opened the door to allow us in.

We filed in, Laura's parents and uncle, Lord Umeqirelle, Miss Olovalur, Laura, her little brother Tam, Liesl, and finally, me.

The guard tried to stop me from taking my magical staff inside, but Lord Umeqirelle vouched for me and told him to let me pass, promising I wouldn't use it for violence.

We walked in quietly, and sat in the back.

The Elfen Council was hearing old business, and it took some time to work their way through the agenda.

I took the opportunity to study my surroundings.

I could see Oak King Faction members in the audience, including several in the front row. They sat tall and proud, and this made me immensely nervous.

The Oak King Faction men were in Elfen disguise, and I could see, in the bright lights of the auditorium, that they not only had on platinum blonde wigs, but false pointed ears, and makeup to make themselves look pale.

If the Elfen Council could be so easily tricked, I would eat my hat.

I glanced at Laura and wondered if she could see the fake makeup and wigs on the men, but she just stared straight ahead, listening.

I leaned to my other side, and in a nearly inaudible whisper, asked Liesl if she could see the disguises.

She nodded that yes, she could see them, plainly.

I hoped the Elfen Council could see it, too. And I wondered if the disguises were so poor, why did the Oak King Faction even bother?

I noticed Chancellor Xilmenor was absent, and I wondered where he was.

I leaned to ask Amrynn, who shrugged.

After listening to the council for nearly two hours, when the members finally turned their attention to new business, I had my answer.

They didn't need to question them.

The way some of the Elfen Council members were talking I could tell that the Elfen Council had already been influenced by the Oak King Faction.

The Elfen Council referred to the "visitors from the elderlands" and indicated the Oak King Faction members in disguise, sitting in the front row. They spoke with reverence of the "special relationship" and the "benefits and rewards" of working with "this new, special alliance."

Then Lord Umeqirelle stood and asked to give a report about what had happened to him and his family. About how his wife and daughter had been held hostage on pain of death, unless Lord Umeqirelle did what the Oak King Faction members had demanded: seduce me and persuade me to move to the Elfen Lands.

The Elfen Council sat unmoving as Umeqirelle spoke for nearly an hour.

When he was finished, he sat down, and looked confident.

The Oak King Faction members in disguise, who sat in the front row, did not move an inch. They sat as still as statues.

What are they up to?

The members of the Elfen Council conferred together, whispering back and forth for some time, before the leader stepped up to the podium.

"We thank Lord Umeqirelle for his words. The special relationship we have with our visitors from the elderlands is well known to the Lord Emissary, and as such, we find his statement puzzling. He knows full well that his wife and daughter were taken to an approved location for a period of rest and relaxation at the request of this very Council. His objections now, before this body, make us question his motivations and judgment."

My face went cold, and my heart dropped.

The council leader continued.

"We understand that a husband on extended work duty may miss conjugal relations with his wife, but to outright misrepresent the purpose of a weekend vacation, well, this council's estimation of Lord Umeqirelle has been cast into serious doubt."

Lord Umeqirelle stood and began to protest. His wife beside him stood as well.

"Madam Councilhead, if I may give a statement...," she started.

"I am *not* in any way misrepresenting...," he began.

Before either of them could finish, though, the hall erupted in what was probably a huge commotion for the quiet and sedate Elfen Folk, but to my eyes and ears it seemed greatly subdued.

The councilhead stood and banged her gavel, then waved her hand and raised her voice: "Silence! Silence! I will have order in this hall!" she demanded. "Lord Umeqirelle, you are out of order! Lady Umeqirelle, I am extremely surprised at your actions here. ORDER!"

The hall did not come to order.

As Lord Umeqirelle tried to speak over the crowd, the councilhead summoned a contingent of guards and motioned for them to remove Amrynn and his wife from the hall.

Amrynn's daughter shrank in her seat, trying to make herself look smaller.

I stared at all of this in utter disbelief.

Lord and Lady Umeqirelle protested loudly as they were led roughly away.

Tam began to weep silently.

"We need to get out of here," Laura's father whispered.

"Not now," the man's brother whispered back, "or we'll have them come down on *us*, and then..."

But the councilhead was speaking.

"This is not acceptable," she warned. "We must consider stricter rules to preserve the order."

The Elfen Council members seated along the table nodded their heads in agreement.

Through it all, the disguised Oak King Faction men in the front row did not move a muscle. Did not react at all.

It was insidious how they appeared to be so outwardly unconcerned at the "obvious lies" that Lord Umeqirelle had charged them with.

By not reacting, they appear to be innocent, even if they're not.

As soon as everything had calmed down, the Elfen Council moved on to talk about the efforts to contain the forest surrounding the volcano, and the water reservoir. As they busied themselves with this, we took the opportunity to exit as quietly as possible: Laura and Tam, their parents and uncle, Liesl, and I.

We walked out slowly and calmly, so as not to attract any undue attention, then made our way out of the hall, out of the Academy, and down the pathway.

We remained calm and silent until we had entered Laura's home and closed the door behind us. Only then did I wonder where Lord and Lady Umeqirelle's daughter had gone. I turned in dismay to ask Laura's father where the child had gone, or been taken, and was halted before I could even begin to speak.

There, next to Laura's father and uncle, stood Laura's mother. She was fumbling with her voluminous skirts, moving the abundant fabric aside to reveal the child, who she'd concealed there as we left the hall.

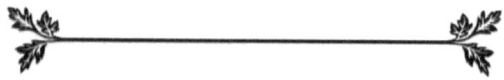

Chapter Nineteen

Home and Hearth

Lord and Lady Umeqirelle's daughter was old enough to understand what had happened to her parents, and she was terrified. She'd only been able to sneak out of the Elfen Academy hall and main grounds because, apparently, Elfen children are taught to hide early on.

This made me sad, yet I completely understood. I'd had to learn this skill myself, quite early, on the streets of New York.

Laura's father and brother sealed the front and rear doors of their house, bringing out seldom-used, but very effective, heavy wooden bars that were set into brackets affixed to either side of each door. In doing so, they effectively sealed off any entry into the house.

The building's windows were small and narrow, and almost looked like they were made for shooting arrows out. I mentioned this to Laura's uncle, and he smiled at me, wiggling his eyebrows up and down. The man was having entirely too much fun with the situation.

Laura, Tam, Liesl, and I all gathered round the little Umeqirelle daughter, who was being cuddled in Laura's mother's lap as she sat by the fire.

Laura brought her a warm scone, split with butter. "Here," she said as she handed the delicious bun to the frightened girl.

Tam handed her a mug of warm milk laced with sugar; the girl took a sip, and smiled for a moment.

We sat around Laura's mother, and kept them company.

"Hey, there," Laura said gently. "What's your name, little lass?"

I'd been told that names of small children weren't usually revealed to people outside their immediately family. There were old superstitions about it. Plus, I learned, magic could be cast around a name. So there was reason to guard true names from unfriendly eyes and ear.

But among friends, revealing a child's name was a sign of trust.

Laura reached out and patted the girl's hand.

The little one smiled and took a nibble of warm buttery scone.

"It's okay. It's safe here," Laura's mother murmured, kissing the top of the girl's head.

Laura whispered to the small child, "My name is Filaurel Ellarian Fazorwyn, but everyone calls me Laura."

The child's eyebrows rose and her eyes widened, and she nodded to Laura.

"Now, what's your name, little miss?" Laura asked again.

The little child murmured, "Lusserina Alea Origwyn, but Marmy and Da call me Lucy."

Laura beamed. "Lucy, that's a fine, fine name. Lucy, welcome to our home."

Lucy's face broke into a small smile that lasted only a few seconds, but was glorious.

We sat and played at Laura's mother feet for some time, and eventually, Liesl offered to hold Lucy while Laura's mother prepared a meal. Laura went to help in the kitchen.

I offered to help, and Laura said, "You don't know the recipes, so come and watch."

We helped make the large meal for all the people who would eat this day in this house.

Laura prepared several vegetable side dishes, while her mother created an enormous rice-and-meat dish.

"What kind of meat is that?" I asked, as the woman stirred a large pot of fragrant meat. The sauce in the pot was plentiful, and as she stirred the meat, a fantastic fragrance rose from the dish.

"It's chicken," Laura's mother answered. "Cooked with spices, and tomato sauce, and a few herbs from our garden out back."

She handed me a small spoon to taste the mixture, and as I lifted a sample into my mouth, I closed my eyes in ecstasy. It was the best thing I had ever tasted.

She made a large pot of red rice, and before covering the boiling mixture, she added the meat to the huge pot, stirred it all well, then setting it to simmer.

I was assigned to make the salad. The ingredients I was given included not just leafy greens, but fruits and nuts. I was handed some herbs, too, with instructions to pluck the leaves and discard the stems. When I had completed this task, I tossed all the ingredients with a wonderful raspberry vinaigrette and, finally, it was done.

"Bring that glorious creation, Holly, and we will feast," Laura's mother instructed, lifting the massive pot of meat and rice with strong arms, and beckoning me to follow.

Laura followed with several smaller dishes of her vegetable creations.

We all gathered at the massive wooden table in the center room. The meal was like nothing else I'd ever tasted.

Laura grinned at my enthusiasm for her mother's cooking.

"Holly," said Tam, "Do you like country Elfen food?"

I could not answer, my mouth was so full. I swallowed too quickly, and began choking. Finally, I coughed and cleared my throat. After all of this, I was finally able to speak. I turned to Tam, and smiled. "Yes," I said, and took another bite.

Everyone at the table laughed merrily.

The food was really REALLY good.

I ate so much my belly was very full, and still I took a few more bites.

Everyone was laughing and jovial, in such good spirits that I wondered whether the food was imbued with some kind of magic.

I asked about this, and Laura's mother blushed when Laura's father squeezed her hand and told me, "the most important magic in the world."

The family time around the table, so large, so massive, was incredibly heartwarming. Such a rare thing, something I had never had as a child, and I was barely out of childhood.

I didn't want it to end.

The dinner lasted several hours, and even then, when plates had been cleared, and pipes lit, when children had left their chairs to sit around the blazing fireplace and listen to old stories told back and forth between grizzled brothers, the family time went on.

"Do you remember the time we went goose hunting and you lost your shoe?" Laura's uncle asked.

"I do indeed, and you always tell this story wrong," Laura's father said, tamping the fragrant tobacco down into his massive carved pipe. "I lost my shoe," he said, "when the bear started to chase me."

"It was when your rifle discharged and you weren't properly braced," his brother countered. "And if I remember correctly, we lost the goose, as well. You were a bad shot back then."

"I lost the shoe because, when I fell backwards from not being properly braced in the bog, the bear found me," said Laura's father.

"The bear found you because you fell on her cub, which had fallen in and been carried downstream," Laura's uncle said. "That bog wasn't even home to that bear. She was living in the caves at the bottom of the hillside, a good half-mile away."

And the jovial disagreement continued, until the whole story had been told.

Then several other stories were told.

Several pipefuls later, Laura's mother suggested toasting marshmellons in the fireplace.

There was a rush for toasting sticks. Some were more coveted than others. Being a guest, I didn't even know where they were stored; Laura finally brought several out for Liesl, Lucy, and me. Luckily, Elfen hospitality being what it was, these toasting sticks were the nicest toasting sticks in the house.

Tam came along, carrying a shorter, blackened stick, his face downcast in disappointment.

"Oh, you," his uncle said, and brought forth a handful of new toasting sticks.

Tam's grin was like sunshine.

All of us kids sat shoulder-to-shoulder in a semicircle, facing the fireplace.

This fireplace was a massive old Elfen design, made for cooking in the olden days, before modern ovens had been invented. The new kitchen proper, where we'd gathered to prepare dinner, was equipped with several ovens and sinks and did not cook by fire. So the fireplace was now in the room where the dinner table was, together with the seats and couches where company gathered.

It was massive. The brick-arched top curved gently across six or seven feet, and the fireplace proper was tall enough that several people could have stood upright inside, if it hadn't been lit.

As it was, it held a blazing fire, with a semicircle of children sitting cross-legged around it, each with four-foot sticks.

At the end of each stick was a homemade marshmellon. These were larger than any marshmallow I had ever seen in either the Fae Folk lands, or the human world: They were the size of large plums.

We skewered them long-ways, and the powdered sugar coating had me licking my fingers carefully before I even stuck mine close to the fire.

The fireplace was wide, and we all easily fit side-by-side, all five of us.

We roasted our marshmellons, each so carefully, and when I tasted that first golden-toasted delicacy, I found I had brand-new room in my belly for half a dozen of the things, even though scarcely an hour had passed since dinner.

Laura's uncle and father sat nearby, giving helpful advice, as if it were a calf-roping contest.

"Hold your stick with both hands, lad, or it'll dip suddenly, and that marshmellon will slip clean off and into the fire."

"Here, let me whittle the point down. You had it too long in the flame, and now it's covered with blackened crust."

"Let me have a taste, son."

"Tam, child, don't hold it so close in the fire. It'll catch the flame."

"Wait, don't wave it like that. It won't put the fire out, it'll just fan the flames."

"Don't zing it back and forth so hard. It'll slip off the stick."

"Did you see where it went?"

"Laura, it's in your hair."

"Here, let me hold the stick."

"You're going to get it stuck to your face like that."

"Wait, let's try to put two alongside each other."

"I think it's done. Look, it's getting black."

And on and on it went.

And us kids got full a second time, enjoying more melty, toasty marshmellons, cooked over the hearth fire, in the warm country Elfen great room.

Chapter Twenty

Midnight Stealth

I fell asleep to the sounds of the adults talking together in low tones.

All us kids bunked in Laura and Tam's shared room, spreading blankets and pillows along the floor, wherever we could find a space.

Their room was large, and it was called "the nursery," as the room where all children slept, together in one room, was called in most Elfen households.

It was very late when Liesl shook my shoulder and awakened me.

"Holly," her whisper was barely audible. "Wake up. We have to leave."

"What?" I was instantly awake. I sat up and stared at Liesl.

What was she talking about?

She was gathering up her things and stuffing them back in her bag, and I began to do the same. I trusted my friend, and she was usually right, so I didn't question it.

"Hurry," she whispered, standing up straight, and slinging her bag over her shoulder.

I finished stuffing my bag full, and grabbed my shoes.

"Where's my staff?" I whispered.

Tam groaned in his sleep, and turned over.

Lucy was snoring gently in the corner.

I glanced over at Laura. She looked asleep, she was motionless, on her back, covered to her chin with her blanket.

"It's over here," Liesl pointed. My magical staff was against the wall, next to the window.

I pulled my shoes on, one at a time. They had laces, so it took a minute to tie them. As I was finishing the second shoe, I heard a mumbled question.

Laura was sitting up. "What are you two doing?" She opened her eyes fully and focused on us. "Oh my God, you're leaving? Is it safe outside?"

"Yes," said Liesl. "Nothing has been out there, since we came back from the school yesterday."

I guess that was yesterday, huh?

Laura pulled on her own shoes, her pants already on. "I'm coming with you," she said.

"No, you're not," I said, getting to my feet.

"Why not?" Laura said, standing up.

"Because we're going home," said Liesl. "Back to Fae Folk lands."

"But why now?" Laura asked.

"Because of what I heard the adults discussing," whispered Liesl. "Hurry up, Holly. Laura, stay back."

"If you're going to walk all the way back to Fae Folk lands, you'll need help," said Laura.

"No, we won't," I countered.

"Do you know how far it is?" Laura whispered, pulling on her jacket and putting her hands on her hips.

I paused for a second. Then: "No, but we'll be fine."

"No, you won't," Laura said. "And if we're walking all the way back to Fae Folk lands, we'll need supplies." She disappeared through the door and into the hallway.

"She's so stubborn," Liesl whispered.

I nodded, staring at Liesl. I wondered what she'd overheard the adults discussing. I was insanely curious, but we needed to get out and on our way before we had a long discussion.

"You ready?" I asked.

She nodded.

I grabbed my magic staff and shouldered my bag, and we crept out of the room and into the hallway.

The nursery was in the back of the house, and we had to pass several other rooms to get out. Rooms where Laura's parents and uncle were sleeping.

We tiptoed, being impossibly quiet.

The house was still and dark, and we could hear the sleepers' deep, slow breathing.

I didn't even glance into the rooms as we passed them. I didn't want to chance it.

Liesl and I crept, slowly, softly, silently, all the way past the other bedrooms, and through the center room; past the fireplace, with its still-cracking and cooling logs; past the marshmellon sticks all neatly stacked by the hearth, until we were at the door.

The heavily and firmly barred door.

"Um…" Liesl whispered.

Yeah. Um is right.

The door was barred, and it looked like Laura's father had somehow locked the thick wooden beam in place.

We'd seen him lift it and secure it there when we'd first come inside. The wooden beam looked like it weighed well over a hundred pounds.

"How are we gonna get out?" Liesl whispered.

Just then, Laura came padding back from the kitchen and saw us.

"Oh, you're not getting through that way," she said. "You have to go through the basement, out the old coal chute."

The what?

Laura had several bags full of food, and she passed one to me, and one to Liesl, and then slung the third over her head and shoulder, so it lay diagonally across her hip.

"Come on, follow me," she whispered.

Liesl and I shrugged and followed Laura. We had no choice now, we had to take her with us. She'd given us food stores. She was showing us out the secret exit.

Okay, this is gross.

The secret exit turned out to be a nine-foot tunnel we had to climb up that was full of cobwebs, squirrel droppings, and slippery dry coal dust. At the end was a metal flap, which was latched on the inside.

Laura held a small flashlight in her mouth, illuminating the outer door, and wiggling the latch free. It wasn't easy, because the latch was metal.

It squeaked.

Laura moved it slowly, by bits.

"Is this going to wake the entire household?" Liesl whispered from behind.

"It might," I murmured.

"This tunnel comes out on the opposite side of my parents' bedroom. If we wake anyone, it'll be... oh."

She stopped, and bit her lip, then shrugged and continued working at the latch. She did it so slowly the squeaks weren't as loud; they were barely-there little noises I hoped would be mistaken for mouse sounds.

It took a while. Laura stopped several times when she heard noises coming from the rooms above us. She'd pause and listen.

But it was only the house settling.

At least ten minutes later, the latch was open.

She careful pushed back the metal door, holding it so it didn't fall and make a loud noise.

She's done this before.

We crept out, and she carefully lowered the coal chute door back into place.

We stood in the shadows of the house, a few feet from the garden.

I turned to Laura.

"Thank you for all you've done for us," I said.

"You've been a dear friend, after just two days," said Liesl.

"And your family is... wonderful," I said. "Last night was incredible. I don't think I'll ever forget..."

"We'd better hurry," Laura whispered. "Let's get a move on. We can talk on the way."

I sighed. Then realized we could not stop her from following us.

"Okay," I said. I turned and walked through the garden and into the woods.

Liesl followed right behind me.

Right behind Liesl, came Laura.

Right behind Laura, came Tam.

And right behind Tam? Came Lucy.

I sighed again and kept walking. We looked like hobbits on a quest.

Chapter Twenty-One
Escape

We traveled south for the first hour, and left civilization behind.

Aspen and Tundra appeared and padded alongside me.

Snowbear rode on Liesl's shoulder, and chattered as we went.

"The Elfen Lands are sparsely populated," Laura said. "They're mostly woodland, with a few farms here and there."

"Fae Folk lands are similar," said Liesl. "Lots of land, not that many people."

"Do you think the Elfen Council is lost to The Oak King Faction?" I asked, getting right to the point of the matter. I hated chit-chat.

"Not sure," Laura said. "But it doesn't look good."

"Liesl, can you tell us what you overheard the adults discussing?" I asked. "That scared you so bad you decided we had to leave?"

"Not just leave, but go home," Liesl reminded me. "Sure. You were already asleep, and I had gone to brush my teeth. Then I was thirsty, so I was in the bathroom for a while. I don't think they knew I could overhear them. In fact, I'm sure they didn't think I could."

We picked our way through the forest as she explained.

"They were huddled near the fire, with their heads together, whispering," Liesl said. "They were discussing how they could rescue Amrynn and his wife. The house was real quiet, and I sat just inside the bathroom doorway, so I could hear everything."

"Was it just my parents? Or my uncle, too?" Laura asked.

"At first it was just your parents," Liesl said. "They mentioned waiting for your uncle's return. Apparently, he'd gone on an errand, sneaking back to gather information."

"Typical," Laura mumbled. "He'd go because he's not on their lists."

I glanced at her with a questioning look.

She explained: "My uncle does gardening work on the Academy lands, usually far from the campus, on the outer ranges. They don't even consider him of consequence. He can usually find things out without them even knowing."

I nodded.

"Anyway," Liesl continued. "Your uncle returned and was telling your parents what he found out." She looked at us. "It wasn't good."

"Did he go find where Lord and Lady U were being held?" Laura asked.

Liesl looked stricken, and her pace quickened. "Yes," she said.

We hurried to catch up.

"Well," said Laura. "Tell us!"

"I..." Liesl hesitated, glancing back at the two smaller kids following us. "Let's stop for a rest here. They look tired."

We stopped in a thicket, sheltered from the more open areas.

Laura handed Tam and Lucy a drink and a scone. "Don't spill," she cautioned, then sat them down and cautioned them not move.

We three huddled six or seven feet away, standing so close our heads were touching. Our noses were within an inch of one another as we spoke in nearly inaudible whispers.

"Okay," Laura murmured. "Spill. What did you hear?"

Liesl closed her eyes, then opened them again. "Lord and Lady Umeqirelle are dead, and so is Chancellor Xilmenor," she said. "And the Elfen Council was sending guards to take Holly and me into custody at dawn."

I couldn't believe my ears. I felt stunned.

Dead?!

It had all happened so quickly.

Laura seemed unsurprised. "I figured something like this might happen. The way The Oak King Faction seemed to be in such tight control of the Elfen Academic Council was frightening."

I couldn't find words to express my horror.

Laura glanced over at Tam and Lucy. "She's an orphan, now," she whispered. Then looked back at Liesl. "I don't know what they will do to my parents and uncle when they find we've escaped, but it won't be good."

Tam got up and came over to join us.

"Laura," he whispered. "I heard you talking."

Laura stared at her little brother.

He continued. "I left a note for mother and father, and set my soldier to go off after an hour. I knew things had to be bad if Liesl was getting Holly out."

We all blinked in surprise.

"So...," Laura murmured slowly, "I guess Mother and Father and our uncle will be warned?"

"They don't know which direction we went," said Tam, "So they'll not be following us. But yeah, they should be able to escape, too."

Laura bent down and gave Tam a long hug. When she straightened back up, there were tears in her eyes.

I looked over at Lucy. "I want to take her safely to the Fae Folk lands."

"She's smart," said Tam. "I think she senses what's happening."

"Then let's get the heck out of the Elfen Lands," I said. "I feel like hurrying."

"Holly," Laura whispered, "You do realize how far we have to travel, right?"

Hmmm...

"Uhhh, how far?" asked Liesl.

"On foot? Days and days," Laura murmured.

I shrugged. "Better than the alternative." I bent down and picked up my pack, then walked over to Lucy. "Hey, ready to go Kiddo?"

The girl looked at me and nodded, rising to her feet.

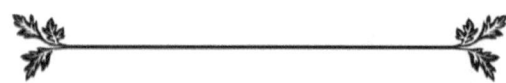

We hiked for the whole day, only stopping to rest twice more, when we'd found concealed spots. These pauses were invariably followed by the removal of stickers and spiders from the little ones, which we did while we walked.

The sun was setting over the trees when we came to the top of a hill in the forest.

"How far do you think we've come?" Liesl asked Laura.

Laura shrugged and looked around. "Those look like the mountains separating us from the Elfen Lands," she said, pointing to a range of peaks far in the distance. "I'd say we've come maybe twenty-five miles? More or less. It's been about fifteen hours since we left."

I scanned the area. "Well, it's getting dark soon. Let's push on for another mile, and look for a place we can hide for the night."

"Agreed," Liesl and Laura both said at the same time, then glanced at each other and laughed.

I had a hold of Lucy's hand while we hiked, helping the small girl to keep up without falling.

Laura kept hold of her little brother's hand for a while, until Tam shrugged it off and took the lead. "I'm not a little kid," he said as he hopped from rock to rock.

We descended into a small tree-filled valley and found an especially overgrown area.

"This looks promising," said Liesl. "Let's go deeper."

We were making our way into the bushes when something or someone jumped onto my back.

I muffled my scream with my hands. We were trying to be quiet, after all. I swung around and caught a small wrist.

It was a halfling.

"You guys again?" I exclaimed softly.

Turns out the thick, overgrown area where we had hoped to hide for the night was next to a halfling village.

Although you couldn't tell anyone lived there, we believed it when they all emerged.

They weren't the same halflings we'd encountered the day before, but they knew of us.

"We had word from our cousins over on the eastern ridges. They held a huge celebration, and told of your great successes in the vineyard," the halfling spokesperson said.

I wouldn't call that a success, but whatever.

I told them as much, but they just laughed and brushed off my concerns.

They insisted we spend the night in their thicket.

"We can't stay the whole night," said Liesl.

"Maybe we can sleep and then leave before dawn?" asked Laura.

"You can stay that long if you want, but Holly and I will be leaving even earlier," said Liesl.

I gripped Lucy's small hand. "And Lucy," I added.

Laura nodded. "Sounds fine to me, you're the boss, Liesl."

The halflings were ecstatic.

We spent most of an hour insisting we could not revel and visit through the night, but had to rest and sleep.

They replenished our supplies with water, nuts, berries, and flatbread. We filled our packs back up, and filled our bellies, then dropped off the sleep.

A deep slumber, as it turned out.

When Liesl roused me, dawn was just pinking the horizon.

"We overslept?" I mumbled.

"Yes, a bit," Liesl whispered. "Hurry, we've got to get going."

I shook Lucy awake beside me, and gave her some water.

We relieved our bladders, washed our faces, and were on our way within a few minutes.

Laura and Tam yawned as we hiked. Liesl shouldered an extra bag of food, and I led the party, holding Lucy's hand as we hiked.

We hadn't gone fifty feet before we noticed a group of halflings following us.

I turned and caught their eye, and pointed back the way we'd come, and said, simply, "No."

The halflings didn't say a word, just looked at the ground.

"I can see you, you know," I said.

They glanced up at me, their eyes pleading.

"No," I said.

"You will need us," said one of the halflings. "We want to help."

Oh, Lord Almighty.

"Fineeeee," I turned and began hiking again.

Liesl hiked alongside me. "Today is Monday. We were supposed to return to Titania Academy in a few hours," she said.

"I know," I said grimly. "I'm not sure how long it'll take us to get back now."

"I wonder what the headmistress will do when we don't return," Liesl murmured, almost to herself.

I wondered, too.

I scanned our surroundings. We were hiking out of the valley where we'd spent the night, and up a forested hill. The Elfen Lands were so heavily forested, we had yet to hike through an area that was not covered with trees.

As we topped the next ridge, I paused, looking down.

"Miles and miles of trees," I murmured.

"At least it looks somewhat clear of bushes," said Liesl. "We could even run for the first part."

I grinned at her. "You want to?"

"Yes!" she answered.

And that's how we found ourselves running, then slipping and sliding, down a slope covered with leaves and trees.

I kept hold of Lucy's hand as I trotted, because she ran slower, even though her little chubby legs moved at a fast pace.

Liesl and Laura passed us, and they were going so fast they were soon sliding on the leaves.

Tam was the first to fall, and as he tumbled, he curled into a ball, and he was soon moving faster than before.

The Laura fell, and she too curled into a ball, gathering speed as she tumbled down the slope.

Liesl slowed to a trot and then a walk, and watched as Laura and Tam tumbled to the bottom.

The halflings started running after us, then jumped and curled into balls, on purpose. They rolled down to the bottom of the slope, giggling madly all the way.

Liesl, Lucy and I carefully made our way to meet Laura and the others.

Tam and his sister were groaning as they slowly got to their feet.

"Ouch," Laura moaned, holding her hip.

"You okay?" I asked, concerned.

"Yeah," she said slowly, "It's just... that was stupid."

I laughed. "Yes," I agreed.

Tam jumped up and ran over. "So much fun!" he exclaimed.

I grinned.

Two different perspectives.

The halflings were happy with their roll down the hillside, too.

"Well," I asked Laura. "Do you want to stop and rest?"

"Naw, I'll be okay. I think I'll just walk it off," she turned and started walking slowly.

I raised my eyebrows as I grinned at Liesl.

And we continued our hike out of the Elfen Lands.

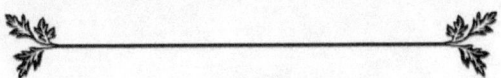

Chapter Twenty-Two
The Dark Wytch

On the third day of our trek, we topped a ridge as dawn was breaking, and we were high enough so we could see the land on the other side of the mountains.

"That looks unimaginably far," I whispered.

"That's Ireland," said Laura.

I blinked.

I had been told the passage to the Fae Folks lands was in Ireland.

"We then, let's go!" I laughed.

We hurried onward, and got in a good five hours of hiking before we stopped for a rest.

Some of the halflings seemed worried about the direction off to our left.

"They want to go around a spot to the east," Laura said. "They said a 'bad person' lives in a cave beyond the second ridge east." She consulted with the halflings in their own language, and seemed to be asking questions.

Some of the halflings seemed eager, but more of them seemed cautious, putting up their hands and moving their heads back and forth.

The message was clear.

No.

Stay away from that place.

Danger.

I was immediately intrigued.

"Do you think we should go check it out?" I whispered to Liesl when we stopped. We both nibbled on berry flatbread and I handed a piece to Lucy, who ate it eagerly.

"We could," Liesl whispered back. "I am insanely curious."

We're going to be way late getting back to the Academy anyway. What can a couple more hours hurt?

I glanced over at Laura, still talking to the halflings.

"I want to know what is scaring those little people so badly."

We continued to eat our lunch, and Laura continued to talk to the halflings. After another five minutes, she came to where we were sitting and leaned over, handing Lucy a bunch of almonds.

"It's a Blackberry Wytch they're frightened of," she said, sitting down.

"A what?" I said softly.

Liesl giggled.

"An old mage that lives in a berry thicket, probably," she said. "Similar to Jess."

"Ohhh. Well, how is that scary?" I asked.

"They seem to think she eats people," said Laura. "But from the way they describe it, it doesn't seem true. I mean, they say she ate a boar and a piglet. Well, heck. My parents had a cookout last fall and roasted a boar over a fire out back."

My mouth began to water. I looked down at the last bit of berry flatbread I held. It was dry, but buttery, with raspberries cooked into it. I'd been eating it for three days now. I would trade a hundred pounds of it just for one pork taco.

I told them as much.

"What's a taco?" Laura asked.

"It's this really thin flatbread they fry, then they fold meat and cheese and stuff into it, and you hold it like this," Liesl said. She tried to demonstrate by cupping her hands and making nibbling motions with her head bent sideways.

I laughed. "This last spring, we'd been back in the human world, the city I spent my first fourteen years in. A street vendor had tacos, and Liesl got to try one."

"It was delicious," Liesl said solemnly. "Intensely delicious."

"You know, Laura, we're friends with a Lacewing Faerie who lives on the border between Central Park, in New York City, that's in the human world, in America, and the Fae Folk lands," I explained. "She's fabulous and has helped me a few times."

Liesl nodded in agreement. "She's kind of a nurse." She glanced at me, then back to Laura. "Holly has a habit of getting injured, and Jess has patched her up before."

Laura grinned.

"It sounds like this Blackberry Wytch is similar?" I said.

Laura shrugged. "I have no idea; I've never met her. I've never even heard of her."

"Well, Holly and I are really curious," said Liesl. "We're thinking of checking her out, you know, just kind of veering east for a couple hours, then getting back on the trail south. What do you think?"

"Sounds okay to me." She glanced back toward the halflings. "I don't think they'll want to come anywhere near her, though."

"Maybe just us, then?" I asked.

"All right," agreed Laura.

We finished resting and eating, and started hiking east, and the halflings became more agitated the farther we went.

Finally, they indicated they would go no farther.

"Wait here?" I asked.

They nodded, looking worried.

"Be careful," they said. And began to lay down a camp.

Liesl, Laura, Tam, Lucy, and I continued our hike to the east. I thought the Elfen kids might be tired after coming so far, then I remembered how the older ones had run horizontally along those walls at the Academy yards. The Elfen were tough cookies.

We passed over two more ridges, and must've gone at least ten miles, when we came to an area with blackened land. Some of the trees were burnt, as well. More light came down onto the forest floor, and it should have been brighter, but it was gloomier.

Storm clouds gathered overhead, full and heavy with unshed rain; they were a dark grey color, and seemed to roil over themselves as they floated by.

"Well this looks kind of creepy," I murmured, looking around.

"Can you see anything?" Liesl asked.

Laura peered through the trees, squinting and straining. After a minute, she stood upright again. "I see nothing."

"Do you suppose this area was in a fire?" Liesl asked.

I turned and stared at her, saying nothing.

She nodded. "Yes. Well, obviously. I guess I meant... recently...?"

A crow cawed loudly overhead, and we looked up to see a flock of them flying over our heads, traveling forward the way we had been hiking.

"Looks like they're going our way," Laura murmured. "Shall we push on?"

We hiked on, following the crows for as long as we could.

They were soon out of sight.

Hiking through the burnt forest was both easier, because the underbrush had been burned away, and harder, because the ground was peppered with blackened limbs that had fallen from the trees.

If I'd though the diseased trees of the northern Elfen lands were bad, I quickly realized they were nothing compared with this charred forest.

It was clear the fire had come through here a while ago, because much of the ash-laden foliage had been rained on numerous times. Still, a burning stink rose from the land.

With every step we took, black soot poofed up from the ground.

We were soon covered with it.

Aspen and Tundra, in their thick white coats, were soon half-covered with it: Their legs were black, and the soot rose to cover their underbellies. They looked like black wolves on their bottom halves, and white arctic wolves on top.

Aspen started to sneeze.

I stopped. "She's inhaling the soot into her lungs. This can't be good for her."

"They're magical, Holly; they should be okay," said Liesl, Snowbear still rode on her shoulder, fast asleep. The soot hadn't bothered her yet.

"Yeah? And what if they're *not* okay?" I was worried. I turned and crouched next to my wolf familiars.

I put my hands on either side of Aspen's head, nuzzling her. "You two should go back to your realm. I'll be fine."

Tundra looked worried.

"I'll summon you if I need you," I said. "You know that. Now go," I commanded.

They popped out of sight.

I glanced at Snowbear.

"You're right," Liesl said. "If she was sneezing from the soot, I'd tell her to go back, too."

Satisfied, I started to hike again.

We soon came over a high rush of trees, all stacked up together.

On the other side was a small cabin.

Grass was growing around it, along with a few live trees.

There were birds chirping in the branches.

"I guess this is the place," said Laura.

I could smell something delicious coming from the chimney.

We walked up to the door and knocked.

I glanced at Liesl next to me. "Just to say hello, right? Just to meet her?"

Liesl nodded, smiling.

We waited.

Presently, the door opened, and an old woman with a wrinkled face peered out, smiling.

"Hello? Who's there?"

She focused on us. "Oh! Visitors!"

She stepped out the door and shook all our hands. "Hello! Hello! How are you?"

She did not seem to be of the Fae Folk world. She wore a colorful array of dress, skirt, apron, several colors of socks, and what appeared to be Army boots. A paisley scarf was tied around her grey skein of hair, and her ears stuck out sideways. They looked larger than normal, and gave her a comical look. Her face was incredibly wrinkled, making her look a thousand years old. She was small, and walked hunched over, using a short brown cane.

"Well, I don't get too many visitors. You children are a sight for sore eyes! Would you like to come inside? I was just roasting a pig for my dinner, you know, they're of a good size, and I have plenty to share..."

We smiled, and nodded. And we all went inside.

Her cabin was crowded with all kinds of things she'd collected over the years, and she had to hunt for five spots to sit in.

She ended up throwing some blankets across the floor, and we sat on those.

The old woman settled herself on a low rocking chair, and smiled contentedly.

We noticed an old black stove, with a pot that bubbled on its surface. The smell of roasting blackberries came from this pot, and so we asked about it.

"Oh, yes: I am making blackberry pie! I use this large pie crust, see?" She indicated the table next to us. I looked and saw the largest pie crust I had ever seen. It could easily hold over a gallon of filling.

"I combine the roast pig and the blackberry filling and get a pie that is the most scrumptious, out-of-this-world meal, finer food than anything else in the whole wide forest," the old woman said.

We chattered happily, smelling the roasting pig, and the bubbling blackberries.

After a while, the old woman sniffed the air. "That is very curious. I think I smell Christmas pie," she said.

"No, I am sure that smell is roast pig," Laura said, laughing.

Chapter Twenty-Three
Blackberry Pork Pie

The wytch started laughing, and she jiggled mightily with mirth. It was infectious, and we all were soon giggling along with her.

The berries bubbled on her old stove.

The pig roasted on the hearth, behind a metal door, giving rise to the most delicious smells.

"No," the wytch laughed, "I am sure I smell Christmas," she insisted.

"I smell berries," said Liesl.

"I smell the pig roasting," said Laura.

Lucy and Tam sat side by side and kind of held on to each other, and it was a long while until I noticed: they were not laughing.

They weren't even relaxed or smiling.

They were nervous and even a little frightened.

I glanced at them, and I was still laughing.

That's weird.

"No, really," the wytch settled down and said. "You know that smell at Christmastime?"

"What do you mean?" asked Liesl.

"The smells of Christmas: cinnamon, cloves, the smell of nutmeg baked into a pie." She put her finger to her face and thought some more. "Oh! The smell of pine in the house, the smell of cranberries cooking, the smell of pig roasting, the smell of apples baking." She beamed at us, "Christmas smells like that."

"You smell that now?" Liesl asked.

"Well, yes," said the wytch. "Plus, I smell the strange smell of doesn't-fit-here-in-this-forest, if you understand me." She suddenly looked around, trying to seek out where the smell was coming from.

"Is... is it me?" asked Liesl.

"What do you mean, Liesl," asked Laura.

"Well, I am new here, and I don't belong in these lands, so it kind of describes me," she said.

I began to feel uncomfortable.

"Holly, you are half Elfen Folk, right?" asked Laura.

"No," I said slowly. "Actually, I am one-quarter Elfen. My mother was half human, although that has been questioned. My father thinks she was pure Elfen, but then Lord Umeqirelle said she was ... half human ..." I trailed off, remembering the Lord Emissary was dead.

"I sense a sadness in your speech, my dear," said the wytch. "Is everything okay?"

"Yes, I guess. Sort of. I can't talk about it now," I said, putting an arm around little Lucy, who had started to lean on me and suck her thumb.

The interior of the wytch's cabin was warm, and the young Elfen child had become drowsy.

"Well," the wytch rose from her seat, "I have to stir the pot on the stove." She made her way over to the bubbling, fragrant mixture.

Picking up a carved wooden spoon, she put it in the pot and began to slowly stir. "Would you children like a drink of mead? I made it myself," she asked.

We all smiled and nodded yes, and a few minutes later she set down the spoon and gather small cups, poured out the dark golden mead, and passed them out.

I was feeling very comfy and cozy.

Lucy had fallen asleep against me.

Tam was looking drowsy.

The wytch settled back down in her chair and looked over at me.

"Actually, child, I do think it is you I smell," she said, winking at me.

"Oh?" I asked. "I bathed just yesterday, I'm sure..."

"No, no, no, it's your essence, my dear," the old wytch said. "You smell of Christmas."

I smiled and looked down.

She continued. "You smell out of place in this forest, though. As if you're far from home and feeling misplaced."

"You can smell feelings?" Liesl said, sounding astonished.

"Well, of course," the wytch answered. "Can't you?" she asked, sounding genuinely curious.

"I cannot," said Liesl.

I shook my head when the wytch looked at me questioningly. "Nope, I cannot either."

The wytch turned her gaze to Laura, who nodded.

What?

Liesl and I turned to Laura is surprise. "You can smell feelings?!" We said in unison.

Laura grinned. "Well of course I can smell feeling. All Elfen can." She nudged her brother, who was next to her and silent. "Tam?"

The boy nodded, then spoke briefly, "Yes."

I would have laughed at the boy's manner of response if I hadn't been so astonished at what he was agreeing to.

I had no idea Elfen Folk could smell feelings. Weird.

"Aha, you see?" said the wytch. "You, young lady, feel out of place." She smiled triumphantly. "But you also smell very strongly of Christmas." She leaned over in my direction and inhaled deeply.

Liesl laughed. "Um, Holly's father is The Holly King himself."

"Is he now?" The wytch sat back, and it was her turn to look astonished.

I smiled. "Yeah, he is," I said casually.

"So tell me, child," the wytch asked. "What is it like to be the daughter of The Holly King?"

"Not as relaxing as you'd think," I blurted out. "But I came here to the Elfen Lands to visit my mother's people. I had thought they would feel like kin."

"Ah," said the wytch. "Your mother may have been Elfenkin, either full or half, but it is clear you take after your father and his people. The Fae Folk. You smell of him. It practically drips off you. Child, you should definitely consider yourself Of The Fae."

I nodded. "I'm beginning to understand that. It's just hard. My mother died when I was very young, and I really miss not having her around. It's like a piece of me is missing. I just came to the Elfen Lands to maybe find some part of that missing piece."

The wytch smiled. "And have you?" she asked.

"Sort of," I said. "I have found Laura, who is becoming a good friend, very fast. And I have Lucy here, who, although I first met her less than a day ago, is becoming like the little sister I never had." I patted Lucy's head. "They are both one hundred percent Elfen, correct?"

The wytch nodded. "That much is obvious."

She looked around. "It is curious, though." She inhaled again. "Did you say you just now traveled through the woods from the Elfen Academy?"

We nodded.

"And did you pass any berry bushes on your way?" the wytch asked.

"Yes, and we picked as many as we could," said Laura. "See? We have them in our bags, to eat later." She opened her bag and then the inner pouch, where she'd stored the blackberries she'd been picking on the way.

The wytch leaned forward and peered inside. "Ahh, yes, I see them. And are the berries you found in your travels through the forest, are they very ripe?"

"Some of them," said Liesl. "Some could have ripened on the vine another week, but we couldn't spare the time to wait for them," she chuckled. "We are actually in a rush to get back home."

"To the Fae Folk lands?" The wytch asked.

Liesl and I nodded.

"I want to put this pie together and give it to you, for your travels." The wytch rose from her chair again, and slowly walked to the stove, and picked up the carved wooden spoon, and began stirring the bubbling berries again.

After a while, she left the stove and, grabbing a thick oven cloth and a pan and fork on her way, walked to the fireplace.

She bent over the hearth, and her voluminous skirts spread as she crouched over the fire. She opened the metal door and stuck the fork in to test the tenderness of the roasting pig.

"Ohh, just right," she said, and plucked a goodly portion of meat into the pan she'd brought.

From where we sat on the floor, we could smell the exquisite scent of roasting pork, and our mouths watered.

"That smells so good," Liesl murmured.

I smiled at her, "Pork is my favorite meat, I could eat it every day."

The wytch closed the metal door carefully, carried the pan of meat to the stove, and busied herself with the huge piecrust.

"You are in for a treat, children." The wytch spooned the meat into the pie crust, then dipped a ladle into the berry mixture, and poured several ladles of it in to join the meat. She stirred the contents of the pie for a minute, then added more meat, and more berry mixture, until it was full.

"Now to add the top," she said, and from an old icebox, she brought out a flat dough top, and placed it carefully over the filled pie crust.

She hummed while she worked.

"You know, child," she glanced over her shoulder at me. "Daughter of The Holly King."

I nodded, getting up and walking over to her to watch her assemble the huge pie.

She continued, "Child, you may not belong in this land, but you are definitely the epitome of your father's line. You smell so strongly of Christmas that your scent is filling this whole cabin."

"Oh," I chuckled. "I think the scent of your cooking is filling it, Ma'am." I smiled.

She shook her head. "I guess I'm so used to these smells, I don't detect them as well as I used to." She picked up two oven mitts and used them to lift the heavy pie, then she turned to the hearth fire again.

"Children, do you mind opening the door? I need to put this in to bake," she shuffled a few steps closer to the fireplace. "I am going to put this right next to the roasting pig, and the smell will go into the pie, making it even tastier." She smiled.

"Sure, let me help you," said Laura, jumping up off the floor.

Lucy and Tam moved toward me, shying away from the wytch.

Liesl remarked, "Boy, they sure are acting weird, huh?"

"Yeah, they definitely are," I said, distracted. I had spied the pan of meat on the stove, the meat the wytch had used to help fill the pie, along with the bubbling blackberry mixture.

I glanced at the pot of berries, and saw it was still bubbling.

I'll burn my finger if I try to taste the berries.

Then I looked back at the pan of meat. It was glistening brown and crusted with delicious looking drippings.

"Here you go, Ma'am," said Laura. "Ooh, that looks like a magnificent pie! Do you need help putting it in?"

"No, I think I can manage it, child, although it *is* very heavy. Here, just let me reach and put it..." the wytch's words were cut off.

"AHHHHH!" screamed Laura, horrified.

I had just reached in the pan of meat and grabbed a morsel.

"OH MY GOD WHAT HAVE YOU DONE!" Laura was nearly hysterical.

I looked back.

Liesl was grabbing Tam and Lucy and backing away from Laura, who had fallen in surprise and horror.

"AAAHHH!" Laura screamed again.

"Really, child, what is your problem?" the wytch asked.

It was odd, because the wytch's manner was so matter-of-fact, in sharp contrast to Laura's panic.

I dropped the morsel of meat and rushed to see what was the matter.

"HOLY HELL!" I cried. I had stepped closer to Laura, reaching for her hand to help her to her feet. I'd happened to glance toward the wytch, who was pushing the pie into the hearth so it could bake. She pushed it slowly, so it could fit in the space next to the roasting pig.

THE ROASTING PIG!

It was not a roasting pig at all! I stared, horrified, at the form of a curled-up halfling child, naked and browning, roasting in the oven.

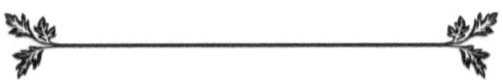

Chapter Twenty-Four
Time Loop

We were horrified. The wytch turned to stare at us, a strangely broad grin on her face. Her teeth showed, and they were blackened, each one. It looked like she has smeared tar over her mouth. She cackled at us.

I turned to look at the pan of meat on the stove, and thought of the morsel I had almost put in my mouth, and felt like throwing up. My stomach heaved, and I had to work to settle it.

I grabbed Laura's arm and tried to pull her up.

The wytch stepped close to Laura, reaching for her.

Laura was hysterical. She flailed and kicked out, and on the second kick, she flipped a small wooden table into the hearth fire, and it caught. On the third kick, she hit the wytch.

Liesl was screaming, "Come on! Let's get out of here!"

Tam was shrieking.

Lucy was crying, her face red, and tears streaking down to her chin.

Laura's kick sent the wytch straight into the hearth fire, almost as if she'd been drawn into it by some unknown force. But the force was Laura's kick. It had been at the perfect angle. She'd been trying to get away from the horror, and had inadvertently kicked the wytch straight into her own fire.

I yanked Laura's arm hard, as I watched in horror.

The wytch screamed in agony as she tumbled down into the large fire and her clothing and hair caught the flame.

Laura screamed and got to her feet.

The fire had consumed the small table, was devouring the wytch, and was spreading so fast it was like a live thing.

"Come on!" Liesl screamed again.

I pulled Laura, and we both ran after Liesl, who was already out the door with the littles.

We all ran outside, and I turned and stopped.

I could hear the wytch screaming for several minutes, then the screaming stopped. By this time, the cabin was completely aflame.

We pulled away from the cabin another twenty feet, because when it became fully engulfed, it was hot and huge.

The trees next to it caught fire and began burning.

The burnt forest around it stood by mutely, as if the trees had seen it all before.

As we backed away even farther, the air near the fire shimmered, and a wave of distilled air blew back from the burning cabin as it collapsed on itself.

Sparks flew up a hundred feet, and we covered our eyes and ran.

A second wave of distilled air buffeted us as we ran, blowing my hair forward and slapping it against my face.

I held on to Lucy's hand as I ran, and Liesl and Laura ran with me, each of them holding on to one of Tam's hands.

Halfway up a rise, Lucy tripped, and I turned and grabbed her, then turned again and ran, carrying her in my arms.

We all ran as if the devil was after us. We ran until we got to the edge of the burnt area, and then we ran some more.

We didn't stop running until we were a long way away.

Liesl stopped to catch her breath, and leaned against a tree, gasping.

"What... what was that...?" I asked, trying to catch my own breath.

"That air... pushing... God," gasped Liesl.

"Oh...," Laura puffed, "I actually know this."

We stared at her.

"They taught us about this last year," Laura said. "I've never seen it happen in real life, and they're supposed to be real rare, but I think that was a Time Loop."

What?

She fished in her pack for her water jug, and generously passed it around to all of us. We each took a sip.

"Good?" Laura asked.

We all nodded.

She packed the small jug back and patted my arm. "Come on, let's get back." She started walking and explaining.

"A Time Loop," Laura said. "That area of the forest looked all burnt, right?"

Liesl and I nodded.

"Well, that's because of the fire just now," Laura explained. "That patch of time was probably frozen, and waiting for us all this time. Might have been a really long time."

"Okay," I said, walking alongside her.

"Well," Laura continued, "When the fire escaped the hearth, it burnt into the rest of the cabin. These things are caused by one of several magical devices, or possible a rare magical stone. Once the fire hit that, it acted as an accelerant, not only of the fire, but of time as well."

"I don't understand," Liesl said as she walked.

"The catalyst warps time and loops it in on itself. So that the burnt forest we had to walk through to get to the cabin, had been burnt by the fire that happened later. We just saw it beforehand."

I felt my mind trying to grasp the concept of the Time Loop. "So, that air buffeting us?" I asked.

"Waves of time doubling back on itself," said Laura. "It's a really good thing we weren't caught up in it, I'd hate to have to relive that hour."

I shuddered.

We hiked on.

Eventually, we got to the halfling encampment, and settled by their fire. They had a vegetable stew going, and had baked fresh flatbread, and several of them had brought along home-brewed tea. After a time with our friends, as the evening wore on, we grew happy again, and content in one another's companionship and in the sharing of food and drink.

By silent mutual agreement, we all agreed never to mention what we'd seen to the halflings, and our respect for their judgement and ways grew by leaps and bounds.

The next morning, we broke camp early, cleaned up our botherment of the forest, and started out again.

We could see the Fae Folk-containing land of Ireland in the far distance, and the hike closer and higher up the mountains felt that much better. I silently kept repeating in my head: *Home.*

The whole next day we hiked, and twice the halflings veered away from a place, insisting we go around a certain hill or valley. Both times, we listened. Liesl, Laura, Tam, Lucy, and I trusted the halflings, and realized we would not have gotten as far as we had without their help. It was a quiet, grateful hike through the forest that day.

Chapter Twenty-Five

The Shadowed Estate

Near the end of the day, we hiked up the side of the mountain, and around sideways a bit, to get around it more easily. These mountains were topped with rocky, snowy peaks and rose up at least twenty thousand feet, and there was no way we were going over the top.

The halflings were now leading us, after we had explained where we wanted to go, they had completely understood and told us they knew of several "shortcuts" and we would "get there sooner" and "love the journey," and so that had been that.

As dusk settled, our path led us to a spot overlooking a wide valley.

At the end of this valley was a castle. It was a huge estate, and it covered a lot of land. We stood there, contemplating this sight a couple of miles away, and I wasn't sure what to think.

Do we go around it?

Do we go past it?

Do we knock on the door and say, "Hello, do you have cookies?"

"What do you think?" Liesl asked.

I shrugged.

"The problem is," said Laura, "that this... place..."

"Estate," I said.

"Castle," Liesl said.

"Haunted Mansion," said Tam, completely unaware of Disney, yet hitting the nail on the head.

"The *problem*," Laura repeated, "is that while we *should* go around it, it looks *extremely* interesting."

I nodded.

"What do the halflings say?" Liesl asked.

The halflings had no idea. Apparently, they had never been beyond the mountains, even into this valley halfway through. They studied the dark estate, and half of them — the older half, as far as I could tell — were wary. The other half of them were curious.

Adventuresome outings can get you in trouble. I well knew this. Heck, we were on one now, and had indeed gotten into trouble.

What should we do?

It was too early to camp for the night.

"We still have more than an hour of good daylight left," I pointed out.

"Okay," said Liesl. "How about we make the descent into the valley, but on the edge. The same path we'd take if we were going around it. We'll be off to the side, but still close, in case we wake up in the morning with the insane idea of checking it out."

So we hiked down the side of the mountain, diagonally, and climbed down to the edge of the valley.

Trouble was, it was marshy.

"Does the spooky castle in the dark valley have a marsh surrounding it?" asked Laura.

"Guess so," Liesl said. "Come on, we need to find high ground to camp on. High, or at least dry."

It took another half-hour, in the dwindling light, to scout out a secluded place to hide for the night.

"Okay," I said, after consulting with the halfling scout. "We are dry here, and the castle is a mile thataway." I pointed east.

Everything spooky is east.

I realized this, and turned to ask the halfling scout what he thought, but he was already gone, folding out his bedroll for him and his son.

I looked around. Everyone was making camp. I shrugged and removed my bag and withdrew my own blanket, too.

Hopefully, things will be calm and uneventful tonight.

The campfire was made, and since we were so close to the estate, we made sure to use dry wood and keep the fire low and clear. We didn't need any visitors drawn by a smoky campfire.

I lay on the field grass, my blanket over me, and stared into the flames.

"Holly? You okay?" asked Liesl.

"I guess so," I said. "I'm actually enjoying traveling through the Elfen Lands. I feel incredibly bad about Lord and Lady Umeqirelle, and yesterday was disgusting, but other than that, I'm great!" I chuckled.

"Yeah, that's about how I feel, too," Liesl said. "The halflings found some bark down here they said was good in tea; I was going to try and make a pot. Want some?"

Liesl had grown up in the Fae Folk lands, where the food and drink were somewhat similar to the British what you'd find in Britain. So she was big into tea.

Me? I preferred a cold Coke. But I appreciated her effort.

"Sure," I said, sitting up on one elbow. "I'd love some of your bark tea. Need any help with it?"

"Naw, I've got it handled," she smiled.

I lay back down.

The sky was getting dark, and the stars were coming out, and they were brilliant. Far more stars in the night sky in the land of Faerie than you could ever see in the human world.

Throughout our journey, I'd been helping a lot with supper, but I felt exhausted tonight.

Lucy came over and curled up against me and yawned.

"Tired, sweetie?" I asked.

She nodded and smiled.

A bit later, Liesl can over with two cups, and I sat up to taste the bark tea. It was surprisingly good. Even Lucy drank hers down. Liesl grinned happily.

A short time later, Liesl returned and handed me and Lucy paper-wrapped grilled mushrooms and onions. "The halflings found these on the edge of the marsh and have declared them edible. See if you like them."

Lucy nibbled on hers, then went back to eating the flatbread I'd given her earlier.

I took her paper-wrapped combination and polished off both our servings.

We bedded down for the night.

Everything was quiet and still.

In the morning, Liesl woke us as the sky was just beginning to turn light.

I was happy to awake, because I'd had dreams of the wytch.

As we all huddled in the cold morning, nibbling on what food we'd scrounged from the night before, I asked the others what they thought about what the wytch had said about me and how I smelled.

"I wouldn't put any weight at all on anything that... person... said," Laura remarked. "She was horrid."

"Agreed," I said. "I just wondered."

Liesl came up and put an arm around me. "Just forget all about it, Holly. You already knew you were your father's daughter through and through. You didn't need some old hag telling you."

"I guess," I murmured.

Lucy sat in my lap as we ate.

Tam walked up to his sister. "Laura, shouldn't we at least go sneak and look at what's going on at that dark estate. What do you think?"

"I think you may be crazy," Laura said, "but I'm curious, too."

"If we do go, we need to be careful not to get caught," Liesl said.

"Always," I said.

So it was decided. We broke camp and slowly snuck over to the east until we could see the castle from the tall marsh grasses.

It was even more dark and foreboding up close.

"What's that?" Liesl asked. "I see people going in and out."

"I wish I had binoculars," I mused, staring at the front of the estate.

It was painted all in black — either that or made of black stone. Even the windows looked dark.

We crept a little closer.

The brush was high, and hid our movements easily. And the people going in and out of the estate didn't seem to pay any attention to their surroundings. They were busy at some task.

"Holly," Laura whispered, because we were so close, "Look."

She handed me a glass ball inside a leather tube. "It's from the halflings. Take a look through it."

I held it up to my eye. Holy cow! I could see the activity at the estate front courtyard clearly, and it appeared much closer.

I started, then looked again at every person going in and out of the estate.

"Liesl," I murmured. "Is that one of the guards from the vineyard shack?" I handed her the makeshift telescope.

She looked through it carefully, taking a long time. Then she said quietly, "It sure is," before handing back the scope.

We backed up a few dozen feet so we could talk.

"That dark estate is an Oak King Faction holding," I said quietly. I looked around. "Where exactly are we again?"

"Nearly to the border," Laura said.

I stared at the huge castle, thinking.

"They were bringing in supplies. Do you think this is their base of operations?" I asked in a low voice.

Liesl looked straight at me, a grim look on her face. "I think it's very likely, yeah."

We had retreated and stayed in the area another day, deciding to investigate this estate.

"The Oak King Faction is almost like a political force," I mused.

"If they're just a political force, why do they have so much influence?" Laura asked. "Why do they have so much power?"

"You mean, why doesn't The Oak King disband them, if he doesn't want them trying to seize power in his name?" I asked.

"Exactly," Liesl pointed at me. "That is the crux of everything, and that is what people have been wondering for a very long time."

I thought for a minute. "I guess we'd have to ask The Oak King that question."

"But The Oak King hasn't been seen for a very long time. It's said to be impossible to get an audience with him," Liesl said.

"So people have tried?" I asked.

"Oh, yeah," Liesl replied. "The Fae Folk Council tried, years ago. They sent several emissaries to request an audience with the king. All were turned away."

Hmmm.

"Turned away?" I asked. "So they never even set eyes on the king?"

"Apparently," said Liesl.

"Well, does anyone know for sure?" I asked. "Did the Fae Folk Council make a public statement about it?"

"I don't think so," Liesl raised her eyebrows. "They're not that forthcoming with information. Their attitude is that their business is their business, and they shouldn't have to answer to anyone, since they're the ruling body. Aside from the kings, of course."

Laura was fiddling with a leaf, deep in thought. She suddenly threw down the leaf as Liesl fell silent, and stood up. "I have a question," she announced.

We both stood and looked at her.

"Why is your school named 'Titania Academy'?" Laura asked.

I shrugged. I think someone had told me once, but I didn't remember.

Liesl grinned. "The school is named after the Queen."

I stared at her. I had never heard anyone talk much about the Queen. She was mentioned very seldom, and it was almost as if she were some ethereal being, possibly even just a concept, instead of a real person.

"The Queen?" Laura asked.

Liesl nodded, then looked thoughtful. "The Queen hasn't been seen in millennia. Legend has it that she entrusted the two kings to rule in her absence. No one knows why she's absent; it's just accepted."

"What's just accepted?" Laura asked quietly.

"It's just accepted that Queen Titania was the first Faerie Being, and exists in legend, mostly," Liesl finished, sounding unsure.

"Wait a minute," I said, my hand up and a small smile on my face. "If Queen Titania is just a legend, and The Oak King hasn't been seen in a long time, it almost sounds like he's fading into legend, too?" I looked at Liesl. She shrugged and nodded.

"So these historical ... figures, sort of, are fading into obscurity, becoming legends, like folktales told to children, because basically they haven't been seen by anyone in a long, long time?" I asked.

"I guess," Liesl said. "No one really knows, Holly."

I looked back toward the dark estate. "I want answers."

"Why am I not surprised?" Liesl chuckled.

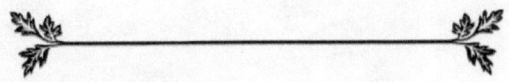

Chapter Twenty-Six
The Halflings

We spent the day discussing everything under the sun, and waiting for nightfall. Because we were going to secretly storm the castle at night.

"Hey, Laura," I asked. "Tell me about the halflings. Because we learned about them last year in school, but I want to confirm everything, because they live here and you know about them, right?"

"Oh, yeah, we actually know a lot about halflings," Laura said as we all sat around a bog fire.

The flames we gathered 'round flickered fitfully.

We'd retreated back into the forest, and the whole area was shrouded in fog.

The castle estate lay miles away.

"Well, what questions do you have about them?" she asked.

"What are their specialties?" I asked. "Do they do anything particularly well?"

"They are great at hiding," said Laura. "In fact, if you don't know a halfling village is there, chances are you will never see it."

Tam piped up: "We had a halfling village a half-mile into our wood, near the house. Father never even saw it."

Laura grabbed her brother around the waist. "None of us is sure it actually existed."

"I'm sure, I saw it," Tam insisted. "The halflings found me, when I was in the wood one time when I ran away. We traded biscuits."

"Okay, so they're good at hiding," I said. "What else? Are they good at sneaking? That's kind of the same thing."

"It's not, actually. But I think they are definitely good at that, too," said Laura. "Tam?" she turned to her little brother. "Go get the halfling leader; tell him we have questions."

"I'm actually already here," a voice said from a few feet away.

I jumped a foot in shock.

"Told ya," said Tam.

The halfling leader was called Terin. He finally told us this after we promised loyalty to the halflings and vowed to be friends forever, and revealed all our names as well as those of our parents and grandparents, as far back as we could.

Sigh.

Terin sat down right between us. He was so small and slight that I started to cover him with my blanket and he just looked like a sack.

"Don't do that," said Terin.

"Sorry," I mumbled, grinning.

"Okay," Liesl said. "So, Terin, you can all sneak? Really well?"

Terin turned his solemn face to Liesl and said in a very serious voice, "If we don't want you to see us, you won't see us."

Tam grinned.

Terin turned to Laura and continued. "We have walked right passed your house, not ten feet from your uncle as he chopped wood, and we were not seen."

Tam laughed, holding his stomach.

Laura's eyebrows shot up and disappeared into her hair.

Terin spoke one last time: "The halfling village close to your house has sent hunters out to gathered food when it rains, and they've gone straight to your school while it was in session, and gone into the kitchens and out again, carrying bags of flour and sugar and jugs of milk, and they were never seen."

Tam was giggling so hard he fell over backward.

"Okay," I said quietly. "You can sneak. Good. I was hoping for this."

Liesl and I exchanged a significant look.

I turned to Laura. "This is what I'd like to do." I picked up a stick and drew on the ground. "First, I say we send a halfling party to scout out the castle grounds. We need to know what the perimeters are, where the doors are, which ones are kept unlocked... all the things."

Terin jumped up. "I will take this mission. I have half a dozen men I will bring with me, and we will go immediately."

"Excellent," I said. "Terin, we will wait here. How soon can you go? Terin? Terin??" I glanced over, and the little man was gone.

"Okay, he's fast," said Liesl.

"Most excellent," said Laura. She turned to me, "Holly, what do you have in mind?"

"Don't freak out, but I want to get inside that place. I want to know what The Oak King Faction is up to."

"You want the halflings to go in? Alone?" Liesl asked.

I stood up and grabbed my magic staff. "Professor Farryn was training me on concealment. I think I can go in with them." I faced a tree and closed my eyes, then opened them. Then I stepped to the side.

"Okay, that was freaky," Laura said. "If you want to talk about freaky."

"You're getting better, Hols," Liesl said, swinging her head, looking around. "Holly?"

I closed my eyes and stepped back the other way.

"Whoa," said Laura.

I sat back down. "Tell me exactly what you saw, I want to make sure that what I'm trying to do is really happening."

"You stood up by that tree, then you closed your eyes and went kind of transparent," said Laura. "I could still see you, but you looked like you were faded away. I could see the trees behind you. Then you stepped sideways and disappeared."

Liesl nodded. "That's what happened."

"Okay, good." I felt satisfied I was going in the right direction with the skill. "I'll practice some more while we wait for Terin to return."

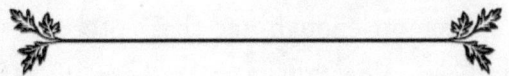

The rest of the day was spent with me practicing, Liesl and Laura helping, and trying to learn concealment themselves — and Lucy and Tam play-wrestling while the rest of the halflings joined in.

By nightfall, I felt ready.

"You really think you can stay invisible after just one day of practice?" Liesl asked skeptically.

I glanced at her. "I took Farryn's lessons for five days, last week, remember?" I said, trying to sound confident.

"Okay, so, six days. You think that's enough?" Liesl asked.

I turned to her. "Are you trying to undermine my confidence on purpose?" I asked.

"I'm trying to make you think. And trying to save your hide from death by overconfidence," she retorted.

"Sheesh. Death? Really?" I looked at her.

Liesl took a slow, deep breath. "Just be careful, Holly."

"I will," I said. "I promise."

"Are we going to just wait for you here, then?" asked Laura.

"Yes," I said, looking around. "I think you guys, and the rest of the halflings, will be okay waiting here. I think this place is remote enough, and that's probably why The Oak King Faction headquarters are here: it's technically still on Elfen lands, but out in the middle of nowhere."

Laura nodded. "We're almost on Fae Folk land, really."

"I wish I could go with you," Liesl whispered.

I stepped close to her and patted her shoulder. "Really, Li, you know I'll be okay. You know it. Don't you?"

"I guess," she said in a quiet voice. "I just hate being left behind."

"I understand that. But you have to be brave," I said. I paused a minute. "Listen, if we don't come back, you should take everyone over the border head to your parents' home, okay?"

Liesl blinked several times, and her eyes looked watery. She nodded, not saying anything.

I hugged her, then Laura came forward and I reached my arm out to include her, too.

"You guys, don't worry. Everything is going to be fine. I have a good feeling about this."

Tam ran up to us. "Terin is back. All of them. They want you to come."

Liesl, Laura, and I hurried over to the halflings.

Terin and his crew were holding court, surrounded by the other halflings, who sat in a double circle around the returning heroes. They listened raptly to the account of their adventures scouting out the castle estate.

I grinned at Liesl, and we sat down to listen, too.

"We approached everything slowly, creeping up, and we saw everything," Terin said. "The men were bringing in boxes and bags, and they didn't see us at all. We check the whole outside, and it was long and far. There were five doors, all locked. I worried how Mistress would get inside tonight, so I stepped inside alongside one of the men carrying a box."

I listened, fascinated. Terin was a good storyteller.

"The inside was very busy. Very, very busy," the halfling said. "But I could take some food after I found their kitchen." He held up a small bag half full of what I guessed were buns or fruit or something. "And I picked up these for Mistress," Terin held up a loop containing several keys.

The halflings clapped and rose to their feet, surrounding Terin and patting his body. This seemed to be the way they showed happiness and respect. Terin shuffled through the crowd of his fellow halflings and came to me.

"For Mistress." He held up the loop of keys. "Castle is kept locked. Now Mistress can get inside," he beamed with pride.

I smiled, taking the keys. "Good job, Terin." I leaned over and kissed the top of his head.

Terin blushed scarlet and nodded, and turned to accept a bowl of stew from another halfling.

Dinner was apparently ready.

We all sat and ate bowls of stew, accompanied by berry flatbread. I stopped myself before I got too full. I wanted to be light on my feet tonight.

I was really getting amped up for the forthcoming recon mission.

I wanted to find out exactly what was going on inside that castle, and if it was indeed the headquarters of the dreaded Oak King Faction.

Chapter Twenty-Seven

Midnight Incursion

We waited until the moon rose and then moved low again. Thank goodness there were lots of clouds; this made the landscape really dark.

Terin, half a dozen other halflings and I made our way across the few miles, and crept over to the ridge next to the dark estate.

I lay on my belly, studying the field before me.

The castle was dark. Not so much as a light in a window lit the grounds. I counted three or four patrols making their rounds outside. They stayed close to the castle, though.

The night was foggy, and thick, and still.

"How many do you count?" I whispered to Terin.

He held up four fingers, and I nodded.

Four. Easy to sneak around.

We had decided, since we were all skilled in sneaking or, in my case, concealment, that we would stick together if possible.

We crept forward on our bellies, and then, when we ran out of low ridge, we rose to a crouch.

I had my magic staff; it was invisible in my hand, but I clutched it with an iron grip.

We inched forward slowly, and, when I glanced toward the halflings I knew were beside me, I couldn't see them. I knew I was also invisible to prying eyes.

Closer...

Closer...

And we were there.

I stepped up next to the stairs leading up to the estate's front doors. The keys Terin had brought me opened every one of the doors, he'd said. I'd decided the best door to use would be the one side door not visible to the outside. This door was behind a wall, and used for the kitchen.

But I wanted to see the whole estate's outside before I went in.

Terin had been told I was to lead, so even though I could not see him or his men, I assumed he was behind me.

I crept along, following the perimeter, stopping and holding my position when I thought a guard was looking my way.

After ten minutes of this, I realized being in a crouch shouldn't matter, so, relieved, I straightened, and continued.

It took a long time to walk completely around, and I didn't really find much out of place. But I felt better knowing the lay of the land.

I approached the hidden kitchen door, and pulled out the keys.

The door opened with the third key I tried, and I slipped in, drawing the door halfway shut. I watched as it opened again slightly, and I knew the halflings were coming in behind me. We crept through the dim kitchen.

The estate was quiet and dark inside. One candle was lit in the front entry hall, and it rested on a side table.

There were three stories, and a center stairway connected them.

Terin had told of hidden staircases, most likely installed so servants could go pass between floors unseen. They were curved staircases in corners, behind walls and, in some cases, hidden by curtains.

I discovered one, and made a beeline for it.

I mounted two flights of stairs, eager to investigate the top two floors.

I started looking around, careful to stay quiet, but when I stood outside the third room of the top floor, I heard voices.

"You've got to give him another dose. It's already nearing the new moon. Really, this cannot wait," a gruff voice said.

The voice that answered was strange, to say the least.

"I don't think he needs it, and I'm worried he's had so much already that he'll never wake."

"That's not my problem," the first voice said.

I wanted so badly to see who was in the room, but the door was shut, and I knew if I opened it to pass invisibly through, whoever was in the room would likely notice.

So I continued to listen.

"Take him outside once a day for five minutes, so no one gets suspicious," the gruff voice was saying.

"Why do you have to get so coarse?"

"Just do what I say, or this'll never get done."

"Fine."

The voices stopped, and the door opened, and I closed my eyes tight, and flattened myself against the wall.

"Okay, I'll make sure."

"Good, you do that," Gruff Voice was saying. "And go check on him right now. Jerich said he needed some tending."

"Is he conscious?"

"No. And his face is still wet. Fix that," Gruff voice demanded, before turning and striding down the corridor.

The softer-voiced man turned and faced down the corridor we were in. I was still flattened against the wall, and I guess so were the halflings.

I gripped my magic staff, in case I needed to use it, but the man just sighed and slowly walked away toward the front stairway.

He didn't see me.

I silently thanked Professor Farryn and his concealment lessons.

The man was getting farther away.

On a whim, I gripped my magic staff and walked after him, following him all the way down both flights of stairs.

He stepped out into the main entry hall, where the candle sat on the side table, its flame flickering in the low light.

With another sigh, the man turned to the right and proceeded down another hall. I followed him, still concealed, still silent.

This is the best skill.

He walked all the way to the end of the corridor, and up to a small door in the side of the wall. Opening it, he descended the stairs that were revealed.

I followed him through the door.

He stopped and glanced up. He had started to pull the door closed behind him, and I had put my hand out, stopping the door from completely closing.

He didn't seem to notice.

The door slowly opened again, and I and the halflings passed through.

I flattened myself against the side of the stairway as the man came back up and firmly closed the door.

He didn't seem suspicious, although I held my breath. He was passing so close.

The door was now closed, and the one old lightbulb hung midway down the stairs, flickering fitfully.

I slowly exhaled in relief when the man started back down the stairs, which were steep and damp. I had to grip the banister tightly to keep from slipping.

The man descended the stairs, with me a few steps behind him.

At one point, he paused and listened, and I stopped, worried he'd heard my footsteps. But he shook his head, mumbled something about "hearing things" and continued his downward journey.

All in all, we descended so far we passed two more fitful light bulbs, and the stairway became even steeper and wetter.

Are the entire house's drips feeding down this stairway?

I knew that couldn't be, yet there was so much water dripping down the stairs that at the bottom it had pooled into a relatively large puddle, and was draining slowly off to one side.

The man reached the bottom of the stairs and turned right, and after a walk down a short corridor, he finally stopped at a bolted doorway guarded by two large, muscled men who almost looked like they had troll blood. Each was nearly seven feet tall.

"Let me in," the man said.

The guard on the right gave him a long look, then slowly turned and unlocked the large padlock, pulled open the hitch, and pushed the door in.

As soon as the door swung open, I could feel it.

Waves and waves of power emanating from the room. Power and something else.

I suddenly clutched my stomach and doubled over, and I felt my concealment flickering.

OH, GOD.

I could not become visible. If they caught me, they would probably kill me.

I closed my eyes and concentrated, and then slowly stood upright.

Thankfully, the two guards had followed the man into the room, and no one had been looking out the doorway.

I was again concealed.

I stood in the corridor and tried to see into the room.

What are they doing?

I took a few hesitant steps, and stood on the side of the actual doorway, and watched as the two guards lifted something from a low table in the corner.

It was a hooded figure, trussed up and wrapped in bindings. The two burly guards lifted this figure until it was upright, then hoisted it up by the arms, and held it between them.

Even next to the tall, burly guards, the wrapped, trussed, hooded figure was utterly massive. It had to be at least nine feet tall, and many hundreds of pounds. The guards both grunted with the effort of carrying it.

The man waved them forward. "He said we have to bring him outside at least once a day; go argue with him if you don't like it."

"Why now? It's the middle of the night?" one guard rumbled.

The man shrugged. "He hasn't been out in a week. We can't wait any longer. You don't want him to get angry at us, do you?"

The other guard grumbled, but they both lifted the figure higher and moved forward.

I stepped out of the way to let them pass.

The burly guards moved surprisingly fast, and hustled the trussed figure up the stairway, dampness and steepness notwithstanding, until they emerged at the top door.

I and my fellow concealed intruders followed, after the man who directed the procession, and who neglected to close the bottom door, which had been previously padlocked.

I surmised the valuable contents of the dungeon room, which had been so carefully locked inside, were contained in the bound figure being taken upstairs.

I followed the line of people down the ground-floor corridor, and out a side door.

The guards carried the covered figure out onto the lawn, taking him several dozen feet away from the estate walls.

"Put him down there," the man said, pointing.

The guard dropped the trussed figure onto the ground. Whoever or whatever was under all the wrappings did not make a sound as it dropped heavily to the grass.

The man walked over to the parcel containing... whoever it was, we could not tell, and gave it a kick.

The kick thumped and the figure inside did not move.

One of the guards grunted. "Think he's dead?"

The man huffed. "No, you idiot," and kicked the bagged figure again, this time much harder.

No response was seen or heard from the thing on the ground.

Out in the fresh air and moonlight, I could again feel the power emanating from both the estate and the collection of people I watched. The guards and the man all stood closely around the trussed-up figure on the ground, and the power I felt thrummed from the entire area.

Maybe the guards have strong power?

I made a mental note to ask Liesl what types of Faerie denizens had the most power, so much power you could feel it, like a hum in the air.

"Kick 'im again," the other guard rumbled.

"No, I will not kick him again; it's doing no good. Look at the grass; it's still yellow."

"Well, hell, then let's take it back down," said the other guard.

The man studied the lump on the ground for a few minutes. Then said, "Loosen the bindings. Get an arm out."

The guard bent and worked at the canvas and rope that bound the figure. It took some doing, but the truss finally loosened, and the guard untied one last flap, and an arm flopped out.

The arm was clothed in more canvas, but the hand was bare.

The man reached and took the arm, and swung it around, trying to get it over, but the body was not moving.

"Move it, swing it over t'other side," he said.

The guards grunted and reached, and flipped the figure over a quarter turn.

The arm swung over, and the man was able to move it to where he wanted.

What on earth is he doing?

I could not see well from my position near the castle wall, so I silently crept forward, and walked around the guards, to see what was going on.

As the figure came into view, I could see just how large it was. It was as big as a horse, wrapped tight in its bindings, and one part was untied, with the huge arm sticking out.

In the moonlight, I saw the hand at the end of the arm was sparkling as if it was coated in gold dust.

As the man grabbed the arm and brought the hand forward, and pressed it into the grass, I could see the stunted and yellow plant suddenly rise up several inches, and turn a deep green color.

The change spread out from the point it started at, slowly reaching forward and covering the entire grounds within a matter of minutes.

As I watched, stunned, the man directed the guards to tie the arm back up, wrap the figure again, and take it back inside, and down to the dungeon.

I stayed outside, and as they disappeared back into the castle estate, and the door slammed shut with a firm bang, I fell back onto the now-lush green grass, and sat there, in stunned silence.

Chapter Twenty-Eight
The Rag Woman

"Get up, Mistress," invisible hands urged me to my feet, and took my hand, dragging me, stumbling, away from the dark estate.

The halflings pulled me along, all the way back across the hillside, across the edge of the marsh, and into the trees to our camp, several miles away.

I had the presence of mind to stay concealed as they did this, but my mind was whirling with a million thoughts, and buzzed with shock with every second that passed.

The halflings brought me to Liesl, and sat me down.

"What?" Liesl said, looking around.

Terin popped back into sight, and said, "I think the expedition somehow broke your friend," and he batted the top of my head several times until I came back into view.

"Holly?" Liesl said. "Hey, you okay?"

I remained silent, staring into the fire with the stare of a thousand lives. I was in shock.

Laura came forward and flicked water in my face. "Holly, wake up," she said. "Come back to us."

Liesl patted my face. "Holly?!"

"We can't risk yelling loudly," Laura murmured.

Liesl then grabbed my arm and gave me such a pinch that my mind was flooded with pain.

"AHHH OWWWWW," I whispered loudly, grabbing my arm and looking over at my friend."

Liesl sat in front of me. "Hey, you okay?"

I stared at her, while my hand clutched my arm where she'd pinched me. "Oh, oh, God, Li. Oh God, they have him, he's in the dungeon, he's... he's drugged or something, I don't know, I can't believe they would do such a thing..."

"Do what?" asked Laura. "Who's down in the dungeon?"

"Holly, what did you see?" Liesl asked.

I turned my head to look at Laura and Liesl. "They... they have a prisoner or something, they ... they untied his body, I think he's still alive. He didn't move, he didn't react ... even when they kicked him, over and over."

"Who? Did you see who?" asked Laura. "Was it just some guy?"

"They... they unwrapped his arm, they took his... his hand, turned him over, and touched his hand to the... to the grass. It turned it green; it revived it," I mumbled.

"Revived what?" Laura asked.

"The grass," I murmured.

"Wait," Liesl said. "They have someone tied up and drugged?"

I nodded. Then I jerked my head up. "Liesl, Liesl!"

"What?"

"I don't know who that was that they have, but we have to find out, we just have to!"

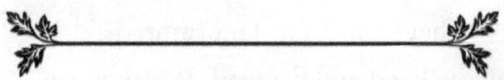

Half an hour later, Laura had brewed some warm berry and apple tea, and had handed out mugs.

None of us could sleep.

I sat there, a blanket around my shoulders, my feet near the campfire, cupping a mug of tea as the steam curled up around my face, warming me.

"You think they've got some guy drugged and tied up and in the dungeon?" Liesl said matter-of-factly.

I took another sip of tea. "I know what I saw," I said in a low voice. "Go ask Terin, if you want to check my facts."

"Oh, Laura is talking to the halflings right now, trust me," said Liesl. "She was more skeptical than anyone."

Laura came back in a minute and sat next to us. "Well," she said, "her story rings true. Terin and the other halflings who went to the castle all described the same thing. They even said there was some kind of dull power coming from the tied-up guy. And that he was huge, big as a troll." Laura's voice was resigned and amazed, all at the same time.

"I can't believe this," Liesl murmured.

I shook my head and yawned. "Neither can I."

Liesl glanced at me. "We haven't had hardly any sleep in two days, especially you, Holly."

"I can't sleep right now, Li. Are you serious?" I yawned again.

"Okay." Liesl looked up at the sky. "I'm pretty sure we have, like, at least a couple more hours until dawn, so how about we just lie down, and you can keep your eyes open and keep talking, and I'll be right here beside you? How's that?"

Liesl lay down next to me; her face was right there. I shrugged and lay down, too. Laura and Tam lay down as well. Lucy had been sleeping already. The halflings took this as a sign, and they all lay down, too.

Liesl handed me my blanket, and I pulled it over me, and yawned.

"I swear, Li, I could not..." I yawned again. "...could not believe what I was seeing. The grass! The grass was yellowed and stunted, and it just, it... it just, like, fluffed up. It changed, Liesl, totally: It turned green and lifted up a bit, like it was recognizing the touch of his hand..."

"Maybe it was some kind of faun," Liesl said sleepily. "Some of the faun strains can do that kind of thing."

I must've fallen asleep, because the next thing I knew, I was opening my eyes. I was lying next to Liesl and Laura, and Lucy was curled up against me.

She must've moved over in the night.

The fire was still warm, but I saw no flame, just a lazy bit of smoke curling up from the blackened, charred logs.

I yawned and sat up, stretching. The halflings were already awake and moving about the camp, making bark tea, putting the food pot back over the fire. Building the fire back up, poking it and adding tinder, until a flame appeared.

The sky was slowly lightening.

I had the weirdest dreams...

I got up and reached for a water jug, and splashed freezing cold water onto my face.

Okay, All right. I'm awake now.

I took a deep breath and closed my eyes.

What had I been dream of?

I hated how dreams mostly faded from my mind upon waking. Sometimes, they stayed. Last night's had been...

OH GOD.

I remembered everything from last night!

I opened my eyes in shock. The halflings had stopped their morning duties and were staring at a figure emerging from the trees right in front of me.

It was a small, old woman, dressed in rags.

I blinked. She was still there.

What was an old woman in rags doing here, in the middle of nowhere?

She was about thirty feet away, and walking slowly toward our camp. Our eyes were locked.

She stared at me, a pleading look on her face, and her eyes were so compelling I could not look away.

I stood there, feeling almost mesmerized, and watched the old woman slowly approach. I noticed she had a small basket with something in it, and her feet were bare.

"Oh, boy, I'm still tired," Liesl stretched and yawned, and looked up at me. "What're you looking at, Hols?"

I glanced down at her and shrugged, then looked back up.

Liesl turned and looked over, seeing the old woman. "Hmmm, company. Seems harmless enough."

The halflings were moving about again, and the tea was now boiling, I could hear the liquid thumping against the metal sides of the little pot.

A halfling came forward with a mug and poured some out, then brought the mug forward and handed it to me.

"Thanks," I said, distracted.

Liesl stood up and accepted the mug the halfling now handed her, and we stood side by side, watching the old woman approach.

When she was a few yards away, I walked up to her. "Hello," I said. "Are you okay?"

She shook her head mutely.

I looked closer as a halfling brought the woman a mug of tea.

"Thank you," she whispered.

"Would you like to come warm yourself by the fire?" I asked.

She nodded, and I led her forward.

Liesl made a place for her with a blanket, and the woman sat down.

We all sipped our tea in the silence of the morning.

I studied the woman over the lip of my mug as I sipped the bark tea. This morning it tasted a bit of honey, and I surmised the halflings had found a hive yesterday as we camped.

She was not as old as I had first thought, although I could not tell her age from looking at her. In the dim light, her face looked wrinkled, but when she turned slightly those wrinkles disappeared.

Her eyes were the color of the sea after a storm, and her complexion was slightly ruddy. Her fingers were delicate and small, yet looked strong at the same time, and I realized the look of strength lay in how she held her hand as she gripped her mug of tea.

She was dressed in rags the color of dirt, varying in shade from sand colored, all the way to medium brown and even grey. I couldn't tell if she wore a dress, or a top and pants, because the material covering her looked jumbled, put together.

She was an incredibly interesting character.

I waited until she had finished her tea., then offered her more.

She nodded, and I poured more into her mug, and she sat sipping the hot brew for a long time.

After a while, I turned to Liesl to talk.

"So, last night was incredible," I said. "They treated this... I guess it was a person, although at first I thought it was an animal, like a horse or a cow or something. Anyway, they treated this person just horribly."

"Was he okay?" Liesl asked.

"I have no idea," I said. "They had him tied up in wrappings, it was the weirdest thing. Almost like a mummy."

"What's a mummy?" Liesl asked.

Laura came up to us just then, holding a mug of tea and a piece of berry flatbread. "Good morning," she yawned.

A halfling came and gave the old woman at the fire a piece of berry flatbread. She took it gratefully, and began to nibble on it.

I turned back to Liesl. "A mummy is a kind of Egyptian um... like, a dead body they've wrapped in cloth, from head to toe."

"So they were carrying a dead body? I thought you said it was really big?" asked Laura.

"No, I don't think it was dead. Wait. I guess it could have been dead." I paused, thinking.

Why did I think it had been alive? I couldn't remember...

"Okay, it could have been a dead body. But they had it in the basement, under guard," I said.

"Maybe it was a wight?" asked Laura.

"Oh, God, I hope not," said Liesl.

"What's a wight?" I asked.

"If it was a dead body, and it was imbued with special magic, it might have... well... they might have been trying to turn it into a wight," said Laura.

"I thought a wight was always a woman?" Liesl said. "Holly, didn't you say you thought it was a man?"

"I don't know, actually. It was covered. Completely wrapped up, except for the arm, they unwrapped that. But it was huge, like a giant. Maybe that's why I thought it was a man," I said uncertainly.

This conversation is not going in the direction I thought it would.

"Excuse me?"

We turned around.

The old woman spoke again, "Excuse me?" she said.

"Oh, hello! Do you need any help?" I asked.

"I... I'm sorry, I couldn't help but overhear what you were discussing," the woman said.

"Yes," said Liesl. "About the goings on down over at the estate? The castle?" Liesl turned to me. "Which is it? A castle? Or just a big estate?"

I shrugged.

"I think it's just an estate," said Laura. "Doesn't a castle require turrets and a keep and a... a drawbridge?"

I shrugged again, then turned back to the old woman. She intrigued me.

"Ma'am, do you know about the prisoner at the dark estate?" I asked.

"I guess it really is a prisoner," Laura said. "If he's tied up. He or she."

"He," I said. "The hand looked like a he."

"My great aunt Luna has the manliest hands I've ever seen, on anyone," said Liesl. "So, you never know."

"True," I replied.

I looked at the woman again.

She took another bite of flatbread, chewed thoughtfully, then cleared her throat.

"I... I overheard you saying... he was tied up?" she said softly.

I nodded. "Tied up, hooded, wrapped up tight. I couldn't tell if he was alive or dead, but I thought he was alive."

"Did he smell?" asked Laura.

"What?!" I asked.

"Dead bodies smell," Laura said.

"Not at first," said Liesl.

"Well, pretty quickly on, though," said Laura. "My great-granduncle, Archiluterres, he died in his sleep, and the next morning…"

"Shhh," I said. She was beginning to gross me out.

I turned back to the woman.

"Yes, he was tied up, and hooded. Completely." I waited for her to speak.

The woman pulled down the scarf on her head, and sat up straighter. "Those men, in that castle, they stole my son. They drugged him and are holding him against his will. For nefarious purposes, I believe."

My jaw dropped.

Chapter Twenty-Nine

Plans of Strong, Brave Deeds

"Your son?" I asked, standing up in alarm. "When did they take him?"

"Not long ago," the old woman said. "It's been so hard without him..." The woman put her face in her hands and began to softly cry.

"Where do you live, Ma'am?" Laura asked. "Where did they take him from?"

The woman's shoulders shook with her sobs, and I put my arm around her to comfort her. As I touched her, I felt a strange feeling come over me, but then it was gone.

The old woman lowered her hands. Her face was wet with tears.

"We lived here, in the forest. In a tree," she said. "They barged in one night and... and took him, as he slept. I was away, foraging..."

Ohhhh... I feel awful. This poor woman...

"How...?" I began. I didn't want to be rude or anything, so I chose my words carefully. "How big is your son? It was dark last night, but I thought the person I saw tied up was really big..."

"My son is big, yes," she said. "He's definitely a big lad." She started crying again.

I hugged her, wrapping both my arms around her.

I felt something odd again, just for a moment, and then it was gone.

"Poor dear," murmured Laura.

I kept thinking of what I'd seen last night. It had been so dark, but I definitely remember the grass changing.

I walked closer to the woman. "Ma'am, can I ask, does your son have any magic that would make grass grow? Is your son part faun? Or all faun?" I asked.

The old woman's eyes brightened, "Yes," she answered. "He is! And he has so much magic in him: full of wonderful magic. He always loved touching plants and grass and making them grow. He would walk across a brown winter field and leave green footprints! He's such a gentle soul." She hung her head, remembering. "He's very dear to me, and I cannot even contemplate my life without him." Fresh tears ran down her face.

"Holly, there are several different types of Faerie Folk that can heighten growth in plants," Liesl said. "Remember? That was in class last year."

"Oh, right," I said, remembering. "Not only fauns, but also dryads and nymphs."

"That's right!" said Liesl. "And naiads, although they mainly stick to water, they can affect the growth of seaweed, palms, and even lily pads," she smiled triumphantly.

I glanced at the old woman, then turned to the others. "I think we should try to rescue her son; from what I saw, they are treating him abysmally."

"But how can we help him?" said Laura. "He's in that castle, surrounded by guards."

A flash of inspiration appeared on Liesl's face. "I know," she said in a quiet voice. "We create a diversion, something big, huge even, to draw every guard out of the castle. Then we go in and get the man. Rescue him."

I stared at my friend. "You make it sound so easy," I said. "You weren't there last night. You didn't see how paranoid those guards are; how huge, too. I'm sure they're part ogre: They were *that* big."

"Then we need a diversion that is over the top. Massive," Liesl said.

"And we need something that could help us defeat the guards who are stationed on the inside. In case they don't leave the dungeon," said Laura.

"Okay, so it's settled," I said in a snarky voice. "We need a huge bomb, and nerve gas."

"What's nerve gas?" asked Laura.

"I don't think we have any bombs," said Liesl. "Or any kind of explosives."

I'd been telling her all about the human world. It looked like she'd remembered some of it.

"The Faerie world doesn't have large bombs," Liesl added, looking thoughtful.

"Then you explain to this poor woman why we can't even try to get her son out," Laura gestured to the old woman in rags.

I sighed.

Think, Holly. Think.

"Diversions don't have to be explosions," said Liesl slowly. "What's a big diversion we could make, just from us?"

"Laura, do you have any magical abilities?" I asked.

"Uhh... not that I know of, what? Do you mean, compared to you? Or compared to humans?" Laura asked.

"Compared to anything?" I said. "What can you *do*?"

"Well, the Elfen Folk can naturally garden, find lost things, fight, we're acrobatic, we can figure out problems... what?" Laura asked.

I had been waving my hands for her to stop.

"I've got it," I said. "I know what we can do, and how we'll do it. Come over here."

I gathered Laura and Liesl and Tam in a huddle, while the halflings played with Lucy.

We consulted and planned and connived and plotted for over an hour.

Finally, we were ready.

"Do you think this will work?" Laura asked.

"No idea," said Liesl.

"Probably not," I said. "But we should still try."

We practiced all morning, and by early afternoon, we felt ready.

"Shouldn't we wait until nightfall?" Liesl asked.

"It'll give us a better chance of catching them by surprise," I agreed.

"Well, fine then," Laura said. She glanced over at the old woman, who'd been weaving a basket by the campfire while we plotted. She was teaching Lucy how to braid dried grasses plucked from a nearby field. It was hard work, and the woman was a patient teacher. Lucy, with her small, pudgy fingers, had managed to weave the circle that would become the base of the basket, and the small disk of straw-colored fibers had a circle of grasses sticking up all in a row, and slanted sideways.

I kept staring over at them, wishing I was there learning at the feet of the old woman.

She had a lot to teach.

We waited until nightfall, and spent the time going over the plan.

I drew with a stick in the dirt, rehearsing it time and again.

Liesl, Laura, and Tam would help the halflings create the diversion, then I and a few of the halflings, including Terin, would go in for the rescue.

Laura was excellent at fighting. Liesl had special skills that she'd use, skills that came naturally to her.

I would do my concealment skills, and be the first one inside. I'd take a handful of the halflings with me.

The diversion was the iffy-est part. I worried it would not be big enough.

"Let's eat and then go," Liesl suggested.

"Agreed," I said.

We settled down to bowls of stew the halflings had prepared.

We were getting too used to camping here, I thought, as I looked out on all of us gathered.

Still, our rescue mission was noble.

We need to get across the border as fast as we can.

The thought came unbidden into my head, and I knew it was a truth I couldn't ignore for much longer.

We set out at midnight.

How the halflings knew it was midnight was beyond me. I had always considered the clock a manmade thing, but the little people seemed to tell the time by looking at the position of the sun and the moon.

At a signal from Terin, we headed out. We broke camp and took all our belongings with us, although we didn't have much to carry.

It was an hour and a half before we got to the estate. It looked the same as it had the night before: dark and brooding, and desolate.

We gathered on the close ridge, an upswing of the forest edge, about fifty feet from the side of the massive building.

The halflings brought everything we needed, gathered along the way. They held large branches of trees that had fallen, and rocks and dirt clods.

"I wish there wasn't a wind tonight," I said.

"It's not too bad," said Liesl. "It'll still be okay, I think."

"Depends on how fast we can get in and out," I murmured.

"True," Liesl said, then patted my arm. "I have faith in you."

Laura shook her head and smiled.

I took a deep breath and studied the perimeter of the grounds. Several guards made their rounds, and yawned, looking very bored.

After ten minutes, I motioned for the halflings to begin.

They moved stealthily forward, taking all their supplies out to the front of the estate, and built a massive pile of flammable brush and wood just beyond the front road area. Then they took their position along the side of the building.

We knew we'd only have a few minutes.

We'd have to be fast, or everything would fail, and all our effort would be for nothing.

I took a deep breath and signaled for Liesl, Laura, Tam to sneak closer with me.

We crept as close as we could, without being caught.

Crossing me fingers, I signaled for everything to commence.

Chapter Thirty

Heroics

I pointed my mouth upwards, cupped my hands around my mouth, and hooted like an owl as loud as I could, three times.

That was the signal: an owl hooting.

Liesl lifted her hands and closed her eyes, and the air suddenly began filling with smoke. It poured out of her fingertips. Her magical ability was *cleaning* the air, and I was fascinated that she could reverse it by creating a smoky haze. Earlier we'd hiked up a short hill, and she'd sucked in as much air pollution as she could, spending almost an hour doing it.

Where she stored it, I have no idea.

The volcano had created a lot of air pollution all over the forest, and the wind had carried it dozens of miles in all directions.

The result was an opaque screen of smoky air that was thick and impenetrable.

Now it was time to light the wood, the huge pile of forest branches and grasses and flotsam and everything that we had dragged with us out of the forest.

Laura and Tam lit the bonfire, and the flames quickly rose more the thirty feet into the air.

Terin, three other halflings and I stepped close to the front door, waiting.

Liesl's smoke filled the air so thickly and so quickly, that it appeared the fire was surrounding the estate.

I lifted my magical staff and brought it forward, slamming it into the front door.

BOOM!

I stepped back, keeping far clear of where it would swing open toward me.

The door opened, and more than a dozen guards rushed out.

Behind them, Terin, the three halflings, and I slipped into the estate.

As we slid farther into the interior, I saw even more guards and castle residents rush out the doors, then come back in, calling help, before rushing out again.

We slipped down the side corridor to the dungeon stairwell.

I still had the keys Terin had lifted.

We arrived at the staircase door, and I unlocked it.

I hollered down the long stairs, summoning the deepest voice I could muster in my best impression of a grown man.

My voice echoed downward, and my call for help must've reached the guards on duty at the bottom, because they came barreling up, running faster than I thought such large men could move, and boiled out of the staircase.

They turned and ran for the outer door, where the other guards could still be heard, yelling.

We slipped down the staircase, taking the slick stairs two-by-two. I gripped the banister tightly, and my hand burned as I descended.

At the bottom door, I brought forth the dungeon key and unlocked it.

The door swung inward, and we rushed in, still concealed.

If there were people inside, I wanted them to see just the door opening, but no one coming in. That way, they would go out, to search for the culprit.

The trussed figure still lay on the table. Otherwise, the room was empty of people. I let out a breath of relief I hadn't realized I was holding.

I took a few minutes to poke the wrapped-up man, to see if he'd move.

To see if he was still alive.

I was rewarded with a groan and slight movement of his head.

"Sir, your mother sent us," I whispered. "We're here to rescue you."

The fellow's hooded head jerk at this news, and he moaned again. I heard him trying to say something.

I tried to remove the hood wrapped over his face.

Terin winked into view at my elbow.

"Mistress, come on! We must make haste or we will be caught," Terin said.

"I have to see," I said, fumbling with the ties.

Terin made a grumble, then fumbled in his pants pocket, then brought his hand up. "Use this, Mistress."

I blinked. He held out a small knife, made of some kind of chipped quartz. I touched the blade: It was razor sharp.

"Careful, it's very keen," Terin said.

That's an understatement.

I slipped the knife under the canvas wrapping, trying to be careful.

"Hold still. This knife is sharp," I whispered.

The figure had been moving a bit, but stilled at my words.

It took a few minutes, which felt like an eternity, but finally, I got the hood off.

A bearded older man with a kind face looked at me groggily, then closed his eyes.

"My... mother sent you... to rescue... me?" he whispered haltingly before opening his eyes again.

I was relieved to hear him talking now. He'd barely been moving the night before. Maybe whatever they'd used to drug him was wearing off.

I nodded.

"Mistress, if we don't leave now, I fear we will be caught," Terin said.

The man glanced over. "Is that... a halfling?" he asked.

"Yes," I said hurriedly.

He struggled at the rest of his bonds. He was wrapped up tighter than anything.

I patted his shoulder. "Okay, just be still and we'll get you out of here," I murmured.

He continued to struggle, then appeared to pass out again.

Maybe the drug's not wearing off, after all. Ugh.

I'd hoped we wouldn't have to carry him, but there was no getting around it. *He must weigh three-hundred pounds!*

He lay still, so we grabbed him and, with all five of us pulling, lifted him off the table, through the door and up the stairs. It was a crazy struggle, but we made it up.

At the top of the stairs, I paused to look around. It had only been a few minutes.

"I think the coast is clear," I whispered.

"The what?" Terin murmured.

"Just come on," I whispered hurriedly back, and, grabbing the figure, I turned to the right, and we headed out the side door.

The area outside the door was deserted. We could hear yelling from around front, and the smoke was still very thick, although the wind had begun to blow some of it off.

I could see the flickering light from the bonfire, against the night. It would take a long time to burn down.

Good.

We carried the trussed man around the corner to the back.

I was still under magical concealment, and the halflings were still sneaking. The only one not under a magical camouflage was the man.

We held him and ran as fast as we could.

We made it to the edge of the trees, and I stopped to look back.

My heart fell.

Guards had spotted us and were coming after us.

"Come on," Liesl cried from deeper in the woods. "Hurry!"

I looked wildly around and couldn't see where my friends were.

"Come on, Terin," I whispered, and we heaved the figure back up, and began to run through the woods.

It was much harder going, the forest ground was uneven, and there were branches and trees and all manner of things in our way. It was hard carrying someone so heavy and trying to navigate the obstacle course nature had put in front of us.

We made it at least a hundred feet into the woods.

Liesl and Laura were running toward us, with some of the halflings.

We were going to make it.

Suddenly, I felt something hit my head, and blood poured down the side of my face, blinding me as I ran.

I stumbled, caught my feet, then stumbled again and went down.

Aspen and Tundra suddenly popped up out of thin air next to me. They growled and lay down alongside me.

The halflings grabbed me and pulled, and I tried to wipe my eyes clear so I could flee.

The wolves whined and rose to their feet.

The guards were getting closer.

"Go, go!" I said. "Carry him to safety!"

The halflings grabbed the man again and tried to lift him and run, but they struggled without my help, and couldn't quite run fast enough.

Bullets were flying passed us. I stared. No, not bullets. *Arrows?*

One hit my arm, and it exploded in pain. I looked to see what had hit me — what the guards were throwing at us.

I saw a small hole in my sleeve, and I peered inside: A tiny fireball, so bigger than a pea, was settled in my bicep.

Tiny fireballs. Huh.

More shots flew near us, some landing in the trunks of nearby trees, leaving black holes.

One hit Terin, and he cried out and fell, clutching his arm.

The halflings who were left dropped the man, and huddled down on the forest floor.

Then another tiny fireball hit me, this time square in the back of the head, and I lost consciousness.

The last thing I felt was a wet wolf tongue on my hand.

The last thing I said was, "Go. Aspen, Tundra: GO!"

The last thing I heard was the pop as both my wolf familiars obeyed me, as they had been trained to do, and leaving this realm of existence, returning home.

They were compelled to obey me, but I knew they hated it, probably more than I hated that we'd been caught.

We had failed.

Chapter Thirty-One
Sadness

I came to as I was being hoisted into the back of a wagon. It seems the guards had thrown me onto the floor, and as I landed, I hit my head.

"OW," I said, opening my eyes.

"Holly! Are you okay?" Liesl cried.

The wagon was dark.

It was still nighttime, and the wagon was near the edge of the forest. I could see the center front of the estate from where I sat. The bonfire was still burning, but the wind had blown much of the smoke away.

I felt dizzy. I touched my head and felt my hair, which was matted with blood. Wrinkling my nose, I looked around.

They had captured Laura, Liesl, Lucy, Tam, and me. The halflings had escaped, I hoped. I worried about Terin; last thing I remembered, he'd been hit and had gone down.

"Did they get Terin?" I asked in a weak voice.

"I don't think so," said Laura. "At least, I didn't see him."

"He got hit and went down," I said. "Right after me." I took a deep breath and was overcome with nausea. I jumped over and leaned my head out of the wagon, and vomited.

"Get in there," a guard yelled. He came forward and clouted me on the head, and I saw stars.

I was flipped back into the wagon.

"Hey, cut it out! She's hurt!" Liesl yelled.

"Well, she can stay where she is, unless she wants us to shoot her again!" the guard yelled back.

I waved Liesl down. "S'okay, s'okay," I said, slumping to the side. "I'll be okay."

"I can't believe how bad this went," Laura mumbled.

I looked over at her. "When were you guys caught?"

"A bunch of guards were in the woods, on recon, I guess," Liesl said. "They caught us as we fled."

Laura looked disgusted.

"I should have noticed them," Tam said dejectedly. I should have known."

"Holly?" said Lucy.

I raised my head. "Hey, sweetheart," I said, reaching for her.

She crawled over and curled up against me.

"I'm scared," said Lucy.

So am I.

"It'll be all right, Luce. I'll take care of you," I said.

Laura patted Lucy's shoulder. "Don't worry, kiddo."

We all fell to the side a bit as the wagon started moving.

"Where are they taking us?" Lucy asked.

"I don't know, but don't worry," I said, wrapping y arm around the little girl. "We'll see soon."

The wagon trundled along.

We eventually fell asleep against each other.

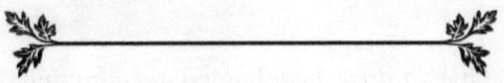

It was hours before the wagon came to a stop, but finally, the lurching and swaying that at first had been so uncomfortable but had helped to keep us asleep — stopped.

"Out," the guard harshly yelled. "Get out!"

I opened my eyes to a red, smoky sky.

What is this?

I sat up. "Aughhh...," I groaned, holding my head.

"Ugh," Liesl said beside me.

"Where are we?" I asked, looking at the sky again. "Is that the volcano?"

"Not sure," Laura mumbled groggily. "I think it's mostly sunset.

I looked around. We were... *Oh, no.*

We'd been brought back to the Elfen Academy.

I groaned again and dropped my head in dejection.

The guards came around to the back of the wagon.

"Hey!" one of them yelled. "You were told to get out of the wagon. Do you need to be told twice?" He brought a large wood branch of some kind forward, and swung it at us.

"Hey! That's mine!" I exclaimed, recognizing my magic staff.

"Heh, yeah, well, girlie, it's mine now." He grinned evilly at me and then looked at the staff.

Suddenly, the staff changed into a snake — a huge, long snake.

"AHHH," the guard yelled and dropped it.

The snake slithered away under the wagon.

I laughed.

The guard whipped his head up to glare at me.

"Get out of the wagon, prisoner scum, NOW!" he growled.

We stood and reluctantly prepared to disembark. I was closest, so I stood and stepped to the edge.

The guard reached out a meaty hand and knocked me behind my knee, and I fell out of the wagon onto the dirt and gravel road.

"OWW," I said, involuntarily.

The others hopped out and tried to help me.

Aspen and Tundra reappeared next to me, and began growling at the guards.

"Pull them back or they'll be killed," whispered Laura. "These guys mean business."

My heart was in my throat as I bent to command the familiars to return to their realm. They reluctantly obeyed, but not before they'd each given my face a lick goodbye.

Lucy was nearly hysterical; they were trying to grab her and hoist her away.

I turned and got to my feet. "That's my little sister," I cried out, lying through my teeth. "Bring her back to me."

The guards finally brought her back, just to shut her up.

Tam stayed silent and stoic through the whole ordeal.

We gathered on the side of the road, bloody and scraped-up.

My head wound had begun to bleed again, after I'd been knocked out of the wagon. My arm was starting to ache from where I'd been shot.

The guards laughed harshly at us and got back into the front, and the wagon moved away, drawn by the sorriest looking dun-colored unicorns I had ever seen.

"Poor beasts," I murmured.

The wagon pulled away, revealing the Elfen guards we'd been handed off to; they stood on the edge of the grass path leading up to the school, a half-mile away.

"Okay, you all must come with us," the nearest Elfen guard said.

I straightened. "Under what authority?" I was getting tired of being pushed around.

He stopped and turned back to me, his face set in harsh lines.

"Under the authority of the Elfen Council. You've been charged with trespassing and theft." He brought up a sheaf of papers and waved them in the air. "It's all right here."

I looked around. For some reason I was feeling incredibly cocky.

"Theft of what? I don't see anything here but us," I spat.

"Just come along," the guard said, brandishing his spear. "Or I'll give you another hole to worry about. This time in your back!"

The other Elfen guards laughed harshly as we fell into line and slowly walked toward the school.

What is it about small-time cops? They always want to hurt you the most.

We walked up the hill under the hot sun, and I watched the sky. What I had first thought were roiling clouds of red fire, turned out to indeed be the sunset against clouds of white and grey. The volcano looked like it was getting more active since the last time I'd seen it.

When was that?

I couldn't remember how many days had passed since we'd last been here.

We were led into a building I hadn't been in before, and I heard Laura's swift intake of breath from behind me.

The message was clear.

This is a bad place.

Chapter Thirty-Two
The Elfen Council

We were put into a bare room and told to wait, so we waited.

And waited.

There were no windows, just one overhead, flickering light that never went off.

We sat on the floor, holding each other's hands and waiting for what seemed like an eternity.

After hours and hours had passed, it was clear they weren't coming to get us until the next day. It had been so long, we knew night must have fallen.

Lucy stretched out on the floor, her face streaked with dried tears.

After a few hours, I lay down, too.

We all finally fell asleep, and slept very fitfully.

It was a long, hard night.

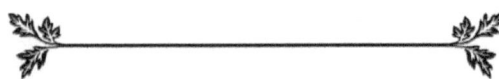

We knew it was morning when the door opened and a guard said, "Wakey wakey. Time to face the music."

We all groaned and slowly got to our feet. I didn't know how early it was, and my body was sore all over. My arm was now numb, my head was crusted with dried blood, and I saw blood on the floor where I'd been lying. Sleeping on a hard surface is never comfortable, and my body let me know it.

"Come on, come on. They're waiting," the guard said in a bored voice.

We filed out.

In the corridor, we were separated. Guards came from several other corridors and grabbed each one of us.

A guard put a rough hand on Laura's shoulder and pulled her toward him.

"HEY!" she said.

Another guard tried to grab Tam and pull him in another direction.

"That's my brother!" Laura protested.

"I don't care," the guard who had her said. "We've got our orders."

Lucy shrieked when she was pulled from me.

"Honey," I called, "Lucy!" I didn't know what to say. Tears fell unbidden from my eyes, and I wiped them away.

We were pulled into different corridors and lost sight of one another.

I was brought to a holding cell. This time, it wasn't just an empty room; this was a long narrow room with bars on the windows and doors.

I tried to opened the door, and I rattled the bars on the window, but nothing would budge.

They left me there for hours.

Finally, the guard opened the door and told me to come.

I was mentally exhausted, and physically hurting. I just wanted this ordeal to be over.

God almighty, I wish I had never left Titania Academy.

I didn't know how many days had passed since I'd stood on Fae Folk soil, but I swore, the second I got back, I was never leaving. I would stay at Titania Academy until forever.

Or nearby. Maybe I could stay the summers with Liesl's family again.

I thought of the Fae Folk lands, how they looked, how they smelled, how they felt. I remembered how the trees reached up to the sky, not like the stunted trees here in these wretched Elfen lands.

I'll get back to Fae Folk lands, and I swear I will never, ever leave.

The guard led me through multiple corridors and finally indicated a door. "Go through and close it behind you," he said, and waited a few feet away, his hands on his hips.

I shrugged and complied, and found myself in a room where the Elfen Council was waiting.

They were all seated at a long table, facing a single chair in front of them.

"Sit," a woman in the center said.

I trudged over to the chair and sat down, glaring at them.

There were fifteen of them. They were all Elfen elders, each one was impeccably dressed and groomed, all of them clean and neat.

I sniffed and wiped my filthy hand across my nose. It came away bloody. I knew I was a mess, but I didn't care. These people had caused so much damage to so many lives I was stunned. They'd killed the Lord Emissary and his wife, leaving Lucy an orphan. They'd succumbed to The Oak King Faction, lending their power to the destruction of the land and the fight against my father and my school.

Since I had been caught trying to rescue the old woman's poor drugged and bound son, I assumed they were complicit in The Oak King Faction's kidnapping and torture of him.

I had no idea what had become of that guy, and I was scared for him.

The woman who we'd left in the forest, would never know what had happened. We never did return with her son.

Who knew what would become of her?

I stared at the fifteen faces, and they stared back dispassionately. It was clear they didn't care at all.

I sat and I waited.

Finally, the woman who seemed to be the spokesperson, spoke.

"Your name is," she looked down at the sheaf of papers in front of her, then looked up again. "Holly Ó Cuilinn?"

I just stared at her. They wanted to hurt me? I was not about to help them.

The woman sighed loudly.

"Miss Ó Cuilinn, I have been fully informed on your whereabouts and activities of the past week."

It's been a week?

"I would like to advise you of a number of things," she said.

Like maybe my rights? Do I have any?

The woman looked back at her papers. "It says here you are accused of trespassing and theft." She looked up. "What do you have to say for yourself?"

I just stared at her.

If she knew what I'd done, I wasn't going to comment. If others had lied about what I'd done, which I was sure they had, I wasn't going to correct her. I didn't care anymore. Maybe the Elfen didn't have Miranda rights, but I was raised in New York City, and by God, I had the right to remain silent, and silent I would remain.

"Miss Ó Cuilinn, now is the time to set the record straight. Confess and we'll go easy on you," the woman said.

I just stared at her.

She sighed heavily again and stood, and began pacing.

"Miss Ó Cuilinn, you may not know this, but you have caused more trouble for this council than we've ever had from any child in a very, very long time."

I just stared at her.

She continued. "I want to make one thing perfectly clear, young lady." She stopped and folded her arms in front of her, and stared at me. "You will *never* return to the Fae Folk lands. NEVER."

I blinked.

Stay in control, stay in control.

She waited for a response.

I just stared at her.

She continued after it was clear I was not going to react.

"Our allies," here she paused and took a deep breath, "have asked us to keep you here in Elfen Lands. This is the land of your mother's side, after all. Even if you are from an out-of-wedlock coupling, your lineage is royal, and your roots are here."

What utter lies. There was no reason under the sun that I should feel rooted here.

I just stared at her.

"And," the woman continued, "Our... allies... have reason to believe that your presence... elsewhere... would be a grossly unfair... advantage... in the upcoming... exercises." She stopped and looked at the ceiling. "Therefore, we will never let you leave. Never. Consider the Elfen Lands to be your new home."

I didn't react. I didn't say anything. I just stared at her.

"Furthermore, we will be fitting you with magical... bracelets... that will keep you from harming yourself. Or anyone else." She gestured to the man beside her, who got up and came forward with two black metal shackles.

He was holding them as if they burned his hands to touch them.

He came forward and murmured to me. "Extend your hands."

I just stared at them.

I refused to help them.

He shrugged and held the shackles in one hand while he hauled off and punched me in the jaw with the other.

His fist hit me with such force my head was whipped around, and I was thrown from the chair.

I landed on the cold, hard floor, my head ringing.

The room stayed silent.

I slowly got back up and, glancing at the man, who had not moved, I sat back down in the chair and slowly extended my hands.

He snapped the shackles onto my wrists so tightly that my hands began to throb with pain. The black metal burned like ice.

I stared straight ahead, showing no emotion at all. I refused to give them the satisfaction.

At least my hands are out in front of me.

If these jerks wanted to team up with The Oak King Faction, then they did not deserve anything from me.

The man returned to his chair beside the spokeswoman's and took a seat.

I pointed my gaze several feet above her head, refusing to meet her eye and ignoring the burning pain on my wrists. I wasn't sure what the shackles would do — if they would keep me from using my Elemental Power or what. Fury roiled inside me, but I kept it bottled up. No matter what, I was *not* going to let them think they'd gotten to me.

The council spokeswoman walked to the door I had been brought through, opened it, and spoke to the guard on the other side.

He came forward and grabbed me roughly, escorting me away and returning me to the cell I'd been in.

I didn't know if the cell was under surveillance, so I didn't say a word. I just sat there, my back against the wall, on the cold, hard floor, until I dropped to my side and fell asleep, dried tears on my face.

And that was that.

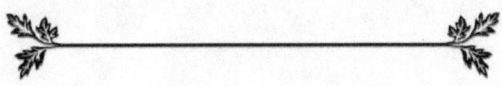

Chapter Thirty-Three

Enough is Enough

I was held in the cell, and couldn't really tell the passing of time very well.

I suspected that several days had passed.

The magic shackles had, indeed, kept me from using my Elemental Power. I had tried on the first day to summon snow and had gotten nothing at all.

Not even one flake drifting down, and the air stayed the same temperature, no matter how hard I tried.

The shackles quickly formed angry red marks on my wrists, as the stinging dulled to a low throb.

Once a day, the door opened and they brought me a bowl of food. It was always the same: some kind of stew that looked very weird. Remembering the wytch's roasting meat, I rejected the food and refused to eat any. This happened three times.

I spent my days lying on the floor, feeling very weak.

At one point, I passed out, and when I woke up, my arctic wolf familiars were asleep against my side.

"Wake up," I whispered. "You have to go. They'll kill you."

Aspen whined against me, and brought her nose to my chest, nuzzling me.

"You have to go...," I said weakly. "Go! Now!"

They popped out of the room.

I sighed and instantly missed them.

On the morning of the fourth day, the door opened, and something was placed just inside the door, before it was quietly shut again.

I stared and watched, wondering what was going on.

After the door shut again, I shrugged, and crawled over to see what had been placed inside my cell.

It was a bottle of water.

Holy heck.

I stared at it.

This is from the human world.

I picked it up and looked at it. It looked like someone had gone inside a 7-Eleven store right there in New York

City, and bought a sixteen-ounce bottle of water, and brought it here.

It was room temperature, and one of those generic bottles of water that are sold cheap. I tried to open it, and found the top was still sealed.

So it's probably not poisoned.

I unscrewed the top eagerly, and drank every bit of it, careful not to lose a single drop. I closed my eyes and tilted my head back. As the last drops dripped into my mouth, I opened my eyes.

What's that?

I squinted my eyes as my stomach rumbled.

There was something written on the bottom of the water bottle. I strained to see the letters. They were very small, and looked like they'd been written hastily.

I turned the empty bottle over, and looked on the plastic bottom.

There was nothing there.

I turned it right-side up again and looked through the small opening at the top. Squinting again, I held it up to the light. I could barely read it... It said ...

"tonight"

I brought the empty plastic bottle down from my eye, and stared in shock into the middle of the room.

My heart thudded.

Is someone coming to rescue me?

For the next fifteen hours, I could not rest. I was weak as a kitten, but I was so invigorated by the message that I stood up and began pacing. I could not sit still.

I hid the bottle, scrunching it down to an inch, screwing the cap back on, and shoving it deep into my pocket.

I wasn't really worried; they never searched me or anything. They never even came into the room.

It was the longest day of my life, that waiting.

Night fell; the barred window showed the daylight leaving.

And I still waited.

I lay on my side, staring across at the wall, thinking of memories of New York City, Aunt Clare, and remembering how I used to steal bread and fruit from the cart vendors.

My eyes were half-open as I dozed, waiting.

Some time later, the door lock clicked.

I immediately sat straight up and stared at the door.

It opened a crack.

A head poked through and looked around.

Lord Almighty.

It was Miss Olovalur, the vice-headmistress of the Elfen Academy!

Her eyes focused on me.

"Come on!" she whispered, her hand appeared, and her forefinger curled: 'COME.'

I needed no further prodding.

I rose shakily to my feet, and walked to the door.

The water had given me more strength, thank goodness.

She took my hand, glancing down at the shackles and wincing, and pulled me out into the corridor, where Liesl and Laura waited.

"Oh, my God!" Liesl whispered, coming and hugging me.

Laura put her arm around me as well.

Liesl had on the same type of shackles I did.

Laura and Liesl were both gaunt and filthy, and Liesl had a cut running across her cheek.

"What did they do to you? I whispered, staring at the cut.

It looked raw and fresh, the blood barely dried on the edges.

Liesl shrugged. "I tried to escape. I think it was day before yesterday."

"Come on, you guys," Miss Olovalur whispered.

We followed her down the corridor and to the door at the end.

She had a passcard and touched it to the door lock, and we heard a click as it opened. We all walked through, and down a second corridor, to the end.

This door opened with her passcard as well, and led to an outside yard.

Grass!

I tamped down the desire to crouch and touch the grass as we walked along the side of the yard, down the fence line, to the end.

It was overcast, the low clouds mingling with smoke from the volcano, so it was very dark in the yard.

We made it almost to the end.

Then...

Floodlights popped on, and we were blinded.

We stopped and shielded our eyes.

Miss Olovalur yelled, "Come on!" and grabbed Liesl's cuffed hands, trying to pull her forward.

A shot rang out.

Miss Olovalur dropped to the ground.

I gasped in horror, and stared at her. A black spot had formed on her forehead, where the miniature fireball had hit her. Her eyes were open, and she look stunned.

She did not move.

We were taken back to our cells, and I spent a day feeling horrible about my would-be rescuer. I mourned the lady, who had been nice before, and incredibly, in trying to rescue me, had become a saint in my estimation.

Poor Miss Olovalur.

I assumed she was dead, but wasn't sure.

I spent the night thinking of her.

On the second day after the failed rescue attempt, the guard opened the cell door, and I was surprised to see that instead of trying to give me another bowl of who-knows-what chow, he was removing me from the cell.

He pushed me roughly ahead of them down a familiar corridor and brought me once again into the Elfen Council chamber.

Liesl and Laura were already there, seated in chairs before the council table.

I was placed in the chair next to them.

I glanced at them, then looked forward at the corrupt committee.

"Well, Miss Ó Cuilinn," the spokeswoman said, "I'm sorry to say that your attempt to escape has resulted in the loss of our school's vice-headmistress."

She stared at me for several minutes.

I stared back, not reacting at all.

My worst fears had been confirmed: Miss Olovalur was dead.

"You and your friends had an ally in Miss Olovalur, but that threat to the Elfen world has been removed." She stared at me, unblinkingly. "Yes, Miss Olovalur is dead. The shot fired killed her instantly."

She kept staring at me.

I decided to stare at the wall above and behind her.

These people put so little value in life. They killed one of their own, an Elfen woman.

Miss Olovalur had been good to us. I felt sorrow at her death, but I showed no outward emotion to this dastardly council.

The woman shuffled some papers in front of her, then placed them back down on the table, sighing loudly.

"Miss Ó Cuilinn, you know, you could be very happy in the Elfen Lands, in time." she looked at me.

Something boiled in my mind.

I thought of Chance, of my school, of my classmates, of Renée, of all the fun we had learning there at Titania

Academy. I remembered Professor Farryn's face. I remembered my father.

I closed my eyes as the tears came.

My father. The Holly King. The most important person in my life.

His face came into my mind.

That merry face, with the white beard, looking exactly like he should: looking exactly like Santa Claus.

His green and white trimmed furry coat.

His smile.

The red holly berries in the green holly leaves, in the garland he wore around himself.

The garland.

I remembered the necklace, the gift from Father that Chance had delivered to me on my fourteenth birthday.

I felt it, suddenly, hanging under my coat.

I brought my shackled hands up to my neckline, and my fingers reached under the cloth, searching for the holly charm.

The woman was speaking again, describing all the great things she thought I would like in the Elfen Lands.

"We have better nature, better forests, more varied magical creatures," she paused, thinking. "Oh! we have unicorns..." She looked at us significantly. "Unicorns! and there are some still wild in the farther forests, too!"

I fumbled for the holly charm, reaching down a few more inches.

Where is it? I know it's there; I can feel the chain...

"And we have griffins, if you ever go mountain climbing...," the woman continued.

Was she for real?

These fools had Liesl and I shackled, for God's sake, and she was trying to describe how great the Elfen Lands were, trying to entice us to stay of our own free will or something?

Nutters.

Ah! I had it. My fingers closed on the holly charm from my father.

"...and we also have a number of rare faeries, the tiny ones... Miss Ó Cuilinn, I am absolutely sure you are going to really love living here!" The woman finished her speech with a big smile.

I stared at her, finally allowing myself to express how I felt. "NOT LIKELY." I grasped the holly charm and rubbed it furiously.

Father...

It felt hot to the touch.

I looked down at the charm.

It was glowing...

It was glowing...

On impulse, I brought the little holly flower charm up to my face, the shackles on my wrists clinking against the chain between them, and kissed it.

The second I kissed it a bright light appeared.

"OH, SO THIS IS WHERE YOU ARE, MY DAUGHTER."

I jumped up. "Father!"

The Holly King had appeared in the room.

I ran to him and fell into his arms.

Chapter Thirty-Four

Reckoning and Return

My father wrapped his arms around me protectively, and I'd never felt so safe in my life. Going from the extremes of incarceration and abuse and shackles, to the absolute safety of my father's embrace was head-spinning.

He held me tightly, squeezing me to him with both his arms. I felt the side of my face smushed into his fluffy white beard, and the feeling was utterly perfect.

I felt giddy with relief.

The room had fallen silent.

Then, I heard the sound of Liesl crying quietly in her chair.

Liesl!

My father raised his head from where it had been resting atop my own, and his body moved a bit as he looked around, taking in his surroundings.

I heard and felt his gasp: That sharp intake of breath was so quick it pushed my own body out a few inches as his chest inflated.

"WHAT IS THIS?!" His voice boomed in the room and refused to be contained.

I think the walls rattled.

The Holly King straightened to his full height, from where he'd been bent over me in a hug. He kept one arm circled round me protectively as he turned to take in everything.

He then bent to examine me in my disheveled state, complete with untreated shoulder, head wound, scrapes and bruises, and the magical shackles.

He gasped again as he examined me.

I kept my arms around him, clutching his robes, my fists gripping him for dear life. I never, ever wanted to leave the safety of his side for as long as I lived.

His eyes narrowed as he focused on the magical bindings on my wrists.

"WHAT IS THIS?" He repeated.

His forefinger lifted the edge of the shackles, then cringed as the metal's burning sensation hit him.

His face screwed up in the angriest expression I'd ever seen on his kind, genial face.

He roared in protest, enraged at what he saw.

With a wave of his hand, the shackles clamped to my wrists flew off and vanished.

His eyes scrutinized me in more detail, slowly examining me head to toe. His face softened in sadness and pity as he studied the wounds on me.

He passed his huge hands over me, brushing down from my head, over my shot shoulder, down my arms, down my legs, and finally, up again to caress my face.

Each inch his hand passed became miraculously cured of all injury and filthiness. It was as if an extreme healing balm spread all over me: Wherever he touched or passed near felt renewed. All the pain and aching left my body in a wave.

When he finished, I embraced him and wept.

The room was silent except for my weeping, and Liesl's soft crying.

The Holly King glanced across at Liesl and Laura, and the sigh that issued forth from him was one of sorrow and empathy.

He stepped to Liesl, and passed his hands over her, healing her and making her whole. Then he stepped to Laura, and smiled at her Elfen face; he passed his hands over her as well, and she was also healed.

The bindings on Liesl's wrists flew off and disappeared.

I clutched at my father's middle, not willing to let go, and stepped everywhere he stepped.

As he finished healing the other two, his arm returned to holding me.

Then he turned to the Elfen Council board members sitting at the long table before us.

His face grew red with fury. His eyes glowed in anger.

"HOW DARE YOU HOLD MY DAUGHTER AND HER FRIENDS AGAINST THEIR WILL? HOW DARE YOU?!"

He sputtered with anger, his words coming so fast they almost blended together.

With a roar of rage, he swept his hand across their table and they were all flung against the wall, pinned there, their feet dangling above the ground.

The council members looked surprised and angry as they hung against the wall, held there by some invisible force. They tried to speak, their faces formed expressions of horror and rage as they found themselves unable to utter a single sound.

The Holly King turned his back on them, and faced us.

"Tell me everything," he said in his normal, quiet, gentle voice.

Liesl and I started talking at the same time.

Father smiled, then put up his hand. "One at a time." He glanced over at Laura, who was hanging back a little. "First of all, who is this?"

"This is Laura, our new best friend," I said. "She is the daughter of the head of security of the Elfen Academy here. She's been a completely fantastic and invaluable ally, Father."

The Holly King looked at Laura and smiled.

"Okay, one at a time," he said. "Tell me what happened."

We spent the next ten minutes filling him in on everything that had happened to Liesl and me since we'd arrived in the Elfen Lands. His expression became more and more shocked as we told our story. His eyes widened especially at how Lord Umeqirelle had been compelled to try to seduce me with Elfen glamour.

When we started to tell him about old woman in the woods and the man bound and held captive in the dark estate, and how we'd tried to help her by attempting a rescue of him, Father gasped, and stopped us.

"Wait. She said she was who? And he was her son?!" He exclaimed. "And his hand made the grass grow?"

"Yes! And she was so sad that he had been kidnapped. She was crying, and told us all about him and how he was a kind of faun and..." I spent the next few minutes telling Father all about the dark castle estate and what I had seen, and how we'd tried to rescue him and what we did that night.

He stopped me again. "Holly," he seemed to gather himself, swallowing back tears. "That old woman... she... she said she's the captive's mother? That was... that was the queen. She is the queen of all the Faerie World."

I blinked.

"But she was just an old woman in rags in the forest," I said slowly. "She looked poor and careworn... covered in..." I stopped, thinking. The more I thought about it and remembered the woman in the forest, who had come out of nowhere, beseeching us to help her rescue her son... I felt shock flood through me, as if a bucket of icy cold water had been poured over my head.

I looked at my father, my eyes wide in complete and utter surprise.

There were unshed tears in his eyes.

"That," I whispered. "...that was... Titania?"

He nodded.

I gulped. "And... does that mean that... the man we tried to rescue... that was...Titania's son? Your brother? The Oak King?!" I asked in shock.

He nodded again.

Suddenly, everything I had seen, everything I remembered about this poor trussed-up captive, fell into place.

OH MY GOD.

I sat down on a chair, in total shock.

Father turned to Liesl and Laura. "Tell me everything else that happened," he asked gently.

And I realized. He needed to know everything. Every single thing.

Liesl and Laura were filling him in about what had happened to them after our failed rescue attempt.

I stood again and found my voice. I joined in with my friends, and informed my father of everything I had also experienced, from the moment I was running with the halflings and carrying the trussed-up, drugged, Oak King, trying to rescue him.

His eyes went wide in shock and anger when I told him the Oak King Faction guards had shot at us, hitting us. Shooting me in the head and arm. Hitting Terin, and all about the miniature fireballs.

Then we told him about how we'd been brought to this place, and how we'd been treated here.

Father's face looked angrier and angrier as we explained everything. Laura and Liesl told how they'd been beaten and starved.

I described how I had refused to eat the food, because of how suspicious I was. This led to a few minutes describing the wytch in the forest and what had happened there.

I told Father of the rescue attempt by Miss Olovalur, and our subsequent recapture and how Miss Olovalur had given her life to try and help us.

After we explained everything, The Holly King straightened from his position of bending to hear us all, and he turned to the Elfen Council members still held in place against the wall.

He admonished them in a voice that was so loud and with words so scathing that we three girls had to cover our ears. And by the time he'd finished, every council member was on the floor, crumpled, and in shock.

The walls were bleeding with feeling, his wrath had been so terrible.

"You have given power and purpose to the enemies of both our peoples," he finished with. "The blood that will be spilled in the coming war, in which both the Elfen *and* Fae Folk lands *and* people will be harmed, that blood is on your hands. Allowing them to hide, convene, and plot, on Elfen Lands, allowing this... this... depraved alliance, between your yourselves, and these criminals, has shamed the Elfen Council. It will never be the same as long as any of you is in power. As long as this alliance remains." He glowered at each of them. "The blood is on your hands now. In the name of the queen, I dissolve this council. It will be made anew, with new, untainted Elfen Kind."

And he turned, and took all three of us into his embrace, and we walked out of the room together.

The Holly King blasted open the door, and we walked out into the corridor.

We went through each and every room.

We found Lucy and Tam, Laura's mother and father and uncle, and several others.

Father healed them, and we walked out into the sunshine.

With a wave of his hand, he tore down the fencing, barbed wire, and guard towers, where the shot had come from that had killed Miss Olovalur.

Then we all walked to the nearby Elfen Academy, and around to the back, to Laura's home.

And there we said goodbye.

"I'll miss you so much," I said, my eyes wet.

Liesl and I hugged all four of them.

Laura's father and uncle were both in such awe that they were meeting The Holly King and shaking his hand, that they could barely stop talking.

"Thank you so much for everything you've done, sir."

"We can never repay you, truly."

Laura's mother hugged my father so tightly he chuckled.

Little Lucy hugged me and refused to let go.

I bent to one knee. "Little lady, Laura's parents will take such good care of you, and spoil you so much, you won't know what hit you!" I glanced up at Laura and her uncle and mother and father. They all smiled and nodded.

I trusted they would take the very best care of Lucy.

Then Father came up to them one last time, and got serious.

"I fear troubled times are ahead," he said. "My brother is still missing. I will try to find him, but I fear he has been moved. The trying times still to come will need strong people, both here and in the Fae Folk Lands. The Elfen Land will need strong leadership, if it is to survive what is coming." He looked meaningfully into each of the adult's faces, and they nodded to him, each in turn.

He was giving them a charge: Take care of your land, and its people. Make things right.

We said our goodbyes and departed Laura's home and family, and my eyes were wet as Lucy and Tam waved at us.

I hoped I'd see them again, but I was very worried about what would happen next.

The Oak King Faction is a force all its own.

As we walked away, I whispered to my father, "They took my magical staff, the birthday present from Liesl and Renée. Can you...?"

He smiled, waved his hand, and as it completed the short arc through the air, my staff appeared in his fist. He handed it to me. "Here you go, my daughter."

I smiled broadly. "Thank you, Father!"

"Now, I can only do that with objects that belong to you," he noted.

I nodded.

Understood.

After we'd left Laura and her family, we traveled together to the dark estate.

My father strode right up to the front doors and stretched out his hand; instantly, they burst open without being touched. He strode in and looked around.

The massive house seemed empty.

Father checked every floor, every room, but everyone was gone.

There were signs that the occupants had made a hasty departure, even food left on plates, and chairs turned away from tables.

We went down the stairs to the dungeon.

It was empty.

Father slowly walked to the table where the trussed-up and hooded man had been kept, where they'd no doubt drugged him.

Tortured him.

Father lay his hand on the surface of the table, tears in his eyes.

He turned and scanned the room, then spoke quietly.

"They've taken my brother away again," he said, his voice catching at the end. "When I find out who is responsible for this, I will make sure the land runs red with their blood," he spoke quietly and with fervor, and his words sounded even more deadly because of his tone.

Without another word, he strode out of the dungeon, up the stairs, and out the door.

We all both followed him, Liesl and I.

He walked out, maybe fifty feet, then turned and waved his hand.

The dark estate where evil deeds had been done, where The Oak King had been held and harmed, where so much evil and sadness had reigned, was utterly flattened to the ground.

The Holly King turned and walked away.

We then traveled to the nearby forest where we'd seen the woman in rags in.

Father knelt in the clearing we'd camped in, and bent his head, communing with Mother Nature, remaining so still and quiet it seemed that everything around him stopped moving, too.

After a time, we heard a rustling of leaves, and the old woman appeared from out of a thicket, dressed in rags.

The Holly King rose and stepped forward, then knelt at her feet and embraced her, and both of their shoulders shook as they cried together.

We returned home to the Fae Folk lands, and I set foot once again on the beautiful green grass of the front lawn at Titania Academy, my heart felt light and happy.

It felt like I'd been holding my breath until I got there.

Until I was home.

I closed my eyes briefly, raised my face to the sunshine, and inhaled the sweet air of the nearby forest and castle.

"HOLLY! LIESL!" Headmistress Ó Baoghill was running down the steps toward us, taking them two at a time, not an easy feat for a woman of her age.

Professor Farryn was right behind her, then came Renée, running fast, and behind them all came Chance.

We were surrounded by other students, who all patted us on the back and welcomed us home.

The headmistress hugged us both tightly, mumbled how sorry she was that she'd allowed this to happen, and smiled with tears in her eyes. Then she thanked The Holly King profusely and repeatedly, shaking his hand over and over, inviting him into the castle for some hot cocoa.

Renée jumped on us both, hugging us tightly and crying. "I was so worried!" She made both of us promise to spend hours telling her exactly what had happened, and I realized we had been gone so long we'd missed over a week of classes. "I promise to tutor you both so you'll be completely caught up," she said, nodding, tears of happiness in her eyes.

"I missed you, Renée," I said.

"Me, too, and God, we could have really used you back there," said Liesl. I nodded in agreement.

Professor Farryn shook our hands, patted us on the back, and congratulated us for surviving.
His smile was broad, and the pride shone from his eyes.

I stood up taller, knowing I had put my skills to good use. Skills that he had helped me hone and perfect. I knew I had a ton more to learn, but I felt I was off to a good start.

I saw Jack smiling and talking with Liesl.

Chance hung back behind the rest of them, and as I shook Professor's hand one more time, my eyes rose and spotted him in the background.

He had a small smile on his face, and his eyes looked wet, and I realized with a start that as the liege of The Holly King, since it was still the beginning of autumn, he had very likely awoken my father a little early, enabling me to inadvertently called the king to me by kissing the holly charm, and basically saving our lives. Again.

I stepped up to him, and he held his arms out to receive me.

I looked into his eyes.

"Oh, Chance...," I murmured.

He bent his head and rested it against mine and embraced me, and I felt his shoulders as they shook with his sobs.

I felt his tears on my neck.

After a while, he stopped crying and, still holding me, began to murmur against my neck.

"I am never letting you go, never, ever, ever, as long as I live, never letting you go anywhere alone, I will stay by your side and accompany you through anything, go anywhere, never letting you go, ever again, I promise...

My heart swelled with love.

We stayed like that a long, long time.

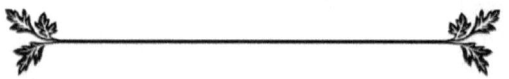

Dear reader~

I'm so glad you read Faerie Born and I hope you loved it. I do hope you'll consider leaving a review. It means so very much to hear what you think.

Get book 4 of the series!

Faerie War

Coming out July 2020!

Here ends Faerie Born, the third book of the Titania Academy series. The fourth book will be called Faerie War.

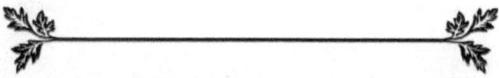

ABOUT THE AUTHOR

Samaire Wynne grew up in a lot of different places, and now happily resides on the East Coast, laboring away at writing stories every day. She is an animal lover with far too many pets, yet she still muses how she'd like to add even more. A lover of all things night and gothic, she also loves to read and reread her favorite books. Owned by a cat named Tyrion, she can be found haunting the shadows and mists that hang low over the hills of southern Virginia.